Also by **L.E.Luttrell**
DRAWING DANGER
THE BREAKDOWN
SMALL SACRIFICES
THE PHOTOGRAPH
THE WAVE

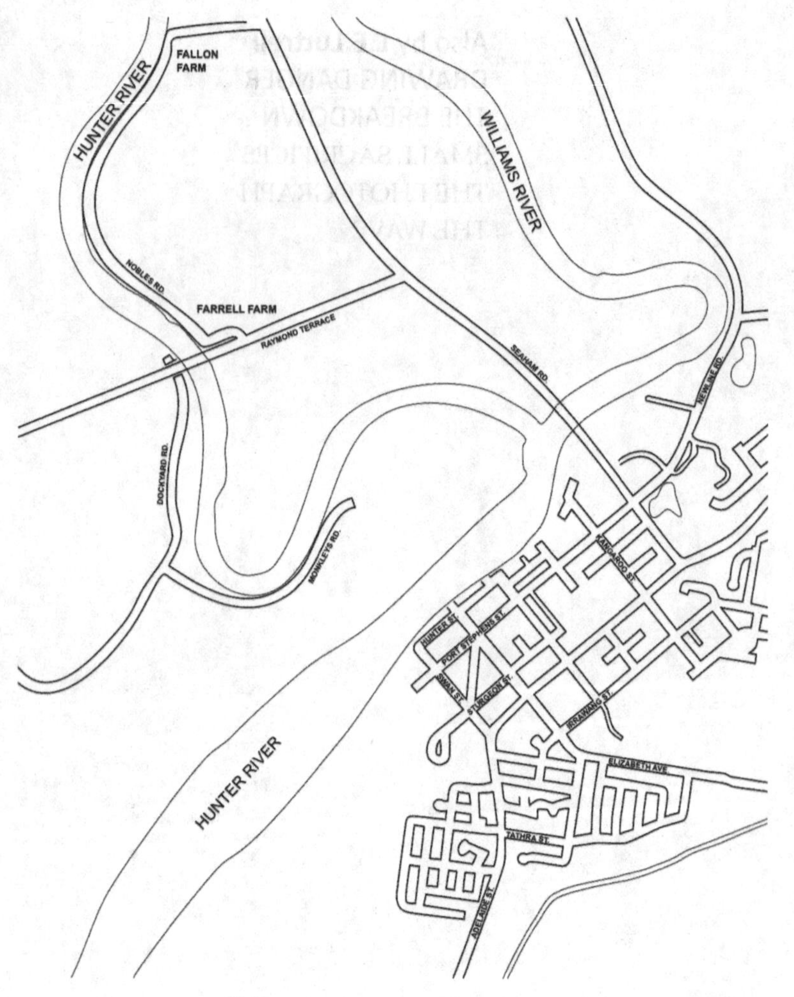

HUNTER RIVER
FALLON FARM
WILLIAMS RIVER
NOBLES RD.
FARRELL FARM
RAYMOND TERRACE
SEAHAM RD.
NEWLINE RD.
DOCKYARD RD.
MONKLEY'S RD.
KANGAROO ST.
HUNTER ST.
PORT STEPHENS ST.
SWAN ST.
STURGEON ST.
IRRAWANG ST.
ELIZABETH AVE.
TATHRA ST.
ADELAIDE ST.
HUNTER RIVER

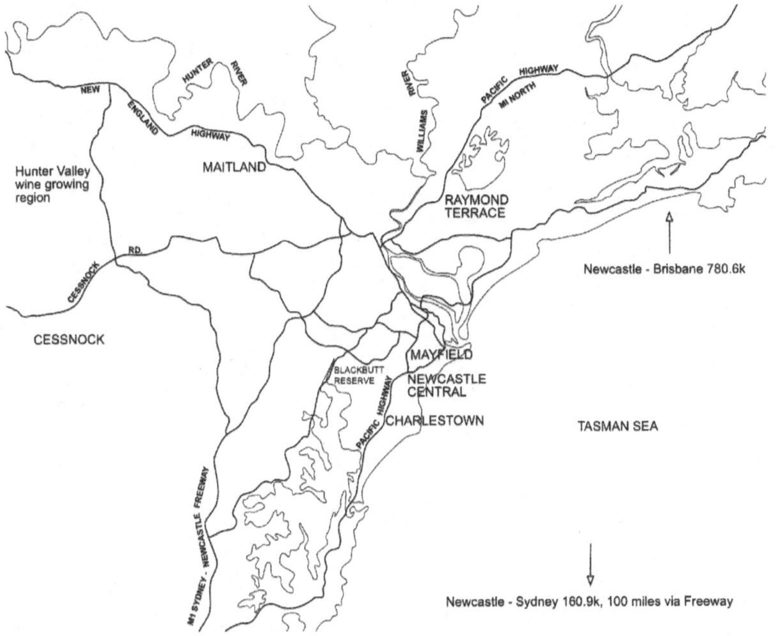

NEW
HUNTER RIVER
ENGLAND
HIGHWAY
WILLIAMS RIVER
PACIFIC HIGHWAY
M1 NORTH
Hunter Valley
wine growing
region
MAITLAND
RAYMOND
TERRACE
CESSNOCK RD.
Newcastle - Brisbane 780.6k
CESSNOCK
MAYFIELD
BLACKBUTT
RESERVE
NEWCASTLE
CENTRAL
PACIFIC HIGHWAY
CHARLESTOWN
TASMAN SEA
M1 SYDNEY - NEWCASTLE FREEWAY
Newcastle - Sydney 160.9k, 100 miles via Freeway

1

Hunter Valley, NSW. Friday April 11th 1975

Liz Farrell slows her car to drive around the bend, conscious the single-track road will take her close to the river's edge. She stops a little further on to take in the sight of the Hunter River which is swollen and raging after days of rain. She shivers and is about to drive off when she hears the roar of a car engine. Looking up she can see a car swerving towards her at speed. The driver and a passenger appear to be waving their arms around. What the hell are they doing? There's no room for the two cars to pass each other.

In a panic Liz puts her car into gear and accelerates towards a gate on her left, in an attempt to move out of the way but the wheels spins on the gravel. *Too late.* The vehicles collide; she can hear the sound of crunching metal and breaking glass echoing in her ears, accompanied by the screech of birds taking flight and someone screaming. She has the sensation of being airborne before landing on something solid. As she lays stunned, she's distracted by the cloudless blue sky above her. She can't remember the last time she looked at the sky like this. She becomes aware that she's on the bonnet of her car; it's edging towards the river and realises her life is in danger. She needs to move before it enters the water. She squeals in pain as she attempts to roll onto her side, something is digging into her forehead causing blood to blur her vision. *Come on Liz*, she chides herself. She makes one last effort to roll clear over the side onto the grass but the pain is excruciating and causes her to lapse into unconsciousness. The car tips and begins to slide into the river; it swirls around for a moment before being borne downstream in the strong current.

2

Newcastle, NSW December 1999

Detective Inspector Frank Bailey is standing outside what appears to be an old mine entrance waiting for the Forensic Anthropologist to emerge. The timber shutters sealing off the mine have rotted over the years but they have now been pulled clear to allow access. He makes a mental note to have one of the team contact the Coal Board to ensure they install a new seal once Forensics have completed their work.

He watches as Detective Sergeant Rachel Sharp approaches him. Newly married, and not long back from her honeymoon, he is still getting used to the change of her surname from Cummings to Sharp and is beginning to wonder if he did the right thing in persuading her to use her married name at work. Already others in the squad have started making little digs about her being 'sharp'.

Rachel has been taking a statement from the man who phoned in about the remains.

'It was the couple's Jack Russell that found the bone,' she says. 'The dog was sniffing around then disappeared off the track. When Bruce Nolan went to find it, the dog re-appeared carrying a bone in its mouth. This bone,' Rachel adds holding up an evidence bag. 'Nolan is a medical student which is how he realised it was a human bone. He followed the dog as it ran back here where he discovered the remains.'

'Okay, if you have all their details go back and tell them they can leave but I'd like them to come into the station to sign a formal statement tomorrow,' Frank says. Rachel nods and moves away.

Although they'd rigged up some battery powered lights, looking around, Frank can see they will soon be running out of daylight hours.

'What can you tell me doc?' he asks when Professor Hayden re-appears a few moments later.

'I can tell you it's the remains of a young woman. I would have to examine what's left of the skeleton in more appropriate conditions to be able to determine her age and roughly how long she's been there. Animals have removed various parts of the skeleton, but the skull and cervical spine have not been moved. There appears to be a number of injuries to the skull, and I can see that the hyoid bone is crushed. The young woman was strangled.'

'Could it have been animals that crushed the bone?'

'No. There is a scarf around the skeleton's neck, which I managed to lift carefully. It's made of one of those almost indestructible synthetic fabrics, and looks like it has been virtually undisturbed since the body was dumped here.'

'So, you believe the young woman was murdered and the body dumped here? Was the scarf used to cause the strangulation?'

'I would say the answer is probably yes to both of your questions. However, from my initial examination I'd say that the scarf was used to cause strangulation and then additional pressure was applied for good measure to ensure death. I don't believe that the scarf on its own would cause such severe crushing to the hyoid.'

'Any idea how long the remains have been there?'

'Initial estimate, I would guess approximately twenty years but I'd need to examine it more closely to give you a more definitive answer.'

'Would there be any chance of getting some DNA from the remains?'

'I can't promise anything, but it's possible.'

'Great. Whoever put her there must know this area well and would've known that it'd be unlikely that the body would be discovered quickly. DNA could help us. Right, Rachel,' Frank says turning to his sergeant who has just returned, 'can you find out if the crime scene techs are on their way. I rang them before we left.'

'Yes sir.'

Young Rachel turns away and checks her mobile for a signal. He knows that like all young ones on the force she carries a mobile phone with her at all times. Something he is reluctant to do, even when he was able to locate where he'd last left it. At five foot four, Rachel is the smallest person on the detective team. When Frank joined the force back in nineteen-seventy-two there had been height restrictions for both men and women – not that there'd been many women. Today, with so-called equal opportunity issues, all that has gone. He'd seen criminals underestimate Rachel and watched as she'd tackled them to the ground with a confidence and fearlessness that many of her male colleagues lacked. He'd recognised her potential and mentored her since she'd moved into the squad from uniforms two years ago. Her recent promotion to detective sergeant was more than deserved.

'There's no signal here sir. I'll have to return to the car.'

'Righto,' he calls back. 'Just make sure they come soon; it'll be getting dark in another few hours.'

Several hours later, as light is beginning to fade, a crime scene technician emerges from the old mine entrance holding up a number of sealed bags. Fortunately, the techs had come equipped with extra strong lights.

'There are several remnants of clothing around the skeleton, probably torn off by animals, as well as the scarf around the neck. And then there is this,' she says holding up a bag which contains what Frank can see is a light-coloured jacket. 'The jacket was lying next to the remains and was covered by the canvas tarpaulin. It appears to be covered in blood splatter, and I found this,' she adds holding up another bag. 'It looks like some kind of leather wallet. It was in one of the pockets of the jacket.'

Back at the forensic lab, Frank and Rachel wait while the technician removes the wallet from the sealed bag. They are hoping that the contents will reveal the identity of the skeleton. He watches as the tech edges a folded piece of paper out of it.

'I think it's one of the old-style driving licences.'

'What's the name on it?' he asks as the tech carefully unfolds it and spreads the licence out on the table.

'Elizabeth May Farrell, date of birth, the thirtieth of May, ninety fifty-three. Address one-five-nine Hill St, Coogee, New South Wales.'

'Elizabeth Farrell. Elizabeth Farrell. Where do I know that name from?' Frank concentrates for a moment and then his face lights up with recognition tinged with shock. 'I've got it,' he says. 'She's the one that went into the Hunter River after a car accident up near Morpeth, back in April seventy-five. Struth, how on earth did she end up in an old mine entrance, miles away. And strangled?'

'Perhaps someone pulled her out of the river, took her back to his place and then later killed her?' Rachel suggests.

'Could be. Hmm. I was involved peripherally on that case. Most of us helped with the search for her. I was stationed at Maitland at the time and my sergeant investigated the accident. I sat in on an interview with the driver of the other vehicle. His wife was badly injured and, in a coma, the first time we dropped into the hospital to see her. She did regain consciousness, but when we were finally able to interview her at the hospital, she couldn't tell us anything.'

'Could her husband have been involved in this at all?'

'I can't see how. Although his car was pretty banged up, he managed to drive his injured wife straight to Maitland hospital and was there for weeks while she was recovering. The Farrell girl went into the river with her car. I wasn't very impressed with the husband though. My sergeant allowed me to sit in on the interview. I thought the man was bunging on an exaggerated act of concern for his wife. He made several references to things about himself. I thought he'd done that in an attempt to gain sympathy from the sarge and deflect attention away from the accident.'

'What sort of things did he say?'

'He made reference to growing up in a local orphanage, being caught in the fifty-five floods as a little kid and his injuries from his service in Vietnam.'

'A *poor me* act then?'

'I thought so at the time. The sarge initially thought the husband might have caused the accident. The couple had been up at Raymond Terrace to finalise things with her lawyer. The wife was due to inherit money from the sale of her parents' property. But then we learned that if she died before probate was completed the husband wouldn't get a penny, so there was no motive for causing the accident where his wife might be killed. That all came later.'

'What? Are you saying he killed his wife after she recovered from her injuries?'

'He attempted to – much later. But that's another story and we weren't involved in the investigation. I'll fill you in on that another time. It doesn't have any relevance to our mystery girl as it didn't happen around here. No, it's more likely to be something like you suggested, or someone who knew Elizabeth Farrell, and had contact with her after she managed to get out of the river. Strangulation is often done in a rage against the victim. I'd say she knew the person who strangled her.'

Turning to the technician Frank says, 'I'd like any DNA you recover from the crime scene evidence processed as soon as possible. Rachel, can you do a search of the records and find the name of the Farrell girl's father. With any luck, the details will all be archived on the computer now. Make contact with him and ask him to come up here as soon as he can. Suggest Monday morning. His name was Charles if I remember correctly. Look him up. I think that was her home address on the licence. Tell him we have possibly recovered some items of his daughter's that we need to be identified. Say nothing about the remains that were found.'

'Yes sir,' Rachel says, turning to leave.

'There is discolouration on the jacket,' the technician continues, 'a tear on the right arm, deterioration probably caused by rodent nibbling and general rotting, but overall, the jacket is in good condition, considering how long it's been there. I would have expected to see further disintegration. It was no doubt protected somewhat by the canvas tarpaulin which again has survived to a remarkable degree. Conditions at the site were fairly dry and sheltered from the elements. I would say it's definitely blood splatters on the jacket. Whether it's the victim's or assailant's blood we won't know until it's tested.'

'How long might it be before you have the results?'

'We've a bit of a backlog at the moment, and with Christmas fast approaching, I couldn't really give you a definite answer on that.'

'Well as soon as you can, thank you. I'll need the things bagged up for the father to look at. I'll send someone to collect them tomorrow morning.'

3

DS Rachel Sharp escorts Charles Farrell into an interview room where Frank is waiting, together with the items they believe belonged to Elizabeth Farrell. He stands to introduce himself.

'I met you briefly many years ago at your mother's farm entrance. A few days after the accident. A sad business,' Frank says.

'Yes,' Charles Farrell replies. 'What's this about? Your Detective Sergeant here told me on the phone that you might have recovered some of Lizzie's belongings. Have they washed up somewhere?'

'In a manner of speaking. Could you look at these items for me Mr. Farrell and tell me whether you recognise any of them?'

Farrell scrutinises the objects in front of him. 'That looks like Lizzie's driving licence wallet,' he says, pointing to the leather wallet. 'I gave that to her as a present when she passed her driving test. And this,' he says peering at the garment in a bag he's picked up, 'looks like a jacket I think she owned.' He turns to another bag, 'Is that a scarf? I don't recognise it, but Lizzie had many scarves, it could've been one of hers.'

'We found this in the wallet,' Frank says, placing the visible driver's licence inside a plastic sleeve in front of Farrell.

'Yes, well that's Lizzie's licence. Where did you find them? The wallet, *jack*et, scarf and licence seem very well preserved for things that have been in water?'

'We thought so too.'

'I don't understand then. Where were they found?'

'I have to inform you that the remains of a young female were found on Saturday afternoon, in an area several miles from the river. These items were found with her. We believe the remains to be those of your daughter.'

'Wha ...what? You've found Lizzie's remains?'

'We believe so.'

'Where was she?'

'We're not at liberty to divulge that at the moment. We have further enquiries to make and we also need to establish, categorically, that the remains are those of your daughter. Can you tell us the name of your daughter's dentist to see if we can make a match with dental records?'

'Golly, um ... our dentist was in Macquarie Street, Sydney. He retired back in the late seventies and I doubt he'd still be alive or that there'd be any surviving records.'

'Could we take a DNA sample from you then? It will be a slower process though. We might not have the results for several weeks.'

'Yes, of course, but if you found these items with the remains, then it is surely going to be Lizzie, isn't it? I just don't understand why she would be found miles from where she went into the river.'

'We are struggling to understand that as well. I seem to recall that your daughter was engaged at the time of the accident and her fiancé was helping with the search?'

'Yes, that's correct.'

'What was his name?'

'Steve Meredith.'

'Do you recall whether Mr. Meredith left the search party at any time?'

'No, I can't really remember. I do know that he went to the other side of the river at one point to take part in the search there. That is, the opposite side of the river to where her car went in. There were other people searching with him though.'

'And you can't recall him being alone during any of those times?'

'I wouldn't know. We searched in different places much of the time. Steve also stayed on when I went back to Sydney. I know a young constable accompanied him when he searched around some of the local properties near the site of the accident. Although we were told it was fruitless, and that Lizzie could not still be alive, Steve didn't want to give up, or leave any stone unturned, so he stayed on with my parents. Why are you asking these questions about Steve?'

Frank ignores his question. 'Are you still in touch with him Mr. Farrell?'

'I haven't spoken to him for many years. He moved to Brisbane. The last contact I had with him was when he rang me to let me know he was getting married. That was about five years after Lizzie died. You don't think he has anything to do with this do you? Steve was completely devastated by Lizzie's death. He sold his catering business shortly after and moved to Brisbane.'

'Hmm. Did he give you a reason for moving away so quickly?'

'He said he couldn't face carrying on with the business without Lizzie. They had built much of it together, although Steve had initially started it with his mother before he met Lizzie. She was studying at university when she went to work with Steve at his new fledgling company. After she was gone, he just felt there was nothing there for him anymore.'

'Do you have any contact details for Mr. Meredith?'

'I had a phone number and address for him, it's at home somewhere in an old address book. I don't know if it would still be valid. It was twenty years ago. I don't even know if he still lives in Brisbane. He could be anywhere.'

'You wouldn't know his date of birth, would you?'

'I know it was in February. I can't remember the date. But he was four years older than Lizzie, so that would mean he was born in nineteen forty-nine. Is that helpful?'

'Yes, thank you Mr. Farrell. Could you dig out that old phone number and address you had for him when you get home, just in case they're still current, and let Detective Sharp have them? I would also ask you not to attempt to get in contact with Mr. Meredith or speak to anyone in the press about this. If you could wait here a moment, Detective Sharp will return to take a DNA sample from you.'

Frank stands and shakes Charles Farrell's hand before he and Rachel leave the room. As they're walking along the corridor, Rachel says, 'Well he seemed genuinely puzzled about his daughter's remains being found away from the river.'

'Yes, I don't think the killer was aware of the wallet in the jacket pocket. It's not very bulky and may have gone unnoticed. I don't think we were ever meant to know the identity of the victim. My money would be on the fiancé being involved somehow. We'll have to check him out and collect a DNA sample from him.'

'Do you want me to check with Queensland Motor Registry to see if he has a current licence, and/or a registered vehicle?'

'I'll do that while you take the DNA sample,' Frank says and turns towards his office.

4

At his home in Sandgate, a coastal suburb of Brisbane, Steve Meredith hears about the remains of an unidentified young woman found in old mine workings in Newcastle, New South Wales, on the ABC national evening news. He switches off the radio, not wishing to hear any more. He is about to pick up his car keys from the kitchen countertop when the doorbell rings. He opens the door to find two suited men standing on his doorstep. *Cops* he guesses even before they open their mouths. He panics for a moment, worried they have come to give him bad news about his son or daughter, but then relaxes. He'd spoken to his daughter fifteen minutes ago, and he'd just spoken to the parents of his son's friend and told them he'd be on his way soon. Perhaps it's about his mother? But surely it would uniform police who would come to see him if that was the case.

'What can I do for you gentlemen?' he asks, a little apprehensively.

'We'd like to ask you a few questions sir,' says one of the men. 'I am Detective Sergeant Ryan from the Brisbane CIB and this is Detective Inspector Bailey from the Newcastle,

New South Wales Police.'

'You're a long way off your base,' Steve says looking at Bailey. 'Why have you come to see me?'

'If you wouldn't mind sir, we'd rather talk inside,' Detective Ryan stresses.

'Fine,' Steve says and turns, leaving the door open for the men to follow. He takes them into the lounge and waves an arm towards the couch. 'I can't be too long though as I have to go and collect my son from his friend's house. So, how can I help you?'

'You were engaged to a Miss Elizabeth Farrell back in nineteen seventy-five when she had her car accident?' DI Bailey begins.

'Yes, that's right. Why are you asking about Liz? Have you found her?'

'Why would you think that Mr. Meredith?' DI Bailey asks.

'Well, you're asking about her for starters, and I was told her body might have snagged on something underwater that one day might release her and that she'd come floating up to the surface.' Steve shudders at the thought. 'Is that what's happened?'

'No, Mr. Meredith. But we have identified some of Miss Farrell's belongings. Could you tell us about your involvement in the search for her back in seventy-five?'

'What do you mean you've identified some of her belongings?'

'Could you just answer the question sir, regarding your involvement in the search for Miss Farrell?'

This was the last thing Steve thought he'd ever be asked to talk about again. Taking him back to the horrors of those ten days. Just thinking about it has brought back a sick feeling in the pit of his stomach and flashes of images that have plagued him for years. He shakes his head to clear them before speaking.

'Well, after checking she wasn't at the Maitland Hospital where the casualties from the other car were taken, we went back to Charles Farrell's parents' house. Liz's grandparents had a dairy farm along the river there. That's where she'd been heading that day. We helped in the search for her along the river and in properties along that stretch of road, although there aren't many houses there. With one of your lot, I visited a woman in a house before the bend in Nobles Road. She'd been in Newcastle the day of the accident and hadn't heard anything. But she let us search her paddocks in case Liz had crawled there. We also looked through the old Fallon Farm. The house was a burnt-out shell but there were a number of outbuildings further into the property. They were all securely locked with additional old padlocks so there's no way Liz called have crawled into any of those buildings. And we found no sign of her in any of their paddocks. Next, we searched the pig arm between the old Fallon farm and Liz's grandparents.'

'And after searching on that side of the river, what did you do?'

'I went across to the other side of the river. After we exhausted all those areas, I helped in the search further downstream, beyond where the Hunter and Williams Rivers meet.'

'How long did you take part in the search?'

'Ten days. I even hired a boat at one point and we

cruised up and down the river looking for any sign of her. But there was nothing. Nothing at all. I watched as they brought her car to the surface a few days after the accident, but as you will know from your records, she wasn't in there either. You know the windscreen on Liz's car was missing right?'

'Yes,' Frank says nodding.

'We were told that the current would have swept her out of the car and downriver.'

'And *you* never found anything, no personal items belonging to Miss Farrell?'

'No. Nothing. Liz's handbag was found in her car as far as I recall. And her small suitcase was still in the boot. The night before we'd been in charge of catering at a wine tasting at one of the big vineyards. We'd stayed at a nearby motel. She wouldn't have had any other belongings with her, so what do you mean when you say you found some of her belongings?'

Ignoring his question Bailey asks, 'How were you feeling throughout this search?'

Steve snorts. Did the detective think he was some kind of therapist?

'What do you mean, how was I feeling? I was bloody devastated! And angry.'

'Why were you angry Mr. Meredith?'

'I believed that the bastard who was driving the other car was responsible for the accident. The police sergeant who was in charge of the investigation got it all wrong. And he wouldn't listen to me.'

The detective nods as though he knows about the scene he caused at the hospital when he argued with the sergeant.

'Can you tell us why you sold your business and moved to Brisbane shortly after the accident?'

'Without Liz there with me my heart wasn't in the business anymore, and I couldn't focus. We had excellent staff and bookings stretching into the following year. It was a great little business, so I put feelers out to an agent and he quickly found me a cash buyer.'

'You did leave rather abruptly though sir. From records we've been able to put together you moved up here immediately after the inquest. Why was that?' Detective Ryan asks.

Steve sighs. He may as well be honest with them.

'To tell you the truth I was having nightmares. I kept seeing images of Liz trapped underwater or bobbing along out in the Tasman Sea somewhere; her body being attacked by sharks or disappearing bit by bit as other creatures nibbled away at her. I thought a fresh start up here might help me shake off the nightmares and that before I ran the business into the ground with my neglect, I should sell it. But on top of that, I was very tempted to go after that Miller bloke and give him a good hiding, so I thought it was best to get right away. I didn't go to the inquest, because I didn't trust myself to be around him.'

'And did you manage to shake off the nightmares when you moved up here?' Ryan asks.

'No,' Steve says shaking his head. 'They carried on for another year or so.'

'Before moving to Brisbane, you lived in Sydney. Did you grow up there? Go to school there?' Bailey asks.

'Yes, I went to school in Parramatta. I always lived in

Sydney. Why do you ask?'

'Just checking all the facts sir. We'd like to take a DNA sample from you Mr. Meredith, if that's okay with you? And could we have the contact details for your mother?'

'Yes, but why would you want a DNA sample from me or need to contact my mother?'

'To eliminate you from our enquiries sir. As we told you, we have found some of Miss Farrell's belongings. Your DNA may be on them, as well as others, so we need be able to isolate your DNA.'

'Okay then. I've got nothing to hide, but I want your assurances that the sample will be destroyed once you've finished looking into this matter.'

5

Frank sits at his desk and examines the crime scene photographs taken where the skeletal remains of the young woman was found. He sighs. There are more questions than they have answers for on this case. It has been confirmed that the remains belonged to a young woman between the age of twenty to twenty-five years old who had not given birth and could have been lying there for as long as twenty-five years. That fitted with Elizabeth Farrell. The height of the woman was approximately five foot four inches. They'd need to check Elizabeth Farrell's height with her father.

Professor Hayden believes the injuries to the skull would have been sufficient to cause death, but someone decided to strangle her to make sure. If the remains belong to Elizabeth Farrell, why dump her body in that location? It had to be someone who knew the area well to be aware of those old mine workings, so far out of the way from the public view. That didn't fit with Steve Meredith. He grew up in Sydney. Frank returns the photographs to the file folder as a knock at his office door interrupts his thoughts.

'We have some new information sir,' Rachel Sharp says.

'Tell me.'

'I've been talking to Steve Meredith's mother. It turns out that Meredith had an uncle, who was a miner. He lived in Cardiff, not that far from the dump site. He used to come up to stay with his aunt, uncle and cousins occasionally in school holidays when he was young. The family no longer live there; the uncle transferred to mining work in the Blue Mountains, outside Sydney, back in the early sixties. But that means Meredith could well have been familiar with the area of Blackbutt Reserve. He would've only been an adolescent at the time, but old enough to remember a secret hidey-hole.'

'Interesting, that brings him back nicely into the frame. I was just puzzling over how a Sydney boy could be connected to the site.'

'That's not the most interesting new development though. The DNA evidence from the skeletal remains has come back. There is no DNA match between the remains and Mr. Farrell. He's not the biological father of the victim.'

'Farrell's not the biological father? Hmm. I think we need another word with him and a chat with his wife.' He looks at his watch and makes a snap decision. 'If we head off to Sydney now, we should catch him as he arrives home from work,' Frank says standing

'You want me to accompany you to Sydney?'

'Yes, of course.'

'Andy and I were planning on going to the pictures tonight, but oh well, just let me make a phone call and I'll be with you sir.'

They make good time on the freeway. The heavier traffic

is heading out of Sydney, commuters returning from a day's work in the city. Something Frank would not ever contemplate doing. The occasional long journey was fine, but to do it every day. A nightmare!

Frank remembers journeys to and from Newcastle to Sydney with his family as a youngster before the freeway was built, where they had to travel on the twisting and winding old Pacific Highway. Journeys that could sometimes take up to five hours in peak times, holiday periods or the occasional Sunday – with "these bloody Sunday drivers" – as his father used to say. The family would play endless games of 'I Spy'. Bored with this on one journey Frank began studying the Sydney bus and train timetables along with the Sydney Street directory which his father kept on the floor under the driver's seat. Frank would choose a destination from either the bus or train timetable and follow its path in the street directory, thinking one day he might like to visit these places. It developed into a compulsive habit when they journeyed down to Sydney to see his maternal grandparents once a month.

Gifted with a photographic memory Frank accidentally memorised all the timetables and routes. When he was a probationary-police constable he let slip his knowledge one day to someone who was trying to work out how to travel to an unknown suburban destination in Sydney. Soon he became famous for his ability to reel off travel information and fellow police officers or administrative staff would either phone him or approach him requesting information. "Ask Frank Bailey, he'll know," they would always be told.

Frank doesn't think he would know now. He is long out of practise, retiring from that unrewarded service when he became a detective. Also, there's the Eastern Suburbs railway line that opened in seventy-nine. That would have changed bus routes surely?

His memory hasn't totally failed him though as he winds his way towards Coogee. There doesn't seem to be many road changes. He passes a bus and recalls that was one that used to go into the city and down to Circular Quay from Coogee. They used to leave Coogee every …

He shakes his head to clear the trivial travel data from his brain and focuses back on the case. It is just starting to get dark as they make the final approach to Coogee. Frank breaks the long silence of the journey and says, 'Of course, there is one other possibility with regard to the victim.'

'What's that sir?'

'That it's not Elizabeth Farrell at all.'

'But who else could it be?'

'Unfortunately, that is the conundrum. Perhaps we should start searching missing person case files back in the seventies. We know the timeline must start from April seventy-five onwards, because of Elizabeth Farrell's belongings. Maybe someone found her things at the edge of the river, because they don't look like they had been immersed in water. Perhaps one of the search party picked them up and pocketed them and they became mixed up with another crime later. It's the blood on the jacket that bothers me. Whose is it? When we receive the full DNA results, we might find those answers. In the meantime, let's see what Mr. Farrell has to say.'

6

'This is an aptly named street,' Rachel says, as they pull up outside the Farrell residence in Hill Street.

'Hmm,' Frank replies as he climbs out of the car. He'd certainly shift some of his excess pounds if he had to walk up that hill every day to reach his house. He doesn't think he could jog it like Rachel, who runs around Newcastle's Hilly Streets regularly.

He knocks on the front door and after some delay Charles Farrell opens it, looking surprised.

'Good evening, Mr. Farrell, I wonder if we might have a word with you and your wife.'

'I'm afraid that might be a little difficult with my wife, Detective Bailey, she passed away from cancer just over a year ago,' he tells them, his voice choking up a little.

'Oh, I'm very sorry to hear that sir. You didn't mention it.'

'No, I realised that after I returned to Sydney. I was so shocked to see Lizzie's belongings and hear what you said, it didn't even occur to me. It was only when I arrived home and remembered that I wouldn't be able to share the news with Kate, my wife, that I recalled I hadn't mentioned it. I still forget that she's no longer here some days and catch myself thinking I must tell her about something. It's not easy after sharing your life with someone for so many years.'

'No, I can imagine.'

'Anyway, come in, sorry for keeping you on the doorstep.'

They follow Charles Farrell through to the kitchen and on to a large double width lounge/dining-room with two sets of sliding doors leading onto a partially covered terrace.

'If you'd like to take a seat here, I'll bring you some iced water. I'm sure you could do with some after that journey from Newcastle.'

'Thank you,' Rachel says nodding.

Outside on the terrace, Frank can see two sets of tables and chairs. One large dining set under cover that are flanked by clear blinds. There is a smaller table and chair set on the open side. *If you fancy sitting in the sun and risking skin cancer.*

Both sets of doors leading to the terrace are open with fly-screen security doors preventing insects coming into the house. So sensible. Frank has no time for the trendies who won't have fly screens "because they're not attractive". Who wants to be bitten alive by mozzies or constantly have flies buzzing around the room?

There is a lovely cool breeze drifting into the room and he forgets where he is for a minute.

'There must be a glorious view of the sea during the day from here,' Rachel says. 'I can just make out the lights of a large ship passing along the coast.'

'Yes, it is rather a wonderful view,' Farrell says, placing a jug of water on the table with some glasses. 'That's why we had the doors and terrace added so we could sit out there soaking it up. These were all individual rooms when we first bought the house back in the fifties, but in the eighties, we took the walls out, opened up all this space and built the terrace. All to take advantage of the view. There used to be an internal staircase leading downstairs to a large play area for the children, but we've turned that into a self-contained flat now. My son Robbie lives down there with his wife – although they join me for meals most nights up here. Anyway, how can I help you detectives?'

'Sir?' Rachel says nudging Frank.

'Sorry, I was miles away. Mr. Farrell, we have received some new evidence today that we'd like to ask you about. Is it possible that you're not the biological father of Elizabeth?' Frank asks him, getting straight to the point.

'What do you mean?'

'It's a bit of a delicate question. Is it possible that Elizabeth was fathered by another man, someone other than you?'

Farrell looks shocked to be asked such a question. He shakes his head vehemently. 'Absolutely not. My wife was a … my wife had not been *intimate* with anyone before we were married, if you take my meaning. Why are you asking that?'

'Because we have received DNA results from the remains we found and it does not match your DNA.'

'Well, it can't be Lizzie then,' Farrell says without blinking.

7

'We have considered the possibility that the remains might not be of your daughter,' Frank tells Mr. Farrell

'It's the only possibility. I can assure you that my wife never had any intimate relations with anyone other than me.'

Frank doesn't know how anyone can be so sure about such matters. With the number of cases he's had to deal with over the years, cheating partners were a common thread that ran through many of their investigations. He'd never personally cheated on anyone but he knew many of his colleagues had, something that always shocked him when he became privy to that type of information.

'Do you still have any of your wife's belongings that we could test for DNA, just so that we can absolutely rule out that possibility? We have to explore all avenues in order to identify this young woman,' he asks Farrell.

'Yes, I have some of Kate's things. I haven't been able to bring myself to throw anything away as yet. It was the same with Lizzie after we lost her. Kate and I hung on to her things for years before we finally cleared out her stuff.'

'Could we have something for testing?'

'I think it will be a waste of your time and money but you're welcome to take something. What would you like? I have Kate's clothes, shoes, or a hairbrush with some of her hair still caught in it. I even have her last toothbrush.'

'The toothbrush and hairbrush would be ideal thank you. We're very sorry to be asking you for this, but I hope you understand we need to be absolutely sure that they're not Elizabeth's remains. A possible theory we have is that one of the search party picked up your daughter's belongings that might've been flung out of her vehicle after the impact, landing in long grass or a bush. They then took them home and that person was later involved in a crime that connects to our victim.'

'That sounds more likely to me,' Farrell says. 'Curious though, that they would throw Lizzie's things in with the remains you found. Maybe to put you off the scent.'

'No, I think whoever dumped the body believed in all likelihood it would never be discovered. What height was your daughter by the way?'

'Bout five foot five. Does that fit with the remains you found?'

'Approximately.' *Give or take an inch.*

Charles Farrell brings them the two items requested and although Farrell has them both in clear plastic bags, Rachel places them inside additional evidence bags.

'Thanks for the water, Mr. Farrell and your wife's belongings. We'll return them as soon as we have completed the tests,' Frank says.

As they are about to leave, Frank has a further thought.

'You wouldn't still have anything of Elizabeth's, would you? Something that we could test for DNA?'

'My wife kept a couple of soft toys Lizzie had as a toddler. They were in Lizzie's room when we finally cleared it out. They've never been washed as far as I know. Would one of those be any use? I still have them.'

'One of those would be ideal, thank you very much.'

The DNA results on what they believe to be Elizabeth Farrell's jacket, wallet and driver's licence finally come in, together with the results of Steve Meredith's DNA. Meredith's DNA is on the jacket and some further traces of his DNA are on the scarf tied around the victim's throat. Frank's chief believes it is enough to have Meredith extradited from Queensland to New South Wales. Frank doesn't agree, as there are other more substantial unknown DNA samples on the same items and he suggests another session of questioning in Brisbane, but the chief insists, so he processes the paper work. They are still waiting on the results of DNA testing on Elizabeth Farrell's soft toy and the mother's belongings. It is unlikely they are going to receive these before Christmas. Frank looks at the results before him:

- Jacket – a DNA match to Steve Meredith and the victim. Two unknown DNAs, but one a familial match to Charles Farrell, which includes the blood, so is likely to be his daughter's DNA.
- Wallet – three DNAs, one matching Charles Farrell, one a familial match, again no doubt the daughter Elizabeth. That would fit with what he said about purchasing it for her. The other DNA was likely the person who handled it when Farrell purchased it.

- Driver's licence - three DNA traces. One a familial match to Charles Farrell. Again, no doubt his daughter. Two unknowns. One possibly from the person who issued it.
- Scarf – Four DNA samples. One matched the victim. One familial trace match to Charles Farrell, probably Elizabeth Farrell again. One unknown that matched one from the Jacket and tarpaulin and one DNA trace matching Steve Meredith.
- Canvas Tarpaulin – Six DNAs. The victim, three familial matches to the victim, and one unknown – the same unknown that was on the jacket and scarf, plus one trace DNA with a familial match from Charles Farrell.

None of the unknown DNAs are a match for anyone listed in their data bases. Frank notes that both the awning, jacket, and scarf have DNA matches from a party other than Steve Meredith. In fact, the scarf is riddled with this other DNA, whereas the DNA on the scarf from Steve Meredith is a miniscule trace by comparison. Similarly, DNA on the scarf, and tarpaulin, which is likely to be Elizabeth Farrell, is also a very small trace.

The victim can't be Elizabeth Farrell. She is likely to still be at the bottom of the Hunter somewhere or became 'shark food' as his old Sergeant had put it. But somehow this victim is connected to her. It's more likely that there is another perpetrator involved. Perhaps the perp had an accomplice in the shape of Steve Meredith? Or maybe it's simply that evidence has been contaminated with the jacket lying across the body under the tarpaulin at some point.

Extradition between states is a lengthy process and Frank would rather Meredith spoke to them voluntarily. It will be Christmas in less than a week which will cause yet further delays over the holiday break. He checks his watch. It's gone 6pm. Hopefully Meredith will be home. Opening the file, Frank picks up the phone and dials Meredith's number, who answers after a few rings.

'Steve Meredith?'

'Yes?'

'It's Detective Inspector Frank Bailey here, from Newcastle. I met you the other week in Brisbane.'

'Yes, I remember. What can I do for you?'

'I was wondering if you'd be willing to come down to Newcastle for a further chat with us. We have some results that we'd like to discuss with you. It'd be very helpful if you could do that.'

'I have a business to run, although we'll be shutting down over Christmas. It'd be impossible to come down before then. I'm travelling down to New South Wales between Christmas and New Year to visit my mother in Orange. I wasn't planning to come through Newcastle, but I could travel across to see you then. Do you have some further news on Liz?'

Ignoring Meredith's question, Frank says, 'That would be great. I'll give you my number and when you know what day might be convenient for you, can you give me a call?'

'Okay, yes. You can't tell me over the phone what this is about? You mentioned results?'

'There's some evidence I'd like you to look at and further questions I need to ask you. That's all I can tell you at the moment. It's better that we meet in person.'

Frank reels off his number and ends the call wishing Meredith a Happy Christmas.

Christmas. As usual the celebrations in his life will be brief. The obligatory Christmas dinner with his sister and her family in Cessnock, pleading work as an excuse for an early departure. Back home for a quiet relaxing read and a whisky or two. He has a book on Australia's involvement in the Second World War to delve into if he's lucky and no more bodies turn up.

They have scoured Missing Persons' reports from as far back as April seventy-five. All missing persons in the Newcastle area in the age range of their victim have been resolved. However, there are quite a large number from the Sydney area. So many that it would take them months to look into all of them. With the millennium approaching there's also the possibility that they could lose all the data if doom and gloom predictions are correct and there is a worldwide computer crash. They've printed out all of the relevant files to have a hard paper copy in case.

Could the victim be from Sydney? Even back in the seventies someone could've driven it in under three hours at the right time of day. Someone from Sydney who knows the area well. Someone like Steve Meredith?

8

Steve Meredith turns up at the station on 27th December for his meeting with Frank. DNA samples from Mrs. Farrell and her daughter Elizabeth have still not come in. Frank is also waiting on further results from the tech lab. Everything had been laboriously slow in the run up to Christmas with excuses such as, 'everyone is waiting for results, and you'll just have to wait your turn. It's not as if you're talking about a fresh body that needs urgent investigation.' As if this victim is less important than others.

'Thanks for coming Mr. Meredith. We'll be taping this interview. You are not under arrest and are free to go at any time, but anything you do say might be taken down and later used in evidence against you.'

'Used in evidence against me? Used in evidence against me for what? What're you on about?'

'Let's just get started, shall we?'

'No, no, no, no, no,' Meredith says shaking his head. 'You need to tell me what this is all about first.'

'I'll get to that, don't worry. First of all, I would like to ask—'

'Stop right there. I'm not going to answer any questions until you answer mine.'

'We're looking into the place where Elizabeth Farrell's belongings were found.'

'Right, and where was that?'

'Blackbutt Reserve. Are you familiar with that area of Newcastle?

'Can't say that I've ever heard of it.'

'We've received confirmation from your uncle's family outside Sydney, that when you used to stay with them at their Cardiff property, they took you there on several occasions.'

'I went to lots of places with them. You can't expect me to remember all of them. I was only a kid.'

'Yes, but this place is very distinctive. Very dense bushland.'

'I do remember some bush walks, but I couldn't tell you what they were called, or even remember where they were,' Meredith says puzzled. 'Are you telling me this is where Liz's belongings were found?'

'I have to tell you that the hidden skeletal remains of an unidentified young woman were found in the Blackbutt Reserve bushland. And yes, items belonging to Elizabeth Farrell were found with these remains.'

'What? How could that be? Where is this place? Is it near the river where Liz went in? Was it Liz you found?'

'We don't believe the remains are those of Miss Farrell. The place where we found them and her belongings is a number of miles from the river. From DNA results we have to hand, it's more than likely that the remains are of another young woman, whose identity is as yet unknown to us. Somehow though, there's a connection to your fiancée.'

'How? I mean, what did you find in this place that belonged to Liz?'

'For the benefit of the recording, I am now showing Mr. Meredith a jacket, a wallet, a scarf and a driving licence,' Frank says, reaching down and lifting the bagged items up on to the table.

'Do you recognise any of these items Mr. Meredith?'

After scanning the items, Meredith says, 'That looks like the jacket Liz was wearing on the last morning that I saw her.'

'Are you sure of that?'

'Yes, pretty sure … or one just like it. I remember giving her a hug and commenting that the jacket was not going to provide her with much warmth. It was pretty cold that morning – the one when I last saw Liz. Is that blood on the jacket? Liz's blood?'

'We believe so. What about the other items?'

'I think that's the wallet she kept her licence in. That's clearly her licence as well. I don't recognise this scarf though,' Meredith says leaning over and having a good look. 'Liz wasn't wearing one that morning. She did wear scarves, but I've never seen that one. It doesn't look like the type of scarf Liz would wear.'

'What do you mean by that?'

'Liz liked silk scarves. That doesn't look like silk. She had one or two cotton ones she wore with sporty type clothes in the summer, plus she had a few woollen scarves for the winter. It doesn't look like cotton or wool either. Liz generally wore clothes made of natural products, like cotton, linen, wool, silk. She said that many of the new man-made fibres irritated her skin. She dressed very plainly, but stylishly. No frills or fancy things. That scarf looks a bit cheap and garish for her tastes.'

'I see. So, you don't recognise the scarf at all? It's not one you have ever seen any other young woman wearing?'

'Look, I see women wearing scarves all the time. I don't take any bloody notice of them. I only know what Liz's tastes were because she mentioned her liking for silk scarves. She once made me look at the fabric and feel the softness of it. That's why I can see that it's not silk.'

'Okay, I get the picture. Moving on, I have to inform you Mr. Meredith that your DNA was found on this jacket which you have identified as Miss Farrell's.'

Meredith pauses for a moment and then shoots back with, 'I can understand that. I just told you I hugged her on the morning she left me and she was wearing a similar jacket. We had more than a hug actually. We had a lingering kiss and I held her for some time.'

Frank clears his throat. 'We also found traces of your DNA on this scarf that you cannot identify.'

Meredith seems genuinely nonplussed. He leans back in his chair and runs his hand through his thick brown hair. 'I can't explain that. I've absolutely no idea how that could've happened. As I told you I've never seen that scarf before.'

'Can you tell me whether you went to the area of Blackbutt Reserve at any time during the search for your fiancée, or at any time in the following five years?'

'No, I didn't have time to be prancing about anywhere else while searching for Liz. All my efforts went into looking for her either in the river, on the river banks or checking properties. If I've ever been to this Blackbutt Reserve, the only time it could ever have been was with my cousins back in the fifties or maybe early sixties. I don't even know where it is. And you know I moved to Brisbane soon after Liz's accident. You're not looking at me for this business about the remains in this place you keep asking about, are you? And what about them? Was the girl murdered? You said the remains were hidden? Where were they hidden?'

'All I can tell you is that the remains were found in Blackbutt Reserve. And yes, the girl was murdered. We know that because we have the main murder weapon.'

'What did the murderer use, a gun, or knife or something else?'

'I'm afraid I can't tell you anymore Mr. Meredith. Thank you very much for coming in. You've been very helpful. You're free to go.'

Meredith narrows his eyes at Frank.

'You should be talking to that Miller bloke, or his wife who was in the car with him,' Meredith says. 'I bet you he's got something to do with this. He was the only one on the scene when the accident occurred. We were told his wife was in a coma, so she wouldn't have taken Liz's stuff. But I wouldn't have put it past Miller to have picked up some of Liz's things.'

'We are looking into that possibility, but it could have just as easily have been someone who took part in the search who picked up Miss Farrell's belongings. Why would *you* suggest Miller in particular?'

'Because we know he lied about how the accident happened.'

'When you say 'we' who are you referring to?'

'Liz's father, Charles Farrell. He and I both know that Miller lied about the details of the accident. Liz's mother Kate, plus Charles's mother and father, Liz's grandparents, also agreed with us.'

Meredith pauses for a moment looking at Frank. 'I don't know if you've read up on the case but Miller claimed Liz was speeding. Liz would never, ever have been speeding along that road. She never drove over the speed limit anyway. She could be quite irritating like that. I used to get annoyed with her sometimes when I wanted her to go faster if we were running late for an event, and she was driving. She'd never put her foot down. I drove down that road where the accident happened with her several times. She always drove it slowly. Very slowly. The pig farmer next door to the Farrell's dairy farm used to allow his few cows out to graze along the edge of the river. Liz wouldn't have taken the risk.'

'Sergeant Pryce from Maitland Police thoroughly investigated the accident at the time. I know because I worked with him briefly on it. He believed Mr. Miller's version of events; the skid marks in the gravel and the accident debris seemed to back up his statement.'

'I told that idiot sergeant that Miller was lying. He should've taken a closer look at everything and listened to Charles and me.'

'Perhaps. You can rest assured that we'll be looking at every possibility, which is why we wished to speak to you. Thanks again for coming in. Detective Constable Tyler will show you out,' Frank says indicating the silent, note-taking young man seated beside him.

'I'm telling you; you're looking in the wrong place. If Miller lied about the accident, then he could've lied about other things as well. Okay, well if that's all you want, I'm off now,' Meredith says standing. 'I hope I won't be seeing you again, unless it's to give me or Liz's family some news about her.'

9

On New Year's Eve, Frank decides to pay a visit to 'Miller's Motors' on Griffith Street. He is greeted by a cheerful young man sporting an ear-to-ear grin. 'Morning sir, can I tempt you into purchasing a car for the New Year? Correction, the new Millennium,' he says bouncing up to Frank.

'No, afraid not. I'm looking for Martin Miller,' he says flashing his identification.

The grin on the young man's face fades, but he remains respectful and polite. 'I'm sorry sir, but Mr. Miller is currently away on his honeymoon.'

'Oh, missed the big occasion, did I? When did he marry and where is he?'

'He married a few weeks ago. He's on one of the islands off the Barrier Reef somewhere. I'm not really sure where. I do know that he won't be back until about the middle of January.'

'Long honeymoon.'

'Well, what can I say?'

'Best not to say anything I would imagine.'

With that avenue closed for the moment Frank returns

to his office to look at the evidence again. Miller would keep. He's virtually dismissed the idea of Meredith being involved. The evidence against him is tenuous at best, and would never be sufficient to mount a solid case against him. They haven't released full details to the public, and Frank is keen for a new press release to be given in the New Year. It might jog someone's memory and bring in fresh evidence or witnesses.

The computers survive into the new millennium. There had been a lot of scaremongering and panicking for no reason. And a waste of bloody paper for all the files that were printed out 'just in case', Frank thinks. He finally has all the results from the lab. The victim definitely had bleached blonde hair at the time of her death. Strands were found all over the scarf and some odd ones still attached to the skull.

The list of missing Sydney women in the time frame have been reduced taking out the non-Caucasians. Now they've been able to whittle the list down to three; three bottle blondes. Three was a much more manageable number. He's put Rachel on to it, who has returned from her two weeks off over Christmas and New Year. If it had been up to him, Frank would have reduced her time off. Rachel is very thorough when she's on duty but she and Tyler are overly fond of their *life* outside the force. Not too keen on putting in the extra hours like him. Especially Tyler.

Frank can't blame them. They at least have a *life* and someone who shares their bed. Unlike him. He shares his bed with a book. Sad, but true. A book that he carefully places on the spare side of the double bed each night when he turns off the lamp.

He'd received the lamp as a Christmas present two years ago from his sister. Its base took up virtually all the space on his bedside cabinet. He kept meaning to replace it with a smaller one – or buy a bigger bedside cabinet, but hasn't got around to either option. A few times he'd tried balancing his book beside the lamp, but no sooner had he turned the light off than he heard the book crash to the floor. Each time he'd turned the lamp back on and leapt out of bed worried he'd damaged the book, examining it carefully before he was reassured his precious volume had survived intact. He'd soon abandoned the bedside cabinet.

Next, he tried leaning over and placing his current read carefully on the floor, but the effort of stretching over (his bed being quite high off the ground) caused a painful crack, felt like he had pulled a muscle or two and he spent many subsequent hours in discomfort. To top it off, when he staggered out of bed to relieve his bladder in the middle of the night, he slipped on the book causing minor damage to both himself and the book. The damage to the book upset him more. His body could mend.

He came to the conclusion that the only safe place for his books was beside him after his bedtime read. He seldom encroached the spare side of the bed after so many years of being very careful not to disturb his wife. Ex-wife. He'd never forgotten the first time she said, 'Can't we buy a bigger bed Frank, I don't like to be touched when I'm in bed.' Considering she didn't like to be touched either in, or out of bed, in addition to the fact that they were *married*, he'd thought her statement rather ironic.

Two years into the marriage she'd announced one day that she was 'finished with all that sex stuff'. *Sex?* He thought he'd been making love to her, but it soon became apparent, from the very first night after taking their marriage vows, that she was not very aroused or responsive. In secret, he'd skimmed books at the library after returning from their honeymoon, hoping to find ways of improving matters, all to no avail.

They'd stuck it out for four long childless years, two of them without physical contact (apart from a peck on the cheek each morning), clinging to their respective sides of the bed, until she informed him one day that she'd found the love of her life and was leaving him. *I thought I was the love of your life when we married* were Frank's immediate thoughts when she'd made her declaration.

He was strangely relieved when she told him that it wasn't a man she was leaving him for, but a woman. When she asked him to sit down so she could explain, he believed she was going to lecture him on his shortcomings as a lover. But she explained that she'd been fighting her sexuality most of her life. She'd always been worried about what other people might think if she announced her preference for women.

'Now I don't care about that. I should never have married you. I only ended up making both of our lives miserable. I thought I'd be fine with a man I loved, and I have always loved you. Like a brother,' she'd clarified.

He'd told he understood, desperately wanting to show that he was a *modern man*, but he hadn't really. He'd worked with women on the force who openly declared their sexuality but he'd never really talked to them about their lives and feelings.

They parted amicably, sold the house and split the furniture. He inherited the bed. For his new house he chose a semi-rural timber clad Federation down a long quiet lane outside the city. The new house is isolated and peaceful, just as he desires. Of a night, as he sits reading, and sipping the odd whisky, the only sounds he can usually hear are the creaking settlement of timbers, relaxing into the evening after a hot day in the sun.

Frank has attempted a few relationships since the marriage split. In his younger years he'd wanted children, but now thinks it's probably too late. He doesn't want to marry again so is quite content to go home alone, which doesn't seem to suit most of the women he's met. There's no one in his life right now. All his energies are directed towards work. He knows other members of the force consider him a 'sad bastard.' And he thinks maybe he is with minor declines in his health; the odd grey strands sprouting amongst his dark hair and the excess weight he carries around his middle. He reassures himself he's not *fat* and that it's only a little extra weight on the odd occasions when he examines himself in the full-length mirror behind his wardrobe door. He promises himself he'll cut back on the unhealthy food, do more gardening and take walks but with his busy schedules it never happens.

He was forced to take action recently though. Several months back he could hear a high-pitched ringing sound. Convinced it was an electrical fault, he scoured the house in search of the culprit, but found nothing. The same sound followed him into work the next day and everyone else swore they heard nothing. When the same loud ringing continued that evening and in the days which followed, he eventually made a doctor's appointment.

'Tinnitus, Frank!' the doctor diagnosed gleefully, patting him on the back as though it was a great achievement. 'Your ears are clear, so it's probably down to your age.'

Age, I'm not old! I'm only forty-eight this year!

'Curable?' Frank asked. The answer was negative.

The Tinnitus diagnosis on top of the 'senior moments' he keeps having recently are beginning to worry him. He wastes precious time and energy searching for things some days. The mobile phone is the worst. Having been issued one for his work, he constantly forgets where he's put it or to remember to charge it. It has a knack of disappearing both at the office, in the car or at home. He admitted to Rachel recently that it was probably his subconscious reluctance to use the phone that causes this rather than a problem with his memory. At home though he has more serious problems which plague him. He can never find the can opener or the single teaspoon his wife gifted him from their cutlery set - 'you don't have milk or sugar in your tea or coffee, and as you're always at work, you only need one,' she'd claimed. But of course, he still needed the teaspoon for his hot drinks and he soon realised that without kitchen equipment like a small whisk – he needed a teaspoon to stir all manner of things. He keeps meaning to buy some new cutlery (his cutlery drawer contains a meagre assortment of mixed bits) and spare can openers, but like all these types of things, the years pass and he still hasn't got around to it. Frank sighs and decides it's time to go home. Maybe cook the steak that's waiting for him in the fridge; have it with the mixed salad he bought last week. A healthy option.

On the drive home, images of chunky chips and slices of bread and butter next to the steak on his plate keep popping into his head. The salad will probably be out of date he reassures himself.

10

The following morning Frank sits at his desk thinking about some of the things Meredith said. That it was chilly on that fatal morning when Elizabeth Farrell parted with him. If that was the case, it's unlikely she would have removed her jacket. The blood on the jacket indicated that it was removed from the Farrell woman post-accident. But how could that be when she went into the river with her car? Unless someone pulled her from the river before the search teams arrived. Or the jacket was somehow separated from her body during the accident.

If someone pulled her from the river and removed her jacket, where was her body? Did they throw her back into the river?

Frank told Rachel that Miller couldn't be involved in taking Elizabeth Farrell's belongings because he'd rushed his wife to the hospital. *If* the jacket had had become detached from the Farrell woman, Miller *could* have picked it up that day, but why would he? And why not mention the fact? Surely, he would have realised it wasn't his wife's jacket? Perhaps in the panic and confusion he wasn't thinking straight.

After putting in a request to archives; he'd looked at what was known about Miller and the accident. One of the interesting things in the accident file he hadn't known about, was that a patrol officer had pulled Elizabeth Farrell over on the morning of the accident. Not because she'd been speeding, but as a routine check. It was usual at such pulls to examine the driver's licence. That could explain why the licence wallet had been found in the jacket pocket. Miss Farrell could've put it there rather than back in her handbag. He knows Miller moved back to Newcastle after his wife left him. June seventy-five, he thought it was and it was not long after that he opened Miller's Motors down on Griffith St.

It's a highly successful business with a solid reputation, trading in used cars. Frank even bought one there himself back in the mid-eighties. They'd also opened a second lot up at Charlestown. It must have been his mate who ran the business while Miller was overseas because the second lot at Charlestown opened while Miller was away. They'd even kept the name, despite probably half of Newcastle knowing what Miller had done.

Frank's Area Command had received information on Miller's return to Australia. If he was involved with their Blackbutt victim, it would've had to have been after his wife left him in June seventy-five, and before August seventy-six when he left for the UK. The times fitted. He was from the Maitland area but had also lived in Newcastle, so he *could* be familiar with Blackbutt Reserve.

Frank's convinced Meredith knows nothing about the victim and has told him the truth. Meredith seemed genuinely astonished about his DNA being on the scarf and was puzzled by some of the questions. Frank decides it's time to request a meeting with the Chief Superintendent Palmer, his boss. Franks calls him the Chief Super to the squad.

At the meeting, Frank manages to convince Palmer to drop the extradition on Meredith.

'We'd have egg on our faces when it comes to nothing and is splashed all over the paper,' Frank tells him. 'I can prepare a statement for you to present to the press.'

Palmer smiles and nods. Frank's boss loves meeting with the press, always keen to be in the limelight, something Frank prefers to avoid. He doesn't like to be recognised by the crims, believing it places him at a disadvantage on investigations.

He thinks there was nothing more tedious than having to take enforced exercise when suspects decide to leg it and he knows there would be more runners if his face was constantly featured in the papers.

After returning to his office Frank spends ten minutes jotting down notes, and then types it up into a sensible structure. He prints off a copy before heading back to the Chief Super's office.

11

The three bottle blondes turn out to be dead ends. Rachel has looked into all aspects of their disappearance and they cannot possibly be their girl. In a follow up meeting with his boss, the Chief Super insists Frank closes the investigation and lists it as 'unsolved'. He tells Frank that their superiors aren't prepared to keep throwing money at the case. They've received the usual crank calls following the newspaper article, but nothing that proves to be a viable lead.

There was one interesting phone call however, from an anonymous woman, who suggested they should look at Elizabeth Farrell. Frank believes the woman definitely knew something, because how else could she have made a connection to the Farrell girl? It had never been disclosed to the press that items belonging to Elizabeth Farrell had been found with the remains. But unfortunately, the woman rang off without leaving her name.

Rachel traced the call to a public telephone in Woolworths at Mayfield. Woolworths told her there was no camera aimed at the phone and people used it regularly to call taxis, so there was heavy foot traffic around that area, which also led to the toilets. It would be impossible to determine who'd made the call.

Frank has one more lead he wants to follow before abandoning the case. He calls on Martin Miller after discovering he's returned from his honeymoon. Miller remains polite, but Frank can sense seething anger brewing just below the surface and wonders what that is about. When Frank asks him whether he had picked up any items of Elizabeth Farrell's following the accident Miller says, 'How could I have done? I presumed everythin' of hers went into the river. Anyway, I grabbed Libby and went straight to Maitland Hospital.'

'We found some of Miss Farrell's belongings with the remains of a young woman discovered at Blackbutt Reserve. Are you familiar with area?'

'You found some of that sheila's things? I thought everythin of hers went into the river with her and the car.'

Frank thinks Miller looks genuinely surprised but notices that he hasn't answered his question about knowing the Blackbutt Reserve area.

'Of course, we checked to see if the remains were those of Miss Farrell's, seeing as her body has never been recovered. But it wasn't her.'

'What did you find that belonged to the Farrell girl?' Miller asks, his face taking on a neutral mask.

If he *was* involved, Miller is putting on a good show, but Frank witnessed him doing that at his interview back in seventy-five.

'I'm unable to tell you that, but there was an item which revealed her identity, so we know she's connected to the remains somehow.'

Miller shrugs and suggests that someone must have found the Farrell girl's belongings and then gone on to murder another young woman, throwing all the items in together.

'That's one theory we've considered,' Frank says.

As he is leaving, Miller asks Frank why he'd come to question him. He turns to Miller and says, 'Someone suggested that we speak to you as you were the last known person to have seen Elizabeth Farrell alive before she went into the river. We've questioned everyone else, so you were my last option.'

'Who suggested you speak to me?' Miller asks.

'You know I can't tell you that.'

12

Several weeks later Frank receives an internal call from the front desk. *'There's a man down here says he has a message for you from the woman who was killed in that hit and run in Mayfield last week. He says he was with her when she died.'*

'Okay, I'll come down now.' Turning to DC Tyler who is in Frank's office he says, 'Can you find out who's dealing with the hit and run in Mayfield for me? Someone's just turned up asking to see me saying they have a message from the dead woman.'

'It's not one of those clairvoyant cranks, is it?' Tyler laughs.

'No clever clogs. He was with her when she died.'

'Why's he only coming forward now then?'

'I don't know. Can you just do what I ask, thank you?'

On entering the reception area Frank spots a nervous looking man sitting alone. He approaches the man saying, 'Good evening, I'm Detective Bailey, you asked to see me?'

'Yeah,' the man says standing. 'My name's Colin Brown. I'm sorry I was so shocked by what happened to that poor woman I only remembered when I woke up this morning that she spoke to me and asked me to pass on a message to you.'

'I'm taking Mr. Brown into an interview room,' Frank announces and presses a button to open a door leading to a long corridor. 'If you would follow me Mr. Brown.'

Once they settle into the room, Frank says, 'So what's the message you were asked to give me?'

'I can't remember the exact details now, but she said I was to tell you to look at the ex-wife in England.'

'Whose ex-wife?'

'That's the strange part – she said "Mar-ee's ex-wife". It didn't make sense to me. How can a woman have an ex-wife?'

Frank knows from *his* ex-wife that she and her live-in-female lover refer to each other as *partners*. He's never heard of anyone referring to their same-sex partner as a 'wife'. There might come a time when same sex couples are allowed to marry though. There's been talk about it for years.

'Are you sure she said Mar-ee?'

'Well, it was definitely something like 'Mar-ee, not Ma-ree',' he said, placing an emphasis on the syllables in different ways.

'And she specifically asked you to pass that on to *me*?'

'Yeah, that's right.'

'Did she say anything else?'

'No, I don't think so. I was in shock that night. I've never seen someone being run over, or had anyone die in my arms like that – well not literally in my arms – I was holding her hand.'

'I'm sure it was a shock. Well in case you do remember anything else, here's my card,' Frank says, handing the card across to him. 'I'll need your details,' he adds taking out a pen and his notebook. 'Didn't you give a statement with all this information at the scene?'

'The police came into the worker's club and asked me lots of questions which I answered, only I forgot about her message; by then I'd been given quite a few drinks. I won't get into any trouble over this will I?'

'No, no, not at all. Well, thank you very much for coming in Mr. Brown,' Frank says standing, to make it clear he wants to terminate the conversation. *Bloody idiots at the scene didn't do a very thorough job of interviewing him.*

Frank learns that Detective Sergeant Paul Lowry is leading the investigation into the hit and run incident and that the woman's name was Susan Kennedy. He meets up with Lowry the following morning to question what information he's gathered. Frank explains about the witness coming forward with the victim's puzzling death message that had been forgotten until yesterday.

'We looked into her background and found some interesting facts,' Lowry begins. 'At her flat in Mayfield, we found a birth certificate for a Susan Alice Searle, born in Melbourne on the twenty-first of April, nineteen fifty-two, which would have made her approaching forty-eight. Her tax file dated back to late June seventy-five when she seems to have moved to Newcastle. There were no tax records existing in her name prior to that.'

'She might've married young and been a housewife,' Frank suggests.

'Not according to our search of records both in New South Wales and Victoria. In October nineteen-eighty she married a William Kennedy, who died following an accident at work in March eighty-six. The marriage certificate was in the flat and she was registered as Susan Alice Searle on that. She remained a widow following Kennedy's death, working occasional jobs until three years ago when she claimed a disability pension. She was still receiving the pension at the time of her death.'

'What was her disability?'

'A back problem. But the most interesting fact is that when we looked into any records of Susan Searle in Victoria, thinking she'd moved up from Melbourne, we discovered that the Susan Searle with the date of birth on the birth certificate in her possession, died in nineteen fifty-five at the age of three from leukaemia. So, her identity was fake. This kid who died was the only Susan Searle in the registry.'

'Ah, that's interesting.'

'Melbourne police traced the Searle family and checked with them for us. They have no idea who she is. Her fingerprints aren't on record anywhere, neither is her DNA, so we have absolutely no idea of her real identity and have been unable to notify anyone in her family of her death. Whatever, or whoever she was running or hiding from, to make her adopt a fake identity, it wasn't anything to do with a law she'd broken. Not that we're aware of anyway.'

'What about other documentation?'

'She's never held a driver's licence in the names she used, nor a passport. The post-mortem revealed that she'd previously had a number of bone fractures and had either given birth or suffered a miscarriage. Although there are no records of children and no evidence of them anywhere in her flat. Searches in hospitals in New South Wales and Victoria brought no results for a Susan Searle receiving treatment. That's the extent of information we've discovered about her. Why do you think she wanted this message to be passed on to you?'

'We received an anonymous phone call following the appeal for information about the remains found at Blackbutt Reserve, from a woman who called from a location in Mayfield. You're telling me Susan Kennedy lived in Mayfield, so she *might've* been our mystery caller. In the phone call she said we should look at Elizabeth Farrell, which was interesting because nothing was mentioned in the paper about items belonging to Elizabeth Farrell being found. What conclusions have you reached about the hit and run?'

'All the witnesses said the car seemed to accelerate towards her. We believe she was intentionally mown down.'

'Hmm. That suggests she knew something and it could be surmised from what has happened that that knowledge placed her in danger. Do you still have the keys for her flat?'

'Yes.'

'Would you mind if I have a look around?'

'No, I was thinking about going there myself today. The place is being cleared out next week, so anything we want needs to be removed soon. If you're free we could head off there now.'

At Susan Kennedy's flat Frank notices she had quality

pieces of furniture, which are a little dated, but that she had clearly looked after. No doubt the remains of her married life. There is a photograph of the woman and her husband on their wedding day sitting on top of a sideboard.

'Did you gain the impression that anyone had been in the place and taken anything at all?' Frank asks Lowry.

'The flat was messy so it was difficult to tell. Clean though. The front door lock looked a bit suspicious, like someone had tried to break in, but the flat was locked up when we came here. I had forensics in to do a quick check around the place. The only fingerprints found were Susan Kennedy's.'

Wearing a pair of gloves, Frank opens the top sideboard drawer and pulls out two photo albums. One is the woman's wedding album. The other has many blank spaces where there had been pictures. The photographs in the album have been stuck in with little corner stickers that are pasted onto the album pages. Leafing through the album he can see all the pictures in the first half a dozen pages have been removed. *Strange.* Photos in later pages mainly shows Susan Kennedy, including ones where she's looking older and must be quite recent. In the wedding photos she is blonde, but later photos show her with reddish brown hair, presumably her natural colouring. A further search of the drawer reveals several photograph wallets containing smaller photos taken at her wedding, the woman with her husband in outdoor settings, or again more recent ones. No older photographs.

'There're gaps in this photo album, as though someone has removed quite a few pictures. Did you take any of them out?' Frank asks Lowry.

'We removed one recent photograph of the victim for our files. We noticed the gaps and thought maybe when she married Kennedy, she removed photos showing previous boyfriends or something. There are no pictures of her when she was a young girl. We think the photos in the album date from after her arrival in Newcastle. We couldn't find wallets with older negatives in them anywhere – only the ones you can see there.'

'Forensics didn't fingerprint the album with the missing photos, did they?'

'I don't think so.'

'I think you should get them to look at it.'

'Okay. I'll take it with me today. I was planning on taking both albums and all the photo wallets.'

'There's something about her that's very familiar in these wedding pictures. Can't put my finger on who she reminds me of, but it's someone I've seen recently. Would you mind if I took one of the wedding snaps? And one of her more recent pictures. It might help me to place where I've seen her likeness recently.'

'Yes, help yourself. We supplied the local press with a recent photo of her.'

Frank pulls out the photos he wants and puts them aside before moving to the coffee table where he'd spotted a note pad. The top sheet is blank but when he lifts it up to the light, he can see impressions of writing from a previous page that have been removed. 'Did you remove a page from this notebook?' he asks Lowry.

'No, the pad was blank, just as you can see.'

'Mind if I take it, there are some impressions showing through that I'd like to look at. It might be just a shopping list or something. But if I find anything of interest, I'll let you know. I'm done here thanks.'

Frank resorts to the good old pencil method to reveal the writing on the pad. Taking a pencil (that he nicked from Rachel's neat container on her desk) he very gently shades across the page. *Eureka!* Some of the writing becomes readable.

He can make out; 'car accident April 1975.' The rest is not readable. Further down the page he is able to reveal 'Fallon fire October …' (date unreadable) then single words that could be names that have also not come through. At the bottom of the page there are a few indistinguishable words until 'photos' and a 'ME' was visible in large print and underlined several times. It's clear that Susan Kennedy had been doing some research.

He checks with Lowry, who tells him no computer or laptop had been found at Susan Kennedy's flat. Nor any internet connection. So, the obvious place Susan Kennedy would carry out research is at a library.

13

No-one recognises Susan Kennedy as a regular borrower at the Mayfield Library. The same is true at the Hamilton Library. Although staff at both libraries immediately admit they recognise her as the woman whose photograph had been printed in the paper. Finally, at Newcastle Central Library he has success.

'Yes, she came in here several weeks back wanting to look up some editions of the Newcastle Herald dating back to the seventies,' one of the librarians tells him.

'And you're sure it was her?'

'Yes definitely, I remember her distinctly as there was a mix up over the microfiche film. When I told her we had all the records for the Herald on fiche files, she became confused and thought I was talking about fish in the sea. I had to explain it to her. I took her to where the Herald records are and showed her how to use the machine. She came in a couple of times actually. The last time was on the day the appeal for witnesses to come forward about the remains you found up at Blackbutt Reserve was printed in the Herald. I watched her stop and read the paper where someone had left the page open on the table. After I saw what happened to her, I phoned the station and gave them the information about her visits. Clearly, they didn't think it important as no-one has made contact with me. Such a terrible thing that happened to her, wasn't it?'

'Yes, now could you show me where those records are please?'

Frank knows he is looking for an article about the Fallon farm fire in October seventy-four. He finds the article which is accompanied by a photograph of a tearful Libby Miller, Martin Miller's wife. Susan Kennedy had written 'photos' in her pad. Is this one of the photographs she was referring to? He moves forward to the accident in April seventy-five and finds an image of Elizabeth Farrell on the front pages. And stops in shock. He understands now why Susan Kennedy had written 'ME' several times. He needs to speak to Charles Farrell again.

Lowry gets back to him with the fingerprint analysis of the album. Only Susan Kennedy's prints have been found, so that's a dead end.

Despite having some new leads, the the Chief Super refuses Frank's request for more time to work on the case. Frank is furious. He's sure that he's on to something now and doesn't want to stop. He considers passing the information he's gathered to Lowry but decides not to. After all, the librarian had contacted the team already. And it concerns his case.

14

The following Sunday, the first day he's had off in almost two weeks, Frank finds himself heading down the freeway to Sydney again. He's arranged a visit with Charles Farrell, apologising and assuring him it won't take up much of his time.

It's the first time Frank has been there in daylight and he's impressed with the view out the back of the house. The men settle at the dining table and Frank produces a photograph of young Susan Kennedy on her wedding day.

'Can you tell me if you know this woman Mr. Farrell?' he asks.

'Call me Charles please,' he says taking the picture from Frank. 'Hmm, there's a slight resemblance to my wife Kate when she was younger. And Lizzie too of course. Lizzie took after her mother. I can see she's not either of them though. Who is she?'

'She was the victim of a fatal hit and run accident a few weeks ago. She went by the name of Susan Kennedy; Kennedy being her deceased husband's name. Her birth certificate stated that her name was Searle, but we know that's not true. The real Susan Searle died at the age of three. So, we don't actually know who she is. When I first saw her photograph, I thought she looked familiar. Then I remembered the photograph I saw of your wife when she was younger; the one that you have on the wall in the hall. I wondered if you might know her.'

'No, I've no idea who she is.'

'I've discovered that she was researching the fire that destroyed the Fallon farm in nineteen seventy-four, and your daughter's accident in seventy-five. Have you any idea why she might be doing that?'

Charles blows out a deep breath and seems momentarily nonplussed. 'Again, I have no idea. That fire was a terrible thing. Wiping out the family like that. My mother phoned to tell us about it after it happened. And a hit and run. Another terrible loss of life.'

Frank nods. 'Did you realise the victim from the other car that collided with your daughter was Libby Fallon, although she was married by then? Her married name was Miller.'

'Yes, we worked it out finally after the inquest. We didn't know prior to that. Nobody told us. At the time we learned that it was a Mr. & Mrs. Miller, but didn't know the woman's first name. At the inquest we were told her name was Elizabeth, so we still didn't realise. It was my mother who put it together. She didn't come to the inquest, but when we spoke to her about it later, she realised it was little Libby who'd been in the other car. She went up to Maitland Hospital to see Libby, but she'd been discharged by then and we had no contact details for her. One of the sisters at the hospital told her Libby's husband had asked the staff not to mention about Lizzie being involved in the accident as he thought it would set back her recovery because the girls knew each other. My mother knew the Fallon family well. She and Maggie Fallon used to go to CWA meetings together, and Lizzie used to play with little Libby when Lizzie stayed up there in the school holidays. I have some pictures of them as youngsters in an album somewhere I could show you if you like.'

'Yes, I'd like to see those. But first, going back to the woman, Susan Kennedy, this is a more recent photograph of her,' Frank says, placing the second photograph in front of Charles Farrell. 'You can see that she is no longer blonde. I don't know if that is her real colouring. We believe this woman was about forty-eight years old. Would you have a photograph of your wife at that age?'

'I have plenty of photographs, but I can tell you this woman doesn't look anything like my Kate.'

Frank has to agree when he is shown photographs of Kate Farrell. In the two photographs he compares he can see Susan Kennedy no longer bears any resemblance to Mrs. Farrell. A shame, as he wondered if there was a distant family connection somewhere. Although that probably would have shown up on the DNA search as they now have both Kate Farrell and her daughter in the data base. He also notices Kate Farrell's smile doesn't quite reach her eyes in the more recent photograph like it does in the photos of her when she's younger.

Perhaps losing a child does that to you, he thinks.

'Would you mind if I borrowed one of the pictures of your wife in her forties? And one of the two girls?' Frank asks Charles. 'I'll return them to you as soon as possible.'

'No that's fine. I have plenty,' Charles says. He pulls photographs out of the albums and passes them to Frank.

'Your wife's family, what were their origins? Were they British immigrants?' he asks.

'No, my wife's maiden name was Katerin Edmonson. They were a Norwegian family who came out to Sydney shortly after the Second World War. They'd lost a number of family members under the Nazis and felt there was nothing for them in Norway anymore, so came here to start a new life. Kate was a young teenager when she moved here. I met her at university in Sydney. She also trained as a pharmacist.'

'And her family? Do they still live in Sydney?'

'Kate's parents are no longer alive. Her one surviving brother Niels and his family live in Sydney. It was Niels who sold the Austin Healey Sprite to Lizzie that she was driving at the time of the accident. I always knew it was a mistake for her to buy it,' Charles says shaking his head.

'Well, I'm sorry to have bothered you again Charles. Our conversation has been very helpful. Just one more question, are *your* parents still alive?'

'My mother is. When my father died seven years ago, mum sold the farm and moved into a house she had built in Maitland. She didn't want to leave the area completely as she has so many friends up there.'

'Okay, thanks for your time. I'll let you know if I have any further information for you.'

'Did you ever discover the identity of the person whose remains you found?' Charles asks as they stand.

'No, unfortunately not. My boss has stopped me working on it now. In official police time that is. I'm still looking into things when they arise in my own time. Like this. I believe there's something connecting the human remains we found, the hit and run victim and your daughter. I just have to figure out what it is.'

'Rather you than me. I don't know how you do it.'

'I don't have much of a personal life. That's how I do it.'

The months roll by and Frank makes no further progress in identifying the remains found last December. He's been busy handling a number of other cases including one that involved serious domestic abuse. The wife had attempted to run away from her violent husband, but he'd discovered her hiding at a friend's house and had almost killed her. The case makes Frank think of Susan Kennedy and he approaches DS Lowry with the suggestion that the Kennedy woman may have moved to Newcastle to escape a violent husband. He reminds him of the old bone breakages that showed up at the post-mortem.

'I had thought of that possibility,' Lowry sighs.

'You could run a picture of her when she was younger, together with a more current picture in the Melbourne press, appealing to the public to see if anyone comes forward,' Frank says. 'Using a birth certificate of someone born in Melbourne suggests that she possibly came from there.'

'Yes, it's worth giving it a shot I suppose,' Lowry concedes.

A few weeks later they have positively identified Susan Kennedy as one Sonja Powell, nee Henderson, born in Melbourne the same month and year as Susan Searle.

Both a former friend and a nurse at a Melbourne Hospital came forward with information. She had been married to a very violent husband, named Ron Powell. In the three years before her escape to Newcastle, Sonja Powell had been treated for a number of injuries, including two miscarriages – one at six months where the baby was stillborn, and various broken bones. Further investigations revealed that Powell died in a Princes Highway multi vehicle accident, just outside Melbourne, in nineteen seventy-nine. So, Powell couldn't have been involved in the hit and run incident.

Frank is pleased that the woman has finally been identified and her surviving family notified. The question of who was responsible for her death is still being investigated separately by Lowry, even though Frank thinks she's connected to his case. Frank's attention keeps returning to the remains found at Blackbutt Reserve and the parting message from Susan Kennedy. The witness who delivered Susan's message must have recollected the name Mar-ee incorrectly or didn't hear it properly. He believes the only way to move forward on the case is for him to travel to England to track down Libby Miller/ Fallon. When he suggests it to the Chief Super he explodes in a rage of fury.

'Go to England? You've got to be out of your mind. As if Newcastle Police could afford to pay for the cost of that. All on a theory you have from the words of a dying woman. It's absolutely out of the question.'

He can't leave it there though. The case keeps gnawing away at him. A young woman has died at the hands of a sadistic killer who thinks he's gotten away with it. She deserves to be identified. And Susan Kennedy? She could well have been another victim of the same killer. There could be more they're not aware of.

Frank puts in a request to take long service leave. He has accumulated a considerable amount of time in both holidays and long service leave. As long as the Chief allows him to pursue matters in the UK on his own time, while he also takes in the usual tourist sites, he is prepared to cover the costs himself.

The Chief Super agrees and so, armed with copies of all the case files, Frank flies out of Sydney in early June. It means he will escape the worst of the local winter in Newcastle and experience Europe at the peak of their summer. He is looking forward to exploring London.

15

London June 2000

With an introductory letter from the New South Wales Police, as well as his police identification, Frank approaches the police department in Kilburn, the station in London who handled the investigation into Martin Miller's attempted murder of his ex-wife and her cousin. They allow him to read their case files and he can't help but admire the tenacity and bravery of Elizabeth Miller. The detectives' notes are brief however and he'd like to know more.

He learns that Elizabeth Miller and her cousin moved to Bristol, the home city of the Fallon family, following the trial and decides that was where he'll head next. Before heading off to Bristol he spends a few days treading the tourist trail around London, seeing Buckingham Palace, The Tower of London, Tower Bridge, Westminster Cathedral and The Houses of Parliament. Sated with these sights, he books a hotel in Bristol, hires a car and sets off.

At Bristol Police Headquarters Frank is passed on to DI George Radcliffe, a veteran of the department, close to retirement. When he tells Radcliffe that he needs to trace Elizabeth Miller, whose maiden name was Fallon, in connection with ongoing investigations in Newcastle, New South Wales, Radcliffe seems shocked and surprised.

'How can this woman help you if she hasn't lived in Australia since the nineteen seventies? Radcliffe asks.

'One of the cases dates back to that period,' Frank says outlining the circumstances and what has led him to England to find Elizabeth Miller.

'I don't know what her current married name is or where she lives, but I know how to contact her uncle – Kenny Fallon. It just so happens, he's my builder. He did a large renovation job on my house some years ago, and his firm is building me a conservatory at the moment. Well at this point they're just doing the foundations. Kenny told me while he was doing my house last time that his daughter, the one who had been attacked in London, had married a New Zealander and now lives out there. He also mentioned that his niece had married again and was living in Bristol. I have his number in my mobile. I could give him a call; he's bound to know her married name and possibly where she lives.'

This was fortuitous news to Frank, and could potentially provide another lead on the case.

'If you give me your hotel and phone details, I'll see what I can do. In the meantime, I'll ring Kenny and ask him if he knows his niece's address. I don't think you should be going there on your own though. I'll come with you. If I manage to obtain her details, what about tomorrow

morning?'
    'That sounds ideal.'

On the way to Elizabeth Carey's house in Clifton, Radcliffe fills Frank in on her background since moving to the city – information he's obtained from Kenny Fallon. She's a widow with two adult children. The eldest, Frank knows from reading the interview transcripts in Kilburn, could be Miller's child.

The house has a driveway but Radcliffe instructs him to park on the street. As he climbs out of the car Frank feels a sense of excitement. All his instincts are telling him he will find all the answers he needs from this woman.

16

Frank reaches out to ring the doorbell of the house in Clifton, when an attractive woman opens the door, briefcase in hand and looks up, startled to see two men on her doorstep.

'Good morning,' he starts, 'Would you be Elizabeth Carey?'

'Yes, that's right. How can I help you?' she asks.

Frank is momentarily rendered speechless by her astonishing blue eyes and beautiful face; beautiful despite an array of faded scars crisscrossing it. Her short, fair wavy hair is swept off her face with no attempt to hide her old injuries. The sun is shining directly onto the front of the house and it's as though she's lit up by halo of magical light. The expression on her face tells him she is waiting politely for him to answer. He shakes his head in an attempt to clear his thoughts, but before he can speak his companion steps forward, holds up his identification and introduces them.

'I'm Detective Inspector George Radcliffe from Bristol CID – and this is Detective Inspector Frank Bailey of the Newcastle, New South Wales Police,' he says. 'We'd like to have a quick word with you if that's alright.'

'Can I ask what this is about? I was just about to leave for work.'

'We'd rather not discuss matters on your doorstep, but if you don't want us to come in, we could talk down at the station,' DI Radcliffe says.

Frank watches as Elizabeth Carey raises an eyebrow and hardens her stare at Radcliffe before turning to him. 'I'm curious as to why the Australian Police are on my doorstep. Is this about my ex-husband?' she asks. 'Because if it is—'

'Mrs. Carey …,' Radcliffe starts impatiently.

'Okay, come in then. Fortunately, I have no appointments this morning.'

Elizabeth Carey leads them into the kitchen/diner and invites them to sit.

'Would you like tea or coffee? As I'm going to miss my morning coffee at work, I'm going to make one here. I'll have to make a quick call to the office though.'

'I'd love a coffee with no milk, thank you, Mrs. Carey,' Frank says.

'Call me Beth please. Mrs. Carey sounds so formal and reminds me of my mother-in-law.'

Frank nods. He'd be more than happy to call her Beth, although he might find that difficult as he tends to automatically address people by their title in his line of work. He wonders when she started using this version of her name.

'Same for me, with milk and two sugars thanks,' Radcliffe adds.

When they finally settle at the kitchen table with their

coffees, Beth Carey says, 'So what is it that you wish to discuss with me?'

Radcliffe nods to Frank and so he opens the conversation.

'Do you mind if we tape this conversation?' Frank asks, removing a mini recorder from his jacket. 'It would help me when writing up my report later and avoid me having to write copious notes.'

Beth shrugs. 'As long as you are not about to say to me "anything you do say may be given in evidence". This conversation is information gathering I take it?'

'Yes, that's correct,' Franks says clearing his throat. 'For some months now, we have been investigating two crimes in Newcastle in New South Wales. One is linked to the unidentified remains of a young woman which had been concealed in an old mine entrance for more than twenty years.'

Beth Carey looks surprised.

'And how on earth would these remains concern me?'

'Documentation found at the site link the remains to the other person who was involved in the car accident on the same day as you and your husband in April nineteen seventy-five.'

Beth raises her arm and interrupts him. 'Hang on a minute, you just referred to another person who was involved in *the* car accident on the same day as me. Are you talking about someone who was involved in *our* accident, the one Marty and I had, or someone who had an accident co-incidentally the same day?'

Frank looks carefully at Beth Carey and realises she still has no idea about the other vehicle or Elizabeth Farrell. He is not sure where to go with this, not wanting to provide information that might cause confusion or provoke misleading information from her. He chooses not to answer her question at this point, but instead asks, 'What do you recall about the accident?'

'What do *I* recall? I don't recall anything about it. But I can tell you what Marty told me, if that's what you want to know,' Beth says, sounding a little irritated.

'That would be helpful,' Frank says nodding.

'Okay. At first, he just said we had a terrible accident, without explaining anything in detail. When I was recovering in hospital and was able to talk again, I asked him what had happened. He said some cows had wandered out in front of the car and we had to swerve to avoid hitting them and rammed into our old farm gate, causing me to go through the windscreen and then land on the gravel. He said I wasn't wearing a seat belt.'

'I see.'

'Did Marty lie about the accident then?'

'Yes, if he told you that then he was lying. It's true that you weren't wearing a seat belt, but there was another car involved in the crash that day. It was assumed that the other person died as a result of the collision. At the time, the police investigation led us to believe that the driver of the second vehicle caused the crash, so your husband was not charged with anything.'

'Ex-husband. Why was it *assumed* the other person died? And who was it?'

'I can't tell you who that person was at the moment, but I can tell you it was a woman and her car went into the river and was swept away. It'd been raining for days and the currents were powerful. I don't know if you remember, but the Hunter and Williams Rivers join shortly after the site of the accident and then eventually flow out to the Tasman Sea.'

'I've seen it on a map, but I don't remember the area much at all. I still have memory issues due to injuries I received in that accident and I haven't been back there since. It was a long time ago. I was only a kid and of course I was known by my childhood name then – Libby.'

'Have you been able to recall *anything* about that day?'

'No, nothing. Only what Marty told me.'

'Can you tell us exactly what he said and what you experienced when you regained consciousness in the hospital? Do you remember that?'

'Oh, I certainly do.'

17

Libby's Story
Maitland Hospital, April, 1975

It was the pain that woke me the first time. It seemed to come from behind me as though someone was holding me in a vice, inflicting agonising injuries on my body. I had no sense of where I was or what had happened to me. I opened my mouth to cry out but I couldn't even manage that. I believe I slipped into unconsciousness again, convinced I was experiencing a bad dream. The next time I woke I could see indistinct shapes moving in the distance. I lay quietly for a while to see if I could make sense of what was happening. I'd heard a strange sound earlier and I could still hear it. I soon realised it was right beside me. I tried to move but the pain was too intense. I tried to call out to the shapes I could see, but something was preventing me from doing so. The only sound I could make was a garbled croak and I almost choked. The next thing I knew I heard a man's voice.

'Libby?' the man said. 'Oh Darl, you're awake. Thank God. I've been worried sick about you.'

I had no idea he was talking to me and was startled by an unshaven fuzzy face looming over me grabbing my left hand. My right hand was attached to some equipment. I attempted to pull my hand free from the man but he was gripping it too tightly. I didn't recognise his face at the time, but the voice; there was something familiar about his voice. And it sent shivers up my spine.

'Now Darl, we were in a terrible car accident and you've had some head and facial injuries. Do you remember anything? The Doc said you might have trouble remembering, but don't worry, he said it'll take time. I'll go and fetch a nurse and see if the Doc is still around.'

I watched him leave the room and could hear him talking to someone. I could only make out the odd word that he said. He mentioned the word "wife" but I didn't know he was referring to me. I had no idea who the man was.

A nurse returned with him a short time after.

'Hello Mrs. Miller,' she said. 'I'm Sister O'Connell. We've been very concerned about you. The Doctor will be along soon and we'll take this breathing apparatus out so that you can speak.' She rubbed my arm. 'I'll be back in a jiffy.'

I could barely take in what she was saying and was so confused. She'd called me Mrs. Miller. Surely that was a mistake; I was convinced they'd mixed me up with someone else.

The man grabbed my hand again and began talking low and softly, telling me how we were married and lived in Sydney, but at the moment I was in a hospital in Maitland, near Newcastle. I didn't fully understand what he was saying. Why was he telling me all this? He kept calling me "darl". While he was talking, I became vaguely aware that someone else had entered the room.

'Good morning, Mrs. Miller,' a voice said. A man in a white coat leaned over me. 'I'm Doctor Jackson. I'm going to remove some things we have connected to you. It might hurt momentarily, but I'll be as gentle as I can. Okay?'

I liked *his* voice. It relaxed me.

The thing he removed from my throat made me cough and splutter. The Sister stepped in and ran a moist cloth around my mouth.

'Now that didn't hurt too much did it?' Doctor Jackson asked.

I attempted to say 'yes, it did' but it didn't sound right.

'Are you in any pain?' he asked.

Again my 'yes' sounded like gobbledegook.

'Ah, I think Mrs. Miller is suffering from aphasia Mr. Miller,' the doctor said turning to the man. 'She's having trouble forming words and possibly understanding what I'm saying. I will have to do some small tests.'

I could understand everything he was saying. Well, almost anyway. What I didn't know was why he was talking to the man instead of me.

'Mrs. Miller, can you blink your eyes for me.'

It was obvious he thought I was Mrs. Miller, so I blinked.

'Good, she understood that. Now can you blink once for yes and two blinks for no to my questions.'

I blinked once.

'Are you in any pain?' I gave him one blink. I was in considerable pain and seemed to be hurting all over.

'Is it your head that's hurting?'

At that moment I had no idea what he was talking about which confused me. I'd understood when he said "blink" so why didn't I understand when he mentioned the word "head". I couldn't remember what part of my body my head was, so I lifted my free hand and attempted to point to the place which was hurting the most. But my arm had a mind of its own and wouldn't go where I wanted it to. Doctor Jackson seemed to understand.

'Are you in pain here?' he asked pointing to what I later remembered was my head. I gave him one blink. 'What about your throat here?' He pointed to the place where he'd removed something. One blink. 'And here?' He pointed to my face. I knew that word without him saying it. One blink. 'Anywhere else?' One blink. There were many more places where my body was hurting. It was taking a great deal of effort to concentrate on what he was saying. I wanted to go to sleep by then. But he carried on.

It took him a while for him to discover that one of my legs, part of my right arm and my nose were also hurting and something that he called a catheter was causing some discomfort. All of these he named very slowly and carefully as though I didn't speak English as he pointed to each of them.

'We've had you on some very strong medication for the past few days to keep you in a deep sleep,' the doctor explained, 'so that you wouldn't feel any pain, but now we'd like to keep you awake to aid your recovery so we'll be giving you lighter pain medication.'

He discussed levels of medication with the sister, and wrote on a chart he clipped to the end of the bed. The sister left the room and returned with a small dish.

'We're going to leave the cannula, fluid lines and catheter in you for the moment,' the doctor explained. He pointed to different things attached to my body. 'Do you understand?' I gave him the one blink. But I didn't understand. I'd never heard the word 'cannula' before and didn't know what it all meant. I blinked so that this man wouldn't think I was stupid. Taking the dish from the sister, the doctor injected some liquid into something beside me.

'This will ease your pain for now. I'll be back to see you later. Sister O'Connell and her team will be dressing your head and face wounds.'

Within a few minutes I felt the pain lessen. I closed my eyes, waiting for sleep. Before I drifted off, I heard the doctor talking to the strange man.

'There seems to be some loss of motor function at the moment, her gross motor skills have been affected, but I'm confident they will gradually return,' the doctor said.

'Whadya mean?' the man asked.

'Your wife will have some trouble with movement. She has exhibited difficulties with arm and hand coordination. She will probably have difficulty walking. The brain will take some time to begin functioning properly again and until it does, we'll not know the extent of any long-term damage that may have occurred.'

'Do you mean she will be stuck in a wheelchair? We live in a flat with no lift on the second floor.'

'No, she has no spinal injuries, just bruising. Once she regains motor function, she should be able to walk, providing the injury to her leg has sufficiently healed. It's only swelling on the knee and some grazes, not a break, so she should be fine.'

'Right. Libby would've knocked her leg on the dash as she went through the windscreen.'

'But the brain function that controls mobility might all take some time. We'll have to be patient. I'll leave you in Sister's capable hands for now.'

'Doctor Jackson?' the man called out. 'Can you tell me whether you think Libby's memory will return to normal? She seems very confused.'

They were talking about me as if I wasn't there, but I had my eyes closed, so they probably thought I was already asleep. I struggled to stay awake, so I could hear what the doctor said.

'That's only to be expected after such severe head trauma. Your wife has sustained fractures, both anterior and posterior – that is to both the front and back of her head. It may take some time, but I am hopeful that her memory will gradually return. However, I have to warn you that often after this type of injury, the brain seems to block out the trauma, so she might never remember the accident, or things that happened before it.'

'Do you think she'll have some brain damage as well?'

'She may very well,' he said. 'Only time will tell.'

My body stiffened with the doctor's answer. I could be permanently brain-damaged! I hadn't understood everything the doctor had said, but I understood that.

'Well I hope she isn't going to be gaga, 'cos I don't know how I'd manage. I couldn't look after her if she was. I need to work.'

'As I said we need to be patient. You have to remember she was very badly injured. She could have died. It will take time. Now, if you have any more questions, I'll have to ask you to walk along with me for another minute or so, I'm due somewhere else now,' Doctor Jackson said. The man followed him out of the room and I didn't hear anything further they may have said to each other.

I woke later to someone calling, 'Mrs. Miller? Libby, can you hear me?'

I didn't answer because I thought it was nothing to do with me. It was Sister O'Connell again I realised when I opened my eyes. She touched my arm while another nurse cranked the top end of the bed into a semi upright position.

'Warrrg?' I was trying to say 'what's going on?', but I stopped because I knew I sounded strange. Words formed in my brain weren't coming out of my mouth correctly.

'We're going to remove your bandages now, to dress your cuts and wounds and see how they're healing. But before we start, I'm going to give you a pill. It's just a painkiller, to help ease the pain. The doctor doesn't want you on morphine injections any longer.'

'Unph?' I didn't know what she meant by morphine injections but I was happy she was giving me something else for the pain. I liked the sister's sing song voice. It had a familiar lilt to it that I couldn't place. Sister O'Connell held a pill close to my mouth.

'Open your mouth now.' I obeyed and the sister popped the pill on to my tongue. She tipped some water into my mouth, but most of it dribbled down my chin with the tablet stuck on my tongue.

'You need to *swallow* the pill with some water,' she said. 'Let's try again.' This time she gently held my mouth shut.

It forced the pill and water to go down my throat.

'That wasn't so difficult, was it?'

It was. I was confused and hadn't understood what she'd wanted me to do. I decided they were right; I must have some brain damage.

'Well, everything is healing very nicely, I must say,' Sister O'Connell said once they'd removed the bandages from my head. 'There's no sign of infection around the stitches. It will clear up quickly now and your hair will grow back in no time at all.'

My head felt cold after the bandages had been removed and I realised they must have shaved my hair off. I wanted to see. I attempted to raise my free arm to feel my head, but once again I had little control over it and it wavered in front of me before I dropped it in exasperation. Why wouldn't it work?

'Best if you don't be touching your head now, Mrs. Miller. After we've finished applying the ointment, we'll re-bandage it, to prevent any problems.'

'Ooghw...' I want to see, I tried to say.

'We'll be as quick as we can and do our best not to hurt you now.'

Sister O'Connell gently applied what she referred to as ointment to the wounds on my head and face, but it was so painful it made me cry out.

'Nurr' – I was attempting to tell them to stop. But I knew they didn't understand because of how strange I sounded.

'Jeez, Libby, you're sporting some beauties there.'

The man who was here before had just walked back into the room, calling me Libby.

'Mr. Miller! Your wife is in great discomfort here.'

'Sorry, it just took me by surprise. I haven't seen Libby's wounds since the accident. Or her shaved head. I didn't know you were gunna do this or I would've stayed. I just needed a break and thought she'd still be asleep.'

I didn't want this man in my room, whoever he was. I turned slowly to Sister O'Connell and started blinking rapidly. Twice. Stop. Twice. Stop. She didn't understand what I was trying to say.

'Oh Mrs. Miller, I'm sorry, we'll have you finished in a jiffy,' she said. 'Then you can spend some quiet time with your husband. He's been so attentive, sitting by your bedside for the past three days.'

That's when I realised they believed this man was my husband and I'd been in the hospital for three days. They finished the dressing, reapplied some bandages and gently eased me back.

'What about some light soup? Would you like that? It would be good for you to start eating and drinking now,' Sister O'Connell said.

I didn't respond because I didn't want her to leave me with the man.

'Nurse Johnson, would you go and ask the kitchen to prepare some soup for Mrs. Miller? Then see if you can get a little of it down her.'

'Yes sister.'

'Are you staying now Mr. Miller?'

'Yeah, for sure, Libby and I have some catchin' up to do.'

'We've given her a light sedative for the pain, so she may not be fully alert after a while.'

Sister O'Connell left the room, leaving me alone with

the man whom they'd called Mr. Miller. He approached my bed and sat down beside me. 'Jeez Libby, with your injuries you might be in the hospital longer than I thought. I've spoken to our landlord, and he seems okay, but I'll have to get back to Sydney soon to sort stuff out.'

I looked at him blankly.

'You don't understand, do you? I know the doc said that you might have trouble rememberin' things, but Libby, we have to get movin' on sortin' everythin' out. You remember about the fire, don't you? That your parents and brother died in last year? Well we've got to get everythin' finalised. You said the Lawyer was completin' the probate, so the settlement should be comin' through soon. As you know there is a sale going through on the property.'

He'd just told me I'd lost my family in a fire! I couldn't remember my family, but discovering I'd lost them brought tears to my eyes. Did I have any other family nearby? And what property was he talking about?

'Look I know it might seem hard. Let me spell it out for you. Your name is Libby Miller. You were called Libby Fallon before we married. We were married in March two years ago. We live in Sydney now. We used to live in Newcastle. Your parents had a small farm near Raymond Terrace where you grew up, from the age of about six.'

Lies, I thought. It had to be lies. I couldn't be married to this man.

'Your family emigrated from England. Your father was a builder, a brickie. It was mainly your mother and brother who worked on the farm. Last October there was a fire one night at your parents' house. Both your parents and brother died in the fire. We were gunna start a business in

Sydney before this happened. Your parents were gunna lend us some of the money for it. But because of the fire, we had to put our plans on hold as they hadn't given us the money yet. We can't have any of their money until probate completes.'

I looked down at the bedding, not wanting to hear any more, but the voice droned on.

'To fill in time while we waited for the money to come through, you were workin' in a college in East Sydney. Look, I'll show you some of your things.' He reached over to the locker beside the bed and pulled out a handbag. 'Your things were put in here for safekeepin'.'

He rummaged in the bag and pulled out a chain with a round metal disc.

'This disc has an elaborate Celtic design on it and in the centre, engraved are the large initials L.F. See. This is yours. These are your initials. Your parents gave it to you for your eighteenth birthday. Although it's not your full name they always called you Libby and you always wore it.'

I looked at the disc, and it *did* seem familiar.

'This is your purse. There's a wedding picture of us – here, look.'

He held the picture over the bed for me to see. It was very small and not very clear, but I could see the couple were smiling happily. Was this me and this man? Surely not?

'I'm sorry there are no pictures of your family at the weddin'. Our weddin' albums were all in boxes at your parents' house. We had a lot of our stuff stored there – in your old bedroom mainly – until we found a bigger place in Sydney. We only moved to Sydney in September last year. Everythin' we had at your parents was destroyed in the fire. This is your weddin' ring. They took it off before you went to the theatre.'

I looked down at my left hand and could see that there was a white band that hadn't been touched by the sun. So, it *was* true. I *was* married to this man! How did that happen? It was really depressing news and I didn't want to hear any more.

'This is your drivin' licence. You passed your drivin' test just after we got married,' he said.

He held out the licence. It showed a name and address, but I barely looked at it.

'Are you telling Mrs. Miller her life story?' the nurse said as she re-entered the room.

'Somethin' like that. Just showin' her our weddin' picture, a necklace, her weddin' ring, and drivin' licence. I thought she might recognise them straight away.'

'Any joy?'

'I think so. Not too sure.'

They were at it again. Talking about me as though I wasn't there – or a complete and utter idiot. It made me angry.

'Would you like to help Mrs. Miller eat some soup?'

'Nah, best if you do it.'

'Better let me sit next to the bed then.'

The nurse tucked a towel, acting as a bib, under my chin, then lifted the bowl and placed it a short distance from my mouth. She dipped the spoon into the watery liquid.

'Open wide then,' she said.

I had a stubborn urge to refuse her instructions, but I opened my mouth and she tipped a spoonful of soup in. How humiliating was this? I was being fed as though I was a baby. The soup quickly dribbled out of my mouth, spilling down onto the towel. I'd forgotten to do that thing Sister O'Connell said I had to do. Close my mouth and swallow I think it was.

'You have to swallow it, Mrs. Miller. I know it might not be super tasty, but it is full of nutrients that you need.'

She placed another spoonful in my mouth and gently held it shut, forcing me to swallow with some difficulty. After several further mouthfuls, which I swallowed unaided, she noticed the tears streaming down my face.

'Oh, I'm sorry Mrs. Miller, is it hurting too much? Shall we leave it for now?'

I blinked twice, but the nurse didn't notice. It wasn't hurting. I was upset to learn that my family was dead, that I was married to this man and I couldn't even feed myself. Who wouldn't be?

'Look, she may be a bit upset about her family,' the man said. 'I reminded her about the fire at the farm where she grew up when I was tellin' her everythin'. I didn't think, but she became teary when I told her.'

'We'll leave it there for now then,' the nurse told me. 'Perhaps you'd like some jelly and ice cream later? That will be more soothing on the throat as well. I'll bring you a bowl this evening.'

She pushed the trolley back along the bed, gathered up the bowl and indicated that she wanted to have a word with the man. She closed the door behind them as they stepped into the corridor. I was left alone and my tears became sobs.

The next time I woke I noticed that my right arm was free of attachments, but the upper part of my arm was still bandaged and I was lying flat again. The room was quiet and dark apart from a weak light coming from the wall, somewhere to my right.

My throat and mouth felt dry and my stomach was making loud grumbling noises. I was feeling … what was I feeling? I concentrated carefully for a few minutes but couldn't catch the word. My brain seemed to be functioning on half measure. I could understand much of what people were saying and could think, but words eluded me and my speech and movements were all wrong. Did I have permanent brain damage from this accident I was involved in? If only I could remember it.

The door opened and the room was flooded with light.

'Good evening, Mrs. Miller. I was just checking to see if you're awake. Would you like that jelly and ice cream now? I'm off duty shortly and I'd like you to have a stab at eating it before I leave for the day.'

It was that nurse again bending over me with a wide smile. She cranked the bed so that it moved into an upright position.

'How about some water first though? You must be thirsty.' She poured a glass of water from the jug on the bedside locker and held it to my mouth. I eagerly sipped the water and swallowed it without support. I *was* very thirsty. That had been one of the words I was trying to remember.

'That's brilliant! Progress. Did you see that Mr. Miller, your wife is now able to swallow without aid?'

Mr. Miller? My eyes darted around the room and I discovered that *the man* was sitting across the room in a chair.

'Yeah, that's great,' he said.

'Mr. Miller will keep you company while I fetch your food,' the nurse said before leaving the room.

'G'day Libby. Did you have a good sleep?'

I looked at him without responding. Until the nurse addressed him, I had no idea he was in the room and it sent shivers up my spine to think he'd been sitting there watching me.

'I had a nap meself, and then went for a smoko. Not that I smoke. Just needed the break.'

He rose from the chair and walked towards me. 'Look, I'm goin' back to Sydney tonight to sort some stuff out. I have to go on the train as the car is a wreck. I'll come back tomorrow though. Don't want to leave you on your own for too long. You might forget who I am again,' he chuckled. 'Anyway, you've got the physio comin' in the mornin' and they don't want me around for that.'

The nurse re-entered the room with a bowl heaped with orange jelly and ice cream.

'Have I got a treat for you!' she exclaimed. 'I asked the kitchen to give me a large portion as you've had no dinner. I hope you can manage it all.'

'I'm off now Libby. I'll see you tomorrow,' the man said. He bent over and kissed the side of my head.

The nurse placed the food on the trolley and sat on the edge of the bed. Once again, she tucked a small towel around my chin.

'Just in case, but hopefully we won't need this,' she said.

I managed to swallow every mouthful she gave me.

The following day I was in a deep sleep when I was woken by Sister O'Connell's voice.

'Mr. Miller, I've been hoping to catch you!' she said. It sounded like they were standing in the doorway of my room and they thought I was still asleep.

'Oh, hi er … Sister O'Connell, isn't it? How was Libby today?'

'She was fine this morning and was able to eat some breakfast, but there was a bit of a disaster at lunch. You didn't tell us that your wife was allergic to seafood. She could have died!'

'What? What happened?' the man asked. He sounded surprised.

'We gave her some fish pie for lunch with some mashed potatoes, but I'm afraid she went into anaphylactic shock. You should have told us about her allergy.'

'Oh God … I'm sorry … I didn't realise – what with everything that's happened, I hadn't even given it a thought. Besides she wasn't eatin' anythin' much up until I left yesterday. I can't believe I almost lost her *again*!' His voice seemed to crack up as though he was about to cry.

'Well, we managed to save her, so there's no harm done,' the sister said, in what sounded like an attempt to comfort him.

The sister was saying I'd had an allergic reaction to the fish they gave me for lunch. After a few mouthfuls I had no memory of what happened. My memory loss was proving potentially dangerous.

'So, Libby's going to be alright,' the man sniffed.

'Yes. She's sedated at present and is sleeping. Hopefully by later tonight she'll be better. Have you hurt yourself by the way? I noticed you were limping when you came in?'

'I wasn't watchin' where I was walkin' and twisted me foot steppin' off a kerb. Is it okay to sit quietly with her?' he said changing the subject.

'Yes, that's fine, but I need to let you know that we'll have to move your wife into a general ward in the next few days, now she's on the mend.'

'Right. That's a shame, I was hopin' we could spend some more private time together.'

'I understand Mr. Miller, but this is a public hospital and the private rooms in this unit are used only for the most serious cases.'

I didn't want him to start talking to me again, so, pretending I was asleep, I kept my eyes closed and eventually drifted off again.

I woke once again in a darkened room. Was he still there? Yes, I could sense his presence, but he'd moved. I'd woken earlier, feeling very woozy to hear him whispering beside me. It was like some form of torture. I'd just closed my eyes again, blanked out his voice and drifted off once more. The curtains were open and although it was dark outside, there was some light filtering in. I closed my eyes and lay unmoving, waiting. I could hear him humming a tune. There was something familiar about it, but I couldn't identify it. He was humming the same tune yesterday.

Realising that contact with him was unavoidable, I opened my eyes and turned my head towards the window where I could see he was sitting in a chair.

'Bout time Libby, thought you were never gunna wake up.'

The man approached my bed, dragging the chair over.

'I've been to Sydney; settled with the landlord, so everythin's okay there. Now we need to get you better, get you outta here and home as soon as possible.'

No! I didn't want to go anywhere with him.

'I'm sorry about what happened with your lunch. It was lucky they were here to save you, can't have you dyin' on me now, can I? Do you wanna drink?' he asked pointing to a jug of water on the bedside cabinet.

I remained silent.

'Okay fine. Well, I'll go and see one of the nurses to see if they are bringin' you somethin' to eat. Somethin' safe.'

He laughed as I watched him leave the room. He'd cleaned himself up and looked smarter in clean clothes and without the hair on his face. His face, now I could see him more clearly, was familiar, but there was something creepy about him which made me shudder. He returned with the nurse who had been on duty last night. She was carrying a plate of food.

'Why don't you let her feed herself?' the man suggested. 'She has to start doin' it sometime. I can't carry on feedin' her like you have when we go home.'

'I think that's a long way off, sir. We won't be discharging your wife until we can see her wounds have healed enough.'

'Sure, but why not let her have a go?'

'Alright, we'll try it, but I'm not sure she's ready for that.'

The nurse moved the mobile trolley along the bed so that it was immediately in front of me. After cranking my bed into an upright position, she took the lid off the food, cut some of it up and laid some things down beside the plate.

'Is Mrs. Miller right-handed sir?'

'Yeah, she is. Look Libby, one of your favourites. Rissoles and mashed potato. She doesn't like peas though,' he said turning to the nurse.

I looked down at the food. Rissoles, mashed potato and peas he'd called it.

'Pick up the knife and fork and start eatin' Libby.'

I looked at the nurse and the man and then down to the plate of food, not understanding what I had to do with the things he called a knife and fork.

'Actually, she doesn't need the knife,' he said, standing and removing what must be the knife from the plate. 'Just eat with the fork Libby.'

He took my hand, wrapped my fingers around the fork and dipped it into the food. 'Now lift the fork and take it to your mouth,' he said.

I attempted to lift the fork, but the food flew off landing on the bed.

'I think I'd better—' the nurse started.

'No! Please let her keep tryin',' the man insisted.

I had another go and this time, although the fork wavered in front of me, it almost made it to my mouth before the food dropped down my front.

'You nearly did it, Libby. Come on, have another go.'

Once again, I struggled with the contents of the fork, but this time the food made it into my mouth. Yes! I smiled triumphantly and some of the food began to dribble back out.

'Well done, Mrs. Miller.'

'Bloody beaut Libby.'

I continued eating. My arm coordination gradually improved as I shovelled food into my mouth. By the time I finished, apart from most of the peas which were too difficult for me to control on the fork, and had disappeared to various parts of the room, I'd managed to eat a good percentage of the food. I felt happy for the first time since regaining consciousness.

18

Bristol June 2000

Beth Carey pauses at this point and asks them if they would like another drink. Frank stops the recording, ejects the tape and inserts a second one.

'I'm making myself one. All this talking is thirsty work.'

Frank had noticed the wobble in her voice a couple of times as she was speaking, so the whole thing was proving quite emotional for her.

'Yes, thank you I'd like another drink. But just water for me thanks.'

'Detective Radcliffe?'

Radcliffe's eyes are closed and Frank is sure he's nodded off. He rouses himself though and says, 'Yes, another coffee would be great, thank you.'

As Beth approaches with the drinks Frank re-starts the tape and says, 'Your husband might not have told you the details of the accident in order to protect you. You were recovering from serious injuries; perhaps he thought it would be too much for you to know the truth?'

'Perhaps. But I think you are crediting Martin Miller

with a thoughtfulness I doubt he possesses. He probably had another agenda in misinforming me.'

'And what do you think that agenda might have been?'

'I think he didn't want me to know that our marriage was on the rocks. The accident, with my memory loss, proved very convenient for him. He was acting like we were still supposedly a loving couple. At that point anyway.'

'So, what happened next?'

19

Libby's Story
Maitland Hospital April 1975

I made excellent progress over the next week – well according to the hospital staff I had anyway. I was still finding everything very difficult, but I could eat unaided, without spilling most of the contents. My brain function had dramatically improved. I was, by that point, able to understand most things. However, I still couldn't speak properly or walk yet. They'd given me physiotherapy sessions and I was determined to walk without props at my next session. I felt so helpless being moved around by Marty and staff in a wheelchair all the time.

I had reluctantly accepted that I was married to the man who came to the hospital each day to see me. After all, you couldn't lie about such things and get away with it could you? He *was* familiar but I couldn't remember anything about our lives together. I found it astonishing that I'd married him in the first place. I must have been desperate to leave home. Marrying at nineteen – I thought that was so young.

In the physiotherapy room I'd mastered walking with the support of the bars. I had yet to walk unaided.

'That's right, Mrs. Miller,' the physiotherapist said at my next session after I'd done a couple of turns. 'Well done. Now attempt to walk back the other way without holding on to the bars.'

This was what I had been waiting for. Could I do it?

I still found it strange to hear someone calling me Mrs. Miller. I turned carefully and considered the distance I had to cover without support. I could feel the sweat forming on my forehead and my heart started beating rapidly; a combination of fear and excitement. Cautiously placing my left foot out, I took one step forward and my leg immediately collapsed under me. I reached up to cling onto the bars to avoid falling to my knees, but a hand grabbed my arm and pulled me upright.

'It's alright Libby, I've gotcha,' Marty said with a huge grin on his face.

'Nooow!' I cried, pushing him away from me with one hand while I clutched the bar with the other. 'I caahn doowit m...my...sef!' I raged at him.

'Crikey Libby, do you know what you just did?'

'What?'

'You just spoke for the first time since the accident!' he said. He looked shocked and then started frowning.

It wasn't the first time I'd spoken. It was simply the first time I'd spoken to him. The first time had been in the bathroom when they'd left me alone to wash. There was a mirror above the sink and so I'd taken the opportunity to see what I looked like. Holding on to the washbasin, I'd pulled myself up and shouted 'Ow noow!' when I saw my reflection. My features were unrecognisable with bandages around my head, several small stitched wound sites dotted around a puffy face and larger wounds across my forehead and down one cheek; my face was a total disaster zone. I'd been hoping that once I saw myself it might trigger some memories, but there was no familiarity in the bits I could see.

Later I realised that I'd produced a half intelligible sound – each day since I'd been practising quietly alone in the bathroom. Most of my words were still not sounding quite right, but I was improving daily. I'd been reticent to speak as I felt embarrassed about how I sounded. The rage I felt towards this man though had finally led to my outburst. Perhaps it was now time to talk openly.

'Sohw?' I asked glaring at him.

'So, it's great news. Another step in gettin' better. We'll be takin' you home in no time.'

'Hmph, ahm not red yet.'

'No, but we're gettin' there girl, we're gettin' there.'

I was *not* ready to go home with him. According to Marty, we'd met when I was eighteen when he'd been labouring for my father. We'd married a year later when I was nineteen. After examining my driving licence, I worked out that I was twenty-one now, and I couldn't imagine sharing the rest of my life with him.

I could acknowledge that Marty was good looking in a rough sort of way, with his thick blond hair and craggy tanned features. He looked a bit like a young man you might see with a surfboard at the beach. But I couldn't stand his voice or the way he spoke to me.

'Mrs. Miller,' the physiotherapist interjected, 'Are you

ready to try again?'

'Yes, onn m…my onn!' I said glaring at Marty.

'Perhaps you could come and sit over here, Mr. Miller,' she said, pointing to a chair near the door.

'Fine. I only wanted to help,' he replied sulkily.

'Yes, but Mrs. Miller needs to do this alone.'

I released my hold on the bars and tentatively took a step forward. My legs supported my weight. Confident, I took another step, then another and before I knew it, I'd reached the end of the bars. I turned and grinned at the therapist.

'Ahh can dowit!' I exclaimed excitedly. To me it was a major achievement.

'Yes, that's fantastic, now come back the other way,' she said.

I repeated the process several more times until I grabbed the bars in exhaustion. Before I could say anything, the therapist said, 'That will do for today, Mrs. Miller, you'll wear yourself out. You've made excellent progress. We'll have a session again tomorrow morning.'

The therapist pushed the wheelchair over to where I was standing at the bars and I staggered out and dropped into it with relief.

'Do you wanna have a go at walkin' back to the ward Libby?'

'I think Mrs. Miller has done quite enough for today,' the therapist said. 'She mustn't overdo it.'

'Okay, I'll take you back in the chair then,' Marty said with resignation. I'd seen his attempts to argue with the therapist over the past week, but he'd learnt that he couldn't win with her.

As Marty wheeled me along, he launched into one his usual monologues. I don't think I'd ever met anyone who talked so much! I blanked him out, remaining silent. I just hoped he wouldn't hang around for too long once I was back in the ward. I wanted to practise using my voice talking to some of the other women. Since being moved into the long ward, Marty thankfully seemed uncomfortable spending too much time there. He often took me outside into the grounds for a walk in the wheelchair and then sat on a bench and talked incessantly to me.

Marty had told me a little about his life growing up in a children's home, leaving there and then moving into a shared house in Maitland, when he first started working for my father. He told me about being conscripted into the army and sent, first to a training camp with living quarters which seemed luxurious compared to the house he shared with mates or the children's home he grew up in. He was then sent to Vietnam. He was discharged from the army after recovering from an injury and two years later started working for my father again, which is apparently how we met. He hadn't met me, he claimed, when he worked for my father in his youth.

He explained how he had to stop doing building work when his old back injury flared up.

He told me that I'd mainly worked in retail shops or various bakeries and how I 'poshed' my voice up to obtain a job in David Jones, an expensive department store in Newcastle (which from what Marty said seemed to have been the pinnacle of my shop girl career).

Once Marty returned me to the ward from these walks however, he clammed up and left. He told me he was staying with one of his old housemates in the centre of Maitland and that it was quite a hike from the hospital.

I'd elected to remain mute when I was first moved into the long ward, not wanting to embarrass myself by uttering strange noises. I communicated with the staff through gesture and actions. I found it incredible though how many people chose to spend time talking to me, without expecting (or probably wanting) any interaction.

Some of the women on the ward seemed to think I offered a form of confessional service as they closed the curtains around my bed and whispered their woes. A couple of the others had introduced themselves to me in passing and hadn't approached me with their problems. I smiled and waved to them. Others just sat down next to me and launched into their spiel.

One woman descended on me saying, 'I knew your mother well from the CWA.' The CWA, she eventually revealed, was the 'Country Women's Association.'

'You know you look just like her,' she'd said at one point. *As if I resembled anyone in this state.*

The woman had talked *at* me for what seemed like hours. The one good thing that came out of her talk was it triggered a memory when she mentioned my mother won prizes for her scones.

I could recollect sitting at a large scrubbed wooden kitchen table eating delicious scones, but I couldn't place my mother, or indeed anyone else at the table with me. When the woman went on to say how sorry she was about the dreadful fire that had killed my mother, father and brother, silent tears streamed down my face. Not that the woman noticed. I was finally rescued by a nurse who interrupted the woman in full flow with, 'Come along Mrs. Grey, we need to get you back into bed now.' With a wink at me, the nurse led the woman back to her bed, which thank goodness, was right at the other end of the ward. The woman had avoided me ever since, so perhaps the nurse had said something to her.

Without me noticing, Marty lapsed into silence at some point on the journey back to the ward from the therapy room. He stopped outside the ward's double doors. 'Libby what do you think about the idea of seeing if you can be transferred to a hospital near where we live in Sydney? It would make life a lot easier for both of us. What do you reckon?'

'Nooow! I wan … say here!' I shouted. I felt safe at the hospital. Outside was the unknown.

'Okay, okay, it was just a thought. I reckon you might be released in another week or so anyway.' He wheeled me into the ward, depositing me beside my bed.

'I'm going to speak to the sister and then I'm off. I'll be back this arvo.'

'Kay,' I said. 'Tank you.'

Marty saluted me and walked off down to the other end of the ward where the sister had a small office.

I glanced around and saw that some of the women were sitting quietly in chairs beside their beds reading, including the young woman in the bed opposite me, whose name was Una. I remained seated for a few minutes until I saw Marty leave the building, then decided I was going to have an adventure.

I liked Una and wanted to cross the room and talk to her. The woman had been friendly towards me without being intrusive. There were no bars to support me, but I was reasonably confident I could do it. Gingerly, I rose from the chair and stepped out into the unknown. Eleven steps later I reached the end of Una's bed and leaned against it. Applause broke out across the ward. I looked around and could see that many of the women and also some nurses were clapping. For me! I blushed with embarrassment.

'Hello,' Una said. 'That was quite an achievement.'

'Tank you.'

'And talking too.'

'Not so well.'

'That will come with practise. Here sit on my chair, I'll take the bed. So, tell me how you got on in physio today?'

I moved forward, fell into Una's bedside chair with gratitude and proceeded to tell her, albeit rather haphazardly, about my physio session. Una seemed to understand everything I said, despite my language inconsistencies. I asked her if she had anything she could lend me to read, explaining that I hadn't been able to read for the past few weeks because of my head injuries and pain, but I now wanted to experiment with some light reading. I'd looked at a chart the physiotherapist showed me when I first went to see her, but none of the words made sense – they were all jumbled up. I'd since managed to read posters and signs dotted around the hospital walls but now, I wanted to see if I could read the text in books or magazines.

Una pulled a couple of magazines from her locker and said, 'Go for it, girl. Magazines would be the best thing; you don't want to be muddling through a complex novel.'

'Tanks. Jus wha I nee.'

I made my way back to my bed, but within minutes I was surrounded by Sister O'Connell and two nurses congratulating me on today's achievements. By the time they left me, lunch was being served and I had no opportunity to look at the magazines. Following lunch, I was so exhausted, I drifted off into a long afternoon sleep.

Over the following two weeks, my speech and mobility improved dramatically. The stitches on my face, forehead and head were removed. Much of the swelling had gone down. I no longer had to have my head bandaged and my scars were healing well although they stood out noticeably. My head was covered in a fine soft growth of new hair which I examined in the bathroom mirror. In the picture Marty had shown me from our wedding day I had blonde hair. No doubt out of a bottle. The new growth was a pale strawberry blonde colour. I liked it and decided I wouldn't colour it again.

Twenty-seven days I'd been in the hospital. It was beginning to feel like home to me, a haven, certainly one that I preferred to the prospect of what awaited me in Sydney. Marty was collecting me that morning. I was sure I was only being discharged at Marty's urging. Although I was dressed ready to leave, I wasn't mentally prepared.

The police had been in to see me a few days before to question me about the accident. There was nothing I could tell them, as I still didn't remember anything about it at all, although I don't think I managed to convey that. A Sergeant Pryce, with a silent colleague, approached me with questions that sounded unintelligible.

With his lips pressed together the Sergeant bombarded

me with questions which flew out of a tiny hole he made in the side of his mouth. From snippets I recalled from our farm, it was a typical strategy adopted by Australian men when they were talking outdoors, particularly in country areas near livestock, to avoid flies entering their mouths. It became habit-forming and they often continued talking in this almost unintelligible way to people when indoors.

I could only tell he was asking me questions by the inflection in his tone and I sat in bed with a perplexed expression. I just said 'huh?' to stifle a laugh.

The Sergeant repeated his questions, this time with his mouth a little more open, but I still didn't quite catch them. And there was no way I could respond to him. He looked and sounded so funny! I tightly clamped my top lip over my lower lip to suppress the threatened laughter that was bubbling up, bowed my head, and turned to the side away from him so he couldn't see my face. I couldn't help but emit constant little noises which must have sounded quite strange.

On his third attempt he raised his voice and shouted a question at me, pausing in between each word. This time he enunciated everything clearly. 'CAN… YOU…TELL…US…*ANYTHING*…ABOUT…THE… ACCIDENT?'

He must have thought I was brain damaged. I managed to say a breathy 'No', all the while continuing to keep my head turned away from the sergeant. I couldn't look at him as I knew I'd burst into fits of giggles.

Sister O'Connell rescued me; no doubt alarmed by his loud manner and asked the sergeant to leave. I heard him say to his colleague as they were walking away, 'It's a shame but I don't think we'll ever get anything sensible out of that one.'

After they left, I'd erupted with laughter until tears streamed down my face and my sides ached.

I wasn't laughing that morning though. Earlier I'd been violently sick. The nurses assured me that it was due to nerves about leaving the hospital to move on to a life I had no memory of. Before Una had been discharged a few days previously I'd confided in her my dislike of Marty and my fears of any form of intimacy with him.

'I don't know if I could stand him touching me Una,' I'd moaned.

'Don't you think you are being a little unfair on Marty, I know you can't remember your life with him, but he's been a very attentive husband, coming to the hospital every day. I'm sure if you explained how you feel, he'd be patient with you and wait until you're ready for any lovemaking. He clearly loves you and he seems very nice.'

I think Una was the kind of woman who saw the best in everyone.

'Does he love me though? There's something that's a bit false about his behaviour towards me,' I said.

'In what way?'

'When I first regained consciousness, he was always there, whispering things in my ear. There was something sinister and creepy about it. Then when the staff came in, he behaved differently.'

'It might be simply that you were still so very ill and woozy from your injuries, that you didn't understand what was going on.'

'Perhaps you're right,' I sighed. 'I certainly didn't

understand much when I first woke up.'

Doctor Jackson had explained that I'd been unconscious when Marty brought me in, then they'd kept me unconscious due to my injuries. He was pleased with the progress I'd made and I'd passed tests they'd given me to check for brain damage. They'd asked me loads of questions, shown me cards with images or symbols I had to recall in sequence and even put some weird plugs on my head. They said my short-term memory was fine. But there were considerable gaps in my long-term memory which they believed would return; given time. I hoped so as there was very little I remembered of my life before waking up at Maitland hospital. Certainly not how Marty explained it. Just the odd memory floating about that I couldn't attach to anything concrete.

I waited with trepidation for Marty to appear looking down at the things he'd brought in for me to wear home which I didn't like. The clothes I'd been wearing on the day of the accident had been binned as they either had to be cut off me or were too damaged by blood, according to Marty. When I asked Sister O'Connell, she confirmed this is what had happened.

In my bedside locker the only clothing items I found were my bra and shoes, a pair of comfy flatties. I wanted to ask Sister O'Connell why there were no pants there but felt too embarrassed.

The skirt was so short I felt embarrassed to be seen in it. Marty said I sounded like a typical 'whingeing Pom', making fun of the fact that I'd been born in England when I'd exclaimed my dislike of the garments. Thankfully, the over-the-knee length coat he'd brought in would hide the skirt when I left.

'Most of your skirts are short Darl, that's how you like them,' Marty had said. 'You have a few long dresses, but they're only summer things. It's the fashion.'

I wasn't happy to be walking around in a skirt that barely covered my underwear. I couldn't imagine dressing like that. And the underwear, that was another thing. The pants were skimpy little things with frilly edges.

'Really?' I'd questioned Marty when I discovered them in the bag he'd brought me. Since being admitted I'd just worn a nightie with no pants and a dressing gown over the nightie that the hospital had supplied. 'I wear skimpy little things like this?'

'Yeah, you always went for sexy knickers and no bras.'

'No bra?'

'That's right, you only put one on the day of the accident because we were goin' to see the lawyer. You always wore a bra to work or around your family. The rest of the time you went bra-less like most of the sheilas your age do today.'

I couldn't imagine this. I could understand wanting to take a bra off after a long day's work, relaxing at home after showering, but to go out without one was unthinkable. I surmised that I must have done this for Marty, but it wasn't something I'd be doing in future that was for sure.

Marty suddenly appeared before me. I'd been so distracted by the gross clothes, that I hadn't seen him approaching.

'Mornin' Libby, you ready to go?'

He was grinning lopsidedly at me. Oh God, here we go.

My heart skipped a beat and I prickled with fear. It was like I was just about to be taken off to serve a prison sentence; stepping into the unknown as a first-time offender.

'Yes,' I replied, applying a smile to my face, 'but I just have to say goodbye to everyone. I won't be long.'

'I'll take your bag and wait outside then.'

After prolonged goodbye chats I could no longer delay leaving. I walked outside the hospital doors into brilliant sunshine. May was supposed to be autumn, but it didn't feel like it. I was stifling in my buttoned-up coat (to hide my short skirt).

Marty led me to a car I didn't recognise. A Ford Falcon, he informed me – one that had seen better days. It had bits of rust on the body plus a few scratches and dents.

'How do you like the new wheels?'

'Is this ours? I thought we no longer had a car as ours was wrecked in the accident?'

'It was. The insurance paid up, didn't they? So I bought this yesterday. I couldn't have you goin' home on the train.'

'Is it roadworthy?'

'Yeah, she's a beaut. Not much of a looker, but she runs real well. Got her in Sydney and drove up in it this mornin. Bit of a gas guzzler though.'

'I think I would've preferred the train, Marty. I feel a bit nervous at the idea of travelling to Sydney in a car.'

'Nah, you'll be right. I'll take it real slow for you. It's not that far; only about three hours.'

Only three hours!

'Do you mind if I travel in the back?' I asked him. I was terrified at the idea of sitting in the front. I didn't want to get into the car at all.

'Nah, whatever your highness wishes.'

Marty opened one of the back doors and I slid in. I spread out across the back seat and said, 'I think I might try to have a sleep; it'll make me feel less nervous and make the journey go quicker.'

'Whatever makes you feel more comfortable Darl.'

I wished he'd stop calling me Darl I thought as I laid across the back seat. Within minutes I drifted off.

20

Bristol June 2000

When Beth Carey pauses at this point, Frank considers how much he should reveal to her. Should he tell her that they met briefly back in Maitland Hospital? He decides to take the chance and see what she makes of it.

'You mentioned that the police came to talk to you at the hospital. I was the silent colleague you referred to. I was accompanying sergeant Pryce that day, although I don't think he introduced us. I was a young constable at the time and I worked with him on aspects of the investigation into your car accident and sat in on an interview with your husband.'

She tilts her head to one side with a quizzical expression.

'When you just said you couldn't understand what the sergeant was saying?'

'Oh my God yes,' Beth says putting a hand to her mouth and laughing. 'That was so awful, you must have thought me terribly rude. I'm sure your sergeant thought I was brain damaged.'

'Well, we both did, to be honest. But I can see that we

were wrong. Why would we have thought you were being rude?'

'When he was mumbling out of the side of his mouth, I was reminded of someone who worked with my grandfather … no sorry, that can't be right. Neither of my grandfather's ever lived in Australia. Anyway, a man who worked for my father talked like that. It always made me burst into fits of giggles whenever I heard him as a child. That's what happened that day. I was struggling to control my laughter trying not to be rude, but he reminded me so much of old Bluey and just took me back to my childhood without realising it …'

Beth stops and her eyes widen. A hand flies to her mouth and her shocked expression reminds Frank of someone who has let slip a four letter swear word unintentionally.

'Is everything alright Mrs. Carey?'

Her hand drops before she says, 'Yes, it's just that the name of the man who worked for my father, just popped into my head. Astonishing.'

'Why is that astonishing?'

'Because I remember so little of my childhood and my life before the accident. I don't know where that suddenly came from. Perhaps hearing an Australian accent for the first time in many years and remembering the way your sergeant spoke triggered it.'

'I can still hear a trace of an Australian accent in your voice,' Frank says.

'Well, I left Australia as an adult. I guess we never lose the accents we take into our adult lives. Clients often remark on it. I can't hear it myself, but my kids make fun of the way I pronounce some things.'

'When you say clients...' Frank trails off.

'I'm a solicitor. Mainly doing conveyancing on house purchases.'

There's no brain injury there then.

'Picking up on what you said about my sergeant, I'd have to agree with what you said. He did have a habit of talking like that and sometimes it was hard to understand him. Especially if you weren't used to it. We often had to ask him to repeat himself. Once he got going each day, he'd start to talk normally though. He grew up on a farm and so perhaps it was a habit he developed there.'

'Yes maybe. After you left, I laughed so much that I almost wet myself. But later I felt dreadful, thinking you must have thought me so rude. I'd had to turn my head away you see so that I wouldn't laugh in his face.'

'Yes, I can see that now, with hindsight. It's a shame his temper got the better of him. If he'd been patient and we'd stayed to speak to you calmly, things might have been different.'

'What do you mean by that?'

'Several things. Amongst his initial questions was one about the other car in the collision. If he'd spoken clearly to you, you would have immediately picked up on the issue of a second car and queried it. Your husband's lies would have been exposed. Also, the way he spoke triggered a memory for you. We might've discovered the source of it. It might have helped you to regain other memories. You say that you have very little recall of your life before the accident. Have you had other instances of where something suddenly comes to you like that?'

'I had a weird incident the other week. I spouted a load

of medieval historical facts that had me flummoxed. I couldn't understand how I'd acquired all that knowledge.'

Beth explains how a situation arose with her daughter Alison and her friend Karen, who were studying medieval history at Bristol University, and how for some time after she puzzled over how she could've known the information.

'But eventually, I worked out that I must have heard it all on a televised documentary, although I don't recall watching one on the subject.'

'Have you recalled anything else?'

'Well, late last year I had a strong memory recall of holding a baby boy when I was about eight or nine years old. My brother was older than me, so it wasn't him. I questioned one of my uncles, who stayed with us in Australia when I was nine, and from what he told me it couldn't have been my family, so I decided it must have been a neighbour's child. But this isn't really what you've come to see me about is it?'

'I think it could all be relevant.'

Beth looks at the clock on the kitchen wall and says, 'Look I have to go into work now. I have some contract exchanges due to take place this afternoon. Is there anything further we need to discuss? And you haven't told me why you want all this information.'

'No, I'm afraid I can't at the moment. But I need to know what happened after your husband took you back to your flat and how you ended up in England. Perhaps we could make an appointment to meet up again tomorrow?'

'Do we really need to? It relates to a period in my life I'd prefer not to have to think about again.'

'It would be very helpful if you could go over things

for me.'

Beth sighs and says, 'Okay, I'll make sure my desk is clear for the morning. Shall we say eight again?'

'That would be fine. Thank you.'

'What is your take on Beth Carey, DI Radcliffe?' Frank asks as they drive away from the Clifton property.

'She seems straightforward enough. But it's early days yet. I'd like to hear what else she has to say. How much are you going to tell her?'

'It depends on what she reveals tomorrow.'

'Do you still think she's linked to your mystery victim?'

'I do. Look, any chance you could get that DNA sample we talked about yesterday afternoon?'

Frank had asked DI Radcliffe whether he could obtain a DNA sample from Beth Carey's uncle without him being aware of it.

'I don't want to cause unnecessary trouble within the family and would like to check the outcomes before we do anything official,' Frank had explained.

Radcliffe had refused saying he wasn't willing to do that to Kenny Fallon. But he was prepared to take a sample from Fallon's son who was actually working in his house.

'With this current heat wave, my wife supplies the builders with endless glasses of water. I'll see if I can grab a glass he's used,' Radcliffe had said.

Frank just hopes Radcliffe is willing to go through with it. He'd told Frank he would have to pay for the sample to be processed himself, through a private lab and had given him the name of one in a place called Filton.

'Yes, okay,' Radcliffe sighs. 'If you drop me back at the

station, I'll pop home and sort it for you. If I'm successful, I'll bring it tomorrow morning. Pick me up at the station about quarter to eight. Same as today.'

'Good morning,' Frank says greeting George Radcliffe the following morning as Radcliffe climbs into the car with grunts and groans.

'There's nothing good about it, as far as I'm concerned. My arthritis is giving me hell today.'

'Sorry to hear that,' Frank says wondering if he should dare ask about the DNA sample. But just as he decides to leave the question until later, DI Radcliffe provides him with the answer.

'This is the sample you wanted. Hopefully you'll get some DNA off that,' he says passing Frank a glass in a sealed evidence bag. 'This can't ever be made official. You understand that don't you?'

'Yes, of course. Thank you,' Frank replies leaning over to place the glass carefully on the floor of the car behind the passenger seat.

He intends to drop that off to the company either today or tomorrow with, if all goes well, a DNA sample from Beth Carey.

Beth Carey greets them with a grimace, 'My daughter hasn't left yet this morning, and so I would appreciate it if we delayed your questions until she leaves. She won't be long. I'll take you into the living room and bring you coffee shortly. Same as yesterday?'

They nod and settle themselves into the comfortable couches the lounge has to offer while Beth Carey closes the door and leaves them. They sit in silence for the next ten minutes listening as a young woman shouts goodbye to her mother and the front door slams. A minute or so later the lounge door opens and Beth Carey walks in carrying a tray of steaming mugs and a plate of biscuits. Frank declines the biscuits, he's been indulging in too many treats since he left Australia, but DI Radcliffe grabs a few before settling back.

Frank starts the mini-recorder, placing it on the coffee table in front of him. 'So,' he starts, 'Could you tell us how things unfolded when your husband took you back to the flat.'

21

Libby's Story
Sydney, May 1975

I woke in the car with a start. 'Where are we?' I asked Marty. I could see we were heading up a busy street.

'We're just driving up William Street in Sydney. You've slept nearly all the way. I told you it'd be alright. Won't be long before we're home.'

It wasn't going to feel like 'home' to me if I couldn't remember it. The thought of sharing any space alone with Marty made me feel quite sick.

He turned right and wove the car around some small back streets, until he pulled into the car park of a long, low rise, modern block of flats.

'This is us, Darl.'

I didn't recognise the place. It looked a little neglected – like the owner had thrown it up and left the tenants to get on with it. 'What floor do we live on?'

'The top floor. Come on. I'm dying for a cuppa after that trip.'

He opened my door, reached in for my bag and waved

at me to hurry out of the car. I followed him through the block entrance and looked at the stairs. I hadn't had to climb any stairs at the hospital and they seemed foreboding. Before I'd left the hospital, I was feeling strong. Right at that moment I felt fragile. I struggled after him up the two flights (there was no lift) to the second-floor landing where there were four doors. I'd had to stop and rest several times while Marty waited impatiently for me. I watched as Marty opened the door to flat nine.

'Home sweet home,' he said and gestured for me to walk in the door before him.

The entrance led into a hallway. I paused, not knowing which way to turn.

'Left is to the bedroom and bathroom. The door in front of you leads to the kitchen and to the right is the living room.'

I opened the door to the kitchen – neutral territory where I'd feel safe. I was pleased to discover that the kitchen wasn't attached to the living room and there was a small table with three chairs in there. I had envisaged an open plan layout that meant no separate space from Marty so it was good to know I could retreat to a space that was not the bedroom. There was a door leading out from the kitchen to the narrow balcony I'd seen from the car park.

I walked across the dirty tiled floor, and glanced through the door. The balcony seemed to run further along to where, I assumed, the living room was. I couldn't see any seating out there so presumably we didn't use it. It faced onto the car park and the road we had come in from. Paint on the metal railings was peeling; it hadn't been maintained for some time. Was that the tenant or landlord's responsibility? I'd noticed some of the railings on other floors looked smarter.

'Is there a laundry in the block we can use?'

'No; but there is a laundromat just around the corner. That's where we do our washin'.'

I looked around the kitchen. There was an electric stove, a large fridge/freezer, a tall double width cupboard and a few low-level cupboards. I couldn't remember ever using an electric stove before, except at the hospital. Mind you, I couldn't remember anything much. I opened the fridge to see it only contained some butter, bread, cheese and milk.

'There's plenty of food in the freezer,' Marty said. 'Most of our meals just go in the oven from the freezer.'

I shuddered at the thought of that.

'How about putting the jug on Darl, while I put your bag into the bedroom. Are you hungry, cos I wouldn't mind some cheese on toast? Also give me your coat. We hang them in the hall.'

I shrugged off my coat and handed it to Marty. He disappeared and I filled what he'd called a jug and I called a kettle – although my memory of them was that they sat on top of the stove. This one was electric, like the one they'd shown me at the hospital. I then set about discovering what was in the cupboards. I found some sugar, loose tea and a teapot, but no strainer. After rummaging around in a drawer, I found the strainer buried under a jumble of cutlery and serving utensils. The tall cupboard multi-functioned as a larder, and was also where all the plates and pots and pans were kept. It was a mess. I was busy examining the state of the pans when Marty startled me.

'Libby, you haven't turned the jug on!'

'Oh sorry, I thought I had.'

'Nor the grill. Look, you have to switch the power for the stove on at the wall first. Then turn the grill on and open the grill door.' He demonstrated how to do this for me. 'Are you gunna be able to do this? Can you remember how to?'

'Yes, yes, I can do it. One of the therapists took me through some simple routines in the hospital, to make sure I understood basic safety in the kitchen.'

I pulled the grubby breadboard from the cupboard and gave it a good wash. I was reluctant to use it while it was still damp as it would make the bread all soggy so I just used side plates (which were thankfully clean) for preparation. With sliced bread it was an easy enough task, but I had to cut the cheese, and my hand was still a little shaky.

Minutes later I congratulated myself on being able to successfully master the task of making cheese on toast and tea. It felt like another significant achievement. I hadn't realised how hungry I'd been after my sickness this morning. The tea was wonderful as well, with not so much milk in it. I'd never really enjoyed the milky slops they served in the hospital. Marty and I were sitting at the table and I decided it was time to find out more information about our lives, plus tell Marty things I had to do.

'I have to find a doctor and let the hospital know his or her name and the address of the practice. They've given me a letter to pass on to whoever I see. You told the hospital we didn't have a doctor in Sydney. Why didn't we?'

'We just hadn't got around to it Darl. We weren't plannin' on stayin' in this area, so there seemed no point in findin' a doctor. We were gunna find one once we decided where we were gunna move to with the new business. Besides, apart from my old injury that I need to see a doctor about occasionally, neither of us were ever ill.'

'Well, I need one now. My doctor needs to know about the accident and my injuries and he or she needs to do a letter to a Sydney hospital for follow up checks.'

'Yeah, okay, fine.'

'So, what is this business we were thinking of starting that you've referred to several times? You never mentioned what it was.'

'We talked about lots of options and the one we finally settled on was a used car yard. I always fancied having a car yard. We went to see a property in Newtown and another one in Leichardt, that were good prospects. They both had three-bedroomed houses, with a garage and a good-sized yard to the front and side of the properties that could hold a good few cars. The one in Newtown had previously been a used car lot that had closed down so that would be the easiest to set up as it had a small office. At the Leichardt one we'd have to build somethin' in the yard but it was all do-able.'

'Why did the Newtown one close down?' I asked him.

'The ol' fella who owned it carked it, and none of his children wanted to take it over. It had been sittin' empty for over a year. They tried to sell it as a goin' business, but no one was interested. When we went to see it, all the cars had gone, and they were just sellin' the property, for a lot less than they were first askin'.'

'We were looking at *buying* these places?'

'Yep. Your father was gunna give us enough money to

get set up with a good deposit on the house and to buy in a load of cars; we were gunna borrow the rest. As a Vietnam Vet I'm entitled to a loan. Your brother Gary was gunna have the farm, so your father was happy to give us some money to give us a helpin' hand. Part of it would have been a loan, the rest a gift. He wouldn't have lent us the money if there wasn't a home attached, and I wouldn't be entitled to borrowin' on just a business, so that's why we were lookin' at places with a house as well.'

'Right,' I said. 'Why didn't we proceed with a purchase? I know you've mentioned it but tell me again.'

'We were gunna collect a cheque from your father the day after the fire – we were due there for lunch. Because of what happened we haven't been able to do anythin'. I doubt those properties would still be available, but I'm sure we'll find another one. Now of course we won't have to borrow any money because of the settlement you'll be gettin' from your family's estate. We could buy somethin' with cash.'

'Would we have enough money for that?' I asked.

'Dunno really, but yeah, I think so. Your parents didn't have a mortgage and the house was insured. They also had savings. There was life insurance on your parents as well. Your brother wasn't insured. No one thinks they are gunna die in their twenties, do they? Then there's the sale of the land, plus the farm animals and farm equipment they auctioned off. The land value is less now than it would have been with a house on it, but the barns and sheds are still standin'. It wasn't like the big cattle stations they have in the outback, but they had quite a good spread, so it still fetched a reasonable price.'

'So how much do you think we are going to receive?'

'You couldn't tell me the final figure after that last trip to the lawyer, as he hadn't completed the sale of the property and hadn't received all the money from the auction. He has the insurance money from the house and your parents' lives though. Altogether it will be well over a hundred thousand bucks.'

I nearly choked on my tea at the figure he quoted. 'Really, that much?'

'Yeah, I'm sorry that you lost your family over it all, but we'll be set now girl. No more havin' to work our guts out for some other bastard.'

I remained quiet for a moment. The knowledge that we were going to profit from my parents' death brought tears to my eyes. I didn't remember them, but I was sure I must have loved them. Everyone loves their parents, don't they? The thought of not having any family around with only Marty in my life was not something I could bear to think about. I would have loved to have had family members who could have visited me in hospital and maybe stayed with after being discharged. I shook my head to clear the depressing thoughts and said, 'Speaking of work, what have you been doing since we came to Sydney?'

'I couldn't work in the buildin' trade any more, due to my old injury. I've had a couple of temporary jobs since we've been here but I'd been mainly claimin' unemployment money. I was on a pension when I first came back from Nam, but then they declared me fit for work. You don't remember *any* of this?'

'No, I told you, I can't remember anything.'

'Anyway, we'd decided to make a new start and were

lookin' at businesses, so it made sense that I didn't work at first, so I could look around at what was available. After the fire, neither of us worked for a bit as there was so much to sort out.'

'Like what?'

'The animals on the farm. The beef cattle weren't too bad as they just fed off the grass, but they had to be moved around into different paddocks. The pigs had to be fed by someone every day. We had to arrange for someone to look after them through your father's lawyer. It was too much for us to do livin' in Sydney and there was nowhere to stay at the farm of course, so we had the lawyer deal with most things, but it all took *months*. Before our accident we agreed that I would start lookin' at places again thinkin' the money would be comin' through soon. Of course, all that had to go on hold, and with bein' up in Maitland for weeks now, I haven't been able to work either.'

'So how have we been able to pay the rent and all our other living costs?'

'You had a job before the accident of course. That kept us goin'. You were owed a week's money when you ended up in hospital, so I collected that. I told them what happened and that you wouldn't be returning. You'd handed in your notice there anyway. I claim unemployment. And I'm sorry Darl but then I had to sell your engagement ring. I needed more money to settle the rent and other things.'

'My engagement ring!' I spluttered.

'Yeah, I didn't think you'd be too upset about it. We've had to pawn it a few times over the past year, but this time I sold it. You weren't that bothered before. Don't worry, you can have a new one when we get the money.'

I swallowed the anger that I could feel rising and changed the subject. I hadn't even known I had an engagement ring, but that wasn't the point.

'So, when are we going to receive this money?'

'You'll have to get on to the lawyer. I've been phonin' him to tell him how you've been doin', but he won't discuss anythin' with me as you're the one the payment will go to.'

'Do we have a phone?'

'Nah, you'll have to use the one in the laundromat around the corner. We thought there was no point in wastin' money installin' a new phone when we were gunna move anyway. This place was just meant to be short term. I would've suggested goin' straight to the lawyer's office in Raymond Terrace when I picked you up from the hospital, but I thought it might be a bit much for you to deal with that and comin' home as well. You can phone him tomorrow. I've got his card here.'

Marty produced a card from his pocket and placed it on the table in front of me. He explained that he'd removed it from my handbag when I was admitted to the hospital so he could keep in touch with the law firm.

'Yes. Okay. Do I have to go up to see him again? He's in Raymond Terrace you said. Is that in Maitland?'

Marty sighed. 'His office is in a suburb, or *town* called Raymond Terrace. It's probably closer to Newcastle. Just off the Pacific Highway. And no, you don't have to see him again. All you gotta do is chase him up for that cheque.'

'When the cheque comes, presumably it will be made out to me. Do I have a bank account?'

'You did have one, but you closed it just before movin'

here to Sydney. You were paid here in cash so it didn't matter. We pay everythin' in cash. You'll have to open a new account. It would probably be better if we opened a joint account. We'll go to the National Bank and do that tomorrow.'

'Okay, but I would also like my own account,' I said.

'You don't need two accounts Darl,' he said. 'The banks will make extra money out of us if you have two accounts. We only need the one.'

I wasn't too pleased with his answer, but decided not to say anything for the moment. I opened the handbag that had been with me at the hospital and pulled out two sets of keys. 'Which of these are the keys to this flat?'

Marty pointed to one set and replied, 'These.' He picked up the set and showed me one of the keys, 'This is door key for enterin' the block, but it's never locked. This one,' he said, showing me another one, 'is the key to our flat door. And this one,' he continued, producing a smaller key off the ring, 'is the letterbox key. The letterboxes are in the entrance hall which is why the door is always left open so the postie can come in.' He removed the post-box key and pocketed it. 'I'll be checkin' the post box each day, so you don't have to worry your pretty little head about it. It'll save you goin' up and down those stairs so much.'

I wasn't happy with this situation, but again remained silent. I doubted he'd said he'd deal with the post for altruistic reasons. He wanted control of the cheque.

'And these keys?' I finally asked, picking up the other set.

'I'm sorry Darl, they were the keys for your parents' house and a couple of the sheds. We won't be wanting any of them now though. The lawyer has asked me to post them to him. He needs this final set of shed keys for the new owner. I'll do that tomorrow. Right,' he said standing. 'Let's go into the lounge where it's more comfortable. You can relax and listen to some music in there if you like.'

I followed Marty into the lounge. The walls, like the kitchen and hallway, were painted white. There was a large couch covered in a cherry red cotton bedspread. I pulled the cover up and noticed the couch had seen better days. It felt quite lumpy when I pressed the cushions. There was also a single lounge chair, in far better condition. It looked comfortable.

'This is my chair,' Marty declared, pointing to the single chair.

I looked around the room and saw a sideboard on which there was a record deck with amp and speakers. It looked like a state-of-the-art piece of equipment. So, we could afford things that suited him. There was a wooden coffee table in front of the couch, which had a shelf underneath stacked with magazines. Apart from an electric heater tucked up against the wall, there was nothing else in the room.

'There are no books. Don't we have any books?'

'Yeah, we did. You took them and the bookcase up to store in your old bedroom at your parents' place when we moved to Sydney. To make our move easier. There's nuthin' left of them now though, with the fire."

'Hmm, and no television?'

'Our old telly broke just before we moved to Sydney and we haven't been able to afford another one since.'

'Radio?'

'Nah, that was at your parents as well and went in the fire.'

'What do we do of an evening then?' I asked.

'My mate comes around and we have a few beers, or I go to his place sometimes.'

'Who is this mate then?'

'Brett. I've known him since high school and we've always kept in touch. He lived in Newcastle when we did but moved to Sydney a few months before us. It's mainly down to him that we decided to move to Sydney. He's like family to me. You'll recognise him when you see him – or maybe not. He was going to move in with us and work in the car yard. Hopefully he still will, when we find the right place. What Brett doesn't know about fixin' cars you could write on a pin head. He's a wizard. Just think, we could buy old bangers, Brett could fix them up and then we'd make a nice big fat profit.'

'Did Brett serve in Vietnam with you?'

'Nah, he managed to escape the birthday lottery call up. Lucky bugger.'

'Does he live nearby?'

'Yeah, just a few streets away. He's the one put us onto this place. He has the same landlord.'

'He must be a good friend then if we were going to live and work with him?'

'Yeah, the best,' he said.

'So, that accounts for you. What do *I* do of an evening?'

'You sit around chattin' to us, listenin' to music or readin' your women's magazines.'

'Hmm. Don't we ever go out?' I couldn't imagine the scene he described. It seemed so unlike anything I might find enjoyable.

'Can't afford it. Now and then we eat out somewhere. We get a take-away meal about once a week. Fish and chips, you know, somethin' like that. Only in your case, you have pie and chips,' he added. 'You never told me you were *allergic* to fish Libby. Only that you didn't like it, so I didn't tell the hospital. Which is why there was a problem that day.'

'I don't know why I didn't tell you. Maybe I didn't know?'

'Maybe. Anyway, I'm gunna put some music on. Brett will be comin' around soon. And you need to sort out what we're havin' for dinner.'

'*I* have to sort out the dinner?'

'Yeah, you always insisted on dealing with our meals. I only organise the take-aways.'

'I am surprised,' I said sarcastically. 'Considering I worked all day and you didn't. Do I ever cook a proper meal?'

'Yeah, sometimes you'd do a roast chicken or somethin' like that. On Sundays, you know, when Brett comes around.'

'So, Brett often eats with us regularly?'

'Yeah, and he will be tonight.'

That's why there were three chairs in the kitchen I realised.

'Okay, I'll go and look at what we have, and leave you to put some music on.' I retreated to the kitchen, incensed at the knowledge that I dealt with the meals when that lazy bugger had done nothing all day. No wonder I didn't cook very often. I wasn't sure how long I was willing to suffer his chauvinistic expectations. I suspected there might be fireworks soon. Perhaps he was taking advantage of the fact that I couldn't remember anything and was trying it on.

The freezer *was* packed with ready-made meals. The idea made my stomach churn. I finally settled on a large lasagne and looked at the cooking times. Too early to put it on yet, but I placed it on the worktop to start defrosting before putting it in the oven. Although it said to cook it from frozen, I didn't like the idea of that. I couldn't remember ever cooking a frozen meal before. I decided to explore the rest of the flat while Marty was busy listening to some of his music. I didn't recognise the artist he was playing, but it was loud and raucous. Not my cup of tea. How did I sit and listen to that night after night?

The bathroom was compact. I spotted a small circular clothes airer hanging over the shower rail with built-in pegs which was probably for underwear. The shower was not in a separate cubicle, but above a bath with a white curtain that was very grubby around its base. Everything else needed a good clean as well. I looked under the vanity unit and finding what I needed, I set about giving the bathroom a good scrub, including the shower curtain which I attempted to clean in situ. I was startled by Marty leaning over me as I scrubbed the toilet.

'I can see you're doin' a great job there Libby, but are you sure you should be doin' this as you've just come out of hospital? And I need to use the dunny Darl, so could you go out for a bit?'

I left the bathroom and turned into the bedroom. There was a double bed, a large built-in wardrobe and a tall chest of drawers. On each side of the bed there was a small bedside cabinet. I wondered which side of the bed was mine and shuddered at the thought of having to share it with Marty. An examination of the bedside cupboard contents confirmed that I slept on the window side. The room smelled stuffy so I opened the window to air it. I began unpacking my small bag, which was on the bed. Not knowing where I kept anything, I opened drawers to examine their contents and discover which were mine.

I rummaged around in the underwear drawer and noticed there were only pants, vests, tights and socks. No other bras. It looked like the one I was wearing was the only one I owned. I'd have to buy some more as I couldn't manage on one bra, otherwise I'd have to constantly wash it out overnight. There was also a small plastic case in the underwear drawer and when I opened it, I realised it was a contraceptive cap. I hoped I wouldn't need to use it soon.

The wardrobe had a double hanging space and some shelving down the right-hand side. There weren't that many clothes on the hangers. I searched through them and found the couple of summer dresses that Marty had referred to, several mini-skirts, (that were definitely going into a charity bag) a couple of long sleeve blouses, a long denim skirt and two pairs of jeans that I assumed were mine as they had elastic on the back of the waist and no zips. I discarded the mini skirt I was wearing and quickly changed into a pair of jeans. The top shelves of the wardrobe seemed to be Marty's and the bottom ones mine. I decided to leave those for another time.

'Are you findin' everything okay?' asked Marty, creeping into the bedroom and startling me.

'Yes, thank you,' I said, determined not to let him know he'd rattled me. 'Marty, I don't seem to have that many clothes here. Is this all I own?'

'Well once again, you stored quite a bit at your parents.'

'Okay. Say no more. Oh, and I've selected a lasagne for dinner. Is that alright?'

'Yeah, that's fine.'

'What is that tune you keep humming?' I asked him. All the time he'd been in the bathroom he'd been humming it.

'It's a nursery rhyme. You know the *'ring-a-ring-of-roses'*. We played it all the time at the kid's home I was brought up in, only we got bored with the version the staff taught us so we made up our version of it.'

'How does that go then?'

He was about to launch into a description when we heard a knock at the door.

'That'll be Brett,' he said. 'Come and say hello to him.'

I followed Marty who had already opened the door and was greeting his friend.

'Libby, this is Brett. Do you remember him at all?' I looked at the man, who was a little shorter than Marty. He had dark brown hair and a bit of belly hanging over his jeans. He was carrying bottles of beer.

'No, sorry,' I said.

'Hi Libby,' Brett said, 'you look er…'

'Very different?' I offered.

'Er… yeah,' Brett laughed nervously. Marty joined in the laughter with him.

'That'll be the short back and sides haircut, and the scars on your puffy face. No offence Darl, but you do look very different without your hair,' Marty said, still laughing.

'Ha, ha, very funny, I don't think. I'll leave you two to your beers and continue unpacking.'

I turned and began walking back down the hall.

'You don't wanna join us for a beer?' Brett asked.

I stopped, turned and looked at them. 'No thanks I don't …' I was about to say, 'I don't drink beer.' But perhaps I did? 'I don't feel like one right now,' I settled on.

The men retreated to the lounge while I returned to the bedroom. They closed the lounge door and put another loud record on the player. No doubt so they could talk without me hearing.

I pulled the blue bedcover back and saw the bed was made up with dirty candy-striped cotton sheets and light blue blankets. The blankets look relatively clean, but the sheets – ugh! I found the idea of getting into those really disturbing. I couldn't do it. Where did we keep the linen? I looked out into the hall and discovered there was a cupboard I hadn't noticed earlier. On inspection, I found several further pairs of candy-striped sheets (must have been on special), sets of candy-striped pillowcases, and other bedding together with towels, stacked haphazardly on the cupboard shelves. There was another type of airer folded in the bottom of the cupboard, with a cylinder vacuum cleaner, boxes, dusters and other bags of stuff. Grabbing a pair of clean sheets and pillowcases I returned to the bedroom, stripped and remade the bed. It took me ages and I felt quite out of breath when I finished.

Satisfied with the bed, I decided to tackle the carpet in the bedroom.

After vacuuming the bedroom, sweeping the kitchen and then the hall which was tiled like the kitchen and bathroom, using a broom and dustpan and brush I'd found in the kitchen, I decided I wasn't capable of washing the floors today. I was absolutely exhausted and aching all over. Perhaps I'd overdone it, but it felt better to have a slightly cleaner house. Especially the bedroom. There's no way I could have slept in there as it was. The cleaning also distracted me from thinking about my situation; namely sharing a bed with Marty.

The doctor at the hospital had said he was confident my memory would return once I returned home and was surrounded by familiar belongings. He was wrong though. *Nothing* was familiar. I was laying on the bed considering this when I heard the lounge door open, footsteps and Marty called out, 'How about that meal now Libby?' I felt like telling him to get it himself, but thought better of it. For the moment.

'Okay,' I called back. 'I'll have to warm the oven, so it will be a while yet. And Marty, can you turn that music down please. It's too loud.'

'That's how I like it. You never complained before, you always liked it loud too.'

'As you know I can't remember that, and I have since incurred head injuries. The music is giving me a headache.'

'Take some of yer painkillers then,' Marty quipped and strode back down the hall. The hospital had prescribed painkillers, but I didn't want to take them if I could help it. I hadn't had any in the past week while I was still in hospital.

I shuffled down to the kitchen and after turning the oven on, fell into a chair, slumped over the table and immediately dozed off, despite the loud music. I woke to the call of my name and someone giving my shoulder a rough shake. It was Marty.

'Is it ready yet?'

'What, oh sorry I must have dozed off. I've been busy cleaning the place, and I'm shattered. I haven't even put the meal into the oven yet.'

Surely he'd seen the meal on the counter-top? Shaking me like that weren't actions of a loving husband. Was he now showing his true colours?

'Jeez Libby, come on. We're starvin'! And you shouldn't have been doin' all that cleanin'.'

'Well bloody well do it yourself then. I'm still not very strong and all that cleaning has killed me. You could have at least given the place a clean before I came home.'

'You're not normally bothered by a bit of dirt. What's all the fuss about?'

'Well, I'm bloody well bothered by it now,' I retorted and stormed off to the bedroom. I was too exhausted to eat anyway and flopped onto the bed, drifting off into a troubled sleep.

When I woke later, I could still hear pounding music coming from the other end of the flat. I was surprised the neighbours didn't complain. I dragged myself up and walked slowly down to the kitchen. I was feeling peckish now and could manage some food. When I entered the kitchen though I could see they'd eaten all the lasagne, the empty container was sitting on the counter, along with their dirty plates. I made tea and toast with Vegemite, and sat at the table. This was not going to be easy I realised and burst into tears.

The rest of the first week passed quickly. Apart from registering with a doctor's practice, and then phoning the hospital with the details, I spent most of the week fulfilling many of Marty's demands, including opening a joint bank account and registering for unemployment.

When I phoned the lawyer, he told me that he'd contacted one of my uncles in England after the police and the hospital had confirmed my condition. My uncle had since called him a few times to check on my progress. The lawyer promised he would attempt to complete the sale by the following week and then wind up the estate.

The following week however seemed like an interminable nightmare. Marty and I began grating on each other's nerves. I concluded that we were totally incompatible. How the marriage had lasted this long, I could only wonder at. We sniped and snarled at each other. Just the sound of my voice seemed to be painful for him. I was betting that he wished I'd never learnt to speak again. He winced each time I opened my mouth, stood up for myself, or made a demand. I'd wanted to go into the city to buy at least one new bra but he insisted that we had to wait until the money came through before we did that. I also wanted to buy some books. I'd read my way through the magazines on offer in the flat and I couldn't stand many more days of sitting alone in the kitchen or the bedroom, but Marty refused, saying there was not enough money to buy books. I suggested joining a library, but he refused that also telling me the closest one was miles away and said, 'I'm not gunna waste time and money usin' up valuable petrol to go traipsin' around Sydney and wait around for you in some bloody library.'

I heard him mumble, 'bloody stuck-up whingein' bitch', one time when he stalked off from me.

Did he view me as stuck-up? I suppose in a way I was, as I often cringed when he spoke. I found him uncouth and uncultured. I couldn't imagine what I ever saw in him. Perhaps there had been a sexual attraction once upon a time. If so, it certainly didn't exist now. For either of us.

He wouldn't let me buy books or papers, but he always seemed to have money for beer. To be fair though, I didn't know if Brett was the one buying the beer. When I insisted that I could go on a bus to the library by myself, he said, 'No. You can't. I promised the doc at the hospital that I wouldn't let you do anythin' out on your own for a bit, as you might have a relapse.' No-one had mentioned anything to me about a possible relapse.

He reminded me that the money would be coming any time now and that we'd soon be busy looking for premises for the car yard. Gone was the chatty Marty I experienced at the hospital. Instead, he was now a surly, irritable character who seldom spoke to me except to discuss household matters or about the money from the lawyer. I felt like I had been released into his custody and that I was his virtual prisoner. I desperately needed to do something to change this.

Marty accompanied me everywhere and had only left me alone in the flat for very brief bursts of time on trips to the bottle shop, the corner shop or fish and chip shop, and so I was surprised when he announced that he was going out to look at some property with Brett on the Saturday morning.

'Shouldn't I come and look at them as well?' I enquired, although secretly I was thrilled at the idea of having some quality time to myself.

'I thought it best if we did a quick shifty first, then if any of them are any good, you can come and see them. It's very tirin' lookin' at places and I know you haven't been too well this week.'

I'd been feeling sick first thing in the morning every day that week and had brought up the food I'd eaten both during the day and evening. I'd begun to worry about what might be wrong and needed to get to the bottom of what the problem was. I had a doctor's appointment on Monday so planned to bring it up then.

They left shortly after and I watched as the car pulled out onto the road. If they were out for hours, it would give me time to examine the hall cupboard thoroughly. I'd managed to search most of the flat in fits and starts when Marty was preoccupied with Brett, or when he popped out briefly. Not that there was much to look through. The sideboard in the lounge I'd discovered held all Marty's personal army papers and some photographs. There were a couple of us, clearly taken a few years before as I looked very young and another larger one of us – with just the two of us on our wedding day. Again, no pictures of my family at the wedding. I couldn't believe how happy I looked in the wedding photo. I'd also found our marriage certificate in the sideboard, which I'd quickly shoved back, not wanting to think about that, but otherwise there was nothing in the sideboard that was mine. I'd looked through all the drawers and wardrobe in the bedroom. They'd told me little.

I had yet to fully explore the bottom of the hall cupboard and discover what was in the bags and boxes there. As soon as Marty and Brett had been gone for ten minutes, I attacked the cupboard. The first bag I pulled out was a type of hessian shopping bag. It contained an extension lead, and a few tools. Moving that to one side I pulled out the next bag. It had an old raincoat, some old worn women's shoes and old slippers. Why would I keep this junk? Behind that was a large shoebox. I opened it and found a lovely pair of brown suede winter boots wrapped in tissue paper. Were they mine? They looked almost new. I pulled one of the boots out and looked closely at it. It had hardly been worn. Why would I keep them in this cupboard I wondered? Okay, when we moved here it might have been warm and I wouldn't have needed to wear them, but why not keep them in the bedroom? Perhaps they were a little big for me like the other shoes I'd found. I removed the other boot, and noticed there was something underneath the tissue paper. I lifted the tissue paper out and found some envelopes. *Bingo!*

The first envelope had been sent to me at a college address. In the envelope I discovered a British passport in my married name. Elizabeth Anne Miller. It was a startling discovery. I knew my birth name was Elizabeth, rather than Libby, they had called me that at the hospital a few times, but I didn't know my middle name and Marty had never mentioned it. It seemed very strange looking at it now with a picture of me before the accident. I didn't think I looked all that much like the person in the photo, but then this woman had a full head of blond hair and no scars. I must have had it sent to my place of work so Marty wouldn't know about it.

With the passport was a copy of my birth certificate. Elizabeth Anne Fallon; born in Bristol, England, on January twenty-ninth, nineteen fifty-four. Parents; Terence John Fallon and Margaret Ruth Fallon (nee Williams). The passport was only a few months old and the birth certificate also looked new. I took out the second envelope, noticing the return address was from a Helen Fallon in London. It was a letter addressed to me here at the flat, sent about eight weeks earlier, not long before the accident. I opened the letter and read the typed contents.

20th March 1975.

Dear Libby,

I am very sorry to hear that things have not worked out with Marty. You must get away if you feel so unhappy. I would be delighted for you to join me in London any time you want. You know you would be very welcome. As soon as the money comes through, just jump on a plane and come over here. 'Take the money and run,' I believe the saying goes! All the family in Bristol would love to see you. We were very distressed to learn of your parents' and Gary's death. You must feel so alone out there now.

Come home and be with your family. Here's my phone number, ring me if you get the chance, or just hop a plane and ring me when you arrive! I can't wait to see you.

Your loving cousin

Helen. Xxx

Underneath Helen had listed her address and phone number, including her work number. Although shocked at the contents I wasn't surprised. This would explain why I found it challenging to be around Marty. I'd planned to leave him when the money was settled from the estate. I wasn't going to start a used car business with him. In a small way, I felt quite sorry for him. He'd grown up in a home never knowing a family, he'd been through an awful war, and the woman he married was planning on leaving him and depriving him of his dream.

I believed Marty would be entitled to half the money from the estate if we split up. Not if, definitely when. I couldn't go on living like this for much longer. I wasn't sure about the law on these matters, and it was unlikely I'd have an opportunity to seek advice. I needed to consult a lawyer, but I had no money. I thought about ringing the family lawyer, and he could charge me out of the estate but I realised I didn't have the number. Marty kept the card in his wallet and always dialled the number when we went to phone him. All I remembered from my brief glimpse of the card was that his name was Samuels and he was in Raymond Terrace, near Newcastle. I didn't even know the name of the firm.

From the contents of Helen's letter, it indicated that I'd been planning on taking *all* the money with me. This did shock me. I didn't believe that was a wise option, Marty would be bound to start looking for me. If the opportunity presented itself, I knew I would take half the money and run. But how to achieve that?

I packed the letter, passport and birth certificate away underneath the boots and returned the box to the back of the cupboard. I needed to think and work out a plan.

22

Marty and Brett returned some hours later with dejected expressions.

'How did it go?' I asked feigning polite interest.

'Biggest load of rubbish you could imagine. If the place was suitable for cars the house was a shit heap. If the house was good, there was no space for the car yard. And none of them had a garage or workshop which we'll need. It was a waste of bloody time!'

'Oh well, there's no big rush is there? It'd be better to find the right place than settle for something that doesn't work for us. Would we have enough money to buy a house and separate car lot?'

'Not in Sydney and I'd prefer our home and business together. That way we can keep an eye on things better.'

'Right. Well, once we receive the money next week you can go out looking every day,' I said, attempting to keep my voice cheery.

'Yeah, but once we have the money, you won't be entitled to claim unemployment. You'll have too much money. I probably won't be able to either. We'd have to start livin' off it, and we don't wanna do that for long as then we won't have enough to buy what we want.'

'Then you'd better get out there looking. Not just on a Saturday. You need to be out there most days.' *And leave me here alone.*

'I can't go out until the postie has been each morning. Brett is at work in the week as well.'

'I can take some time off if you want,' Brett volunteered. 'I'm owed some holidays.'

'That settles it then. After the post comes in the morning, you can get out there looking at places,' I said.

'Yeah, okay, we'll do that.' Marty agreed.

On Monday morning I attended my first doctor's appointment, which Marty surprisingly allowed me to do alone. He was keen to remain at home waiting for the postman. I explained about my injuries in the accident, and how the hospital wanted me referred to a Sydney hospital for follow on consultations. The doctor told me that he would call the hospital in Maitland to obtain my medical records before making referrals. Finally, I told him about my vomiting bouts, my initial thought of being pregnant and the shows of blood I'd had, both in the hospital and at home, after which the doctor suggested I complete a pregnancy test to eliminate that possibility.

I handed the test to the surgery nurse before returning to his consulting room.

'The test is positive Mrs. Miller. You are pregnant. It would appear that you must have fallen pregnant before your accident. Quite honestly, I'm surprised that you didn't miscarry following the accident. Or that the hospital didn't discover the fact.'

Much of what the doctor said after that passed me by in a blur and I stumbled out of the surgery in shock. Why hadn't the hospital realised I was pregnant? I'd raised the fact that I wasn't having proper periods; just small shows of blood, with Sister O'Connell. She said periods often stopped or became irregular after severe traumas and injuries like I'd experienced.

I was at a loss as to what I could do. What about my plans to escape back to England? That seemed almost impossible with Marty so vigilant with the post box. He would insist on accompanying me to the bank with the cheque. The bank. That was the first thing I needed to do. Open my own account.

I rushed off to the bank and managed to open a new account in just my name with the few dollars I had in my purse. I made enquiries about how I might convert money to English pounds and was advised that the best way to do it would be with traveller's cheques and a small amount of cash. The staff member I spoke to at the bank informed me that I would have to order both the traveller's cheques and cash a week in advance. *A week!* I groaned with despair. My situation was impossible.

I returned to the flat feeling quite depressed. Marty wasn't home; he must have gone out to look at properties. That meant the cheque hadn't arrived that morning. I made myself a cup of tea and sat thinking at the kitchen table. I decided I wouldn't tell Marty about the baby. I had no idea what his reaction would be to such news anyway. Did he even want children? The subject of children had never come up in our conversations.

It was evening before Marty and Brett returned. Brett had taken a week off, so that meant he would be around every day. They were carrying a bag of what I assumed were more bottles of beer, judging by the sound of clinking glass. From the reek of alcohol as they passed me in the hall, I suspected they'd been drinking in a bar already. The smell made me feel quite ill. I was noticing that all sorts of different smells were affecting me – which of course must have been due to the pregnancy.

'How 'bout puttin' some dinner on Libs girl?' *Libs girl? That was a new one.*

'Yes, I'll see to it,' I sighed. I needed to keep Marty thinking that I was going along with his plan and not cause too much friction.

Marty turned before entering the lounge, 'Oh and what did the doc say was wrong with you?'

'He confirmed that I probably have a stomach bug, my body recovering from the accident and just adjusting to different food. He suggested I should probably have a healthier diet,' I lied.

'Nuthin' wrong with what we eat!' Marty shouted and walked into the living room. He slammed the door and proceeded to do his usual thing of playing loud music.

I turned the oven on, found a Shepherd's Pie in the freezer and placed it on the worktop. No point in putting it in the oven yet. The electric oven was so slow to heat up. I could hear peals of laughter coming from the lounge. Again. I wondered what they found to laugh about so much. Were they laughing about me?

I'd realised that Marty hadn't been calling me 'Darl' for the past week. Much as I disliked hearing him say it, he had used it as a term of endearment. *Careful what you wish for.* Now his manner to me was somewhat abrupt, and more perfunctory. I tiptoed along to the lounge door and leaned over to listen. It was difficult to make out the conversation with the loud music and I could only catch snatches of what they were saying.

I caught Marty saying the words 'hoped', 'brain damaged' and 'put her in a home.'

Had Marty hoped I was going to be brained damaged so he could shove me in a home?

Brett said, 'What', 'gunna' 'do' and 'her' with words missing in between.

'She's … me nuts. Whingin' … I'll … rid of her.'

I could easily fill the gaps in for parts of that. He'd told me I was driving him nuts. The last part sounded like he was wanting to get rid of me. Get rid of me how?

Brett asked Marty what he meant.

I heard Marty say 'give her seafood' with indistinguishable words in between until 'settled in our new place.' I also heard him say 'off the balcony'.

Brett then laughed. Did he think this was funny – or did he think Marty was joking?

I retreated shakily to the kitchen. I hadn't ended up brain damaged as he'd hoped so now it sounded like he was either planning to push me off the balcony or give me some seafood somehow, after we'd bought a place and set up the car yard. Was it drunk talk or was he serious? He knew that I was allergic to seafood after what had happened in the hospital, he had mentioned my allergy in a conversation, so that could only mean that he was planning an attempt to kill me. My God! Did he know that I'd been planning to leave him before the accident? Wouldn't he have said something? No, of course he wouldn't. He wanted the money, just as I'd wanted it. God, what a pair we were.

I couldn't imagine how Marty could accidentally get me to eat seafood, unless he forced it down me or disguised it in something. He'd have to start preparing food to do that. I shuddered at the thought and instinctively placed my hand on my stomach – the baby! I had to ensure its protection. Perhaps I ought to tell Marty about the pregnancy after all. Surely, he wouldn't attempt to kill me if he knew I was having his baby? I took deep breaths and tried to calm my pounding heart. I couldn't let Marty know that I'd heard anything he'd said.

I jumped up and put the meal into the oven. Everything had to seem normal. When the Shepherd's pie was almost ready, I put a pan on the stove to cook some frozen mixed vegetables to accompany the pie. I served myself a small portion of food, although I wasn't all that hungry. I had to eat for the baby. I knocked on the lounge door and told the men that the food was ready. I had no intention of plating their food and serving it to them. I hadn't done this for them for days now.

'Where's our dinner Libby?' Marty demanded as per usual, when he came into the kitchen.

I pointed to the stove and said nothing.

Marty paused and looked at me in silence while I stared defiantly back at him. I waited for a string of expletives to be shouted, which I'd had some nights – depending on how much he'd drunk, but instead he laughed and set about dishing up two platefuls of food and then returned to the lounge.

After washing up the saucepan, utensils and my plate, I retreated to the bedroom. I wished I had something to read, to escape into. I felt so isolated and alone. No friends to talk to. According to Marty, I had no close female friends. The few I'd had in Newcastle had moved to Melbourne. He might have lied about that. I couldn't remember anyone anyway and no one in Sydney had come around the flat to see me, so perhaps he was right. I moved over to the edge of the bed and did my usual thing of turning on my side so that I would have my back to Marty when he eventually came to bed. I was becoming more accustomed to sleeping with him beside me, but I didn't sleep easy, worried every night he might try to touch me. Thankfully he'd not attempted to have sex with me in the past two weeks since I'd been home. I just hoped that he would continue to respect my fragility and not make any demands. It was about the only thing he seemed to be thoughtful about.

I was vaguely aware of the flat door slamming some hours later, hearing Marty relieving himself in the bathroom before undressing and crawling into bed. I tensed and held my breath waiting, but Marty was snoring within minutes and I relaxed into sleep again.

At eleven the following morning Marty insisted I come down to the letterbox with him, dressed ready to go to the bank if the cheque had arrived. He'd slept in, was edgy with a hangover and had been sniping at me all morning.

He opened the box and on discovering it was empty, began shouting.

'That bastard lawyer! He must be lyin'. He hasn't sent

the cheque! You're gunna have to phone him again Libby to chase him up. I want that money!'

I noticed that Marty used 'I' when referring to the money. I remained silent. Marty continued swearing and ranting and was only interrupted by a man, that neither of us had noticed, standing inside the front door.

'Excuse me mate, could you keep your voice and language down a little. And while you're here, I would ask that you stop playing your music so loud. It's totally over the top and I can't hear my television or radio over the noise that comes through the walls.'

The man, who must have been our neighbour, looked indignant, but was not being aggressive in his approach. Unlike Marty's reaction.

'Why don't you just fuck off *mate*, I'll play my music as loud as I bloody want,' Marty retorted taking a step towards the man.

The man opened his mouth to reply and I could see the situation might escalate into further unpleasantness with Marty's mood, so I stepped in, 'Come on Marty, leave it,' I said. 'Let's go and phone the lawyer.'

I grabbed hold of Marty and moved towards the door. The man stepped aside and I mouthed a silent 'sorry' as we passed him.

'Who does he bloody well think he is?' Marty continued as we walked along the street.

'He's a neighbour who's unhappy about the noise level of your music Marty. You do play it very loud. I don't like it either. I've asked you to turn it down several times. I'm surprised he, and other neighbours, haven't come knocking on our door to complain.'

'Well, they can all get stuffed, as far as I'm concerned.'

I chose not to react to Marty's mood and walked on in silence to the laundromat.

As usual Marty dialled the lawyer's number even though I asked him for the card to do it myself. I tried to look over his shoulder to see the numbers but he was blocking me. When I managed to speak to him, the lawyer confirmed that he'd only posted the cheque the previous afternoon and it would take a few days to be delivered. I told Marty this after hanging up. Now it was too late for me to phone the lawyer in secret and ask him to deal with the money another way.

'About bloody time too,' Marty sulked.

'Is Brett coming around today? Are you going to look at any places?'

'Yeah, we're gunna try some new areas today. Maybe a bit further out south or west where the properties are cheaper.'

Marty's mood seemed to pick up at the idea of finding a place and he chatted more convivially on the walk back to the flat.

Once Marty left to collect Brett, I waited twenty minutes to make sure they didn't return and locked up, planning to go to the bank. On impulse I stopped outside the door of flat number ten and knocked. I surmised that this must be where the man we'd encountered earlier lived. It *was* him and he seemed surprised, but friendly when he opened the door.

'Hello there, how can I help you?'

'I just wanted to apologise for what happened earlier,

and to say I'm sorry about the music as well.'

'It's not your fault. I can see that. Thanks for the apology. What happened to you?' He indicated my face and the scars that I frequently forgot were still prominent on my face. At least now all the swelling had gone.

'Oh,' I said, 'I was in a serious car accident up near my parents' house.'

'In Sydney somewhere?' he asked.

'No; near the Hunter River outside Newcastle. I was in Maitland hospital for several weeks. I don't remember anything about the accident, and I was in a coma for a few days. I went through the windscreen and had a rough landing on a gravel road.'

'Ouch! Maybe it's a good thing that you don't remember the accident.'

'Probably. To be honest I don't remember anything much about my life before the accident, including my husband and living here. We've lived here since last September, after moving down from Newcastle. Do you know me? Have we met before?'

'No, I only moved in about a month ago. It was very peaceful and quiet at first – until the last couple of weeks that is. Now I know why it was so quiet; you weren't here. Crikey, that must be bloody difficult, not even knowing your husband.'

'Yes, it's been ... complicated. It's like living with a stranger. The other day, when I was looking through some things, I learned that I'd planned to leave him anyway and return to England when the settlement came through.'

'Settlement, you mean from your accident?'

'No, from my parents' estate.'

I explained about the fire that killed my parents and brother and how I wanted to return to England to be near other family members.

'I'm sorry to hear about your loss,' he said. 'And I can understand why you would want to go back to England. It's probably the best thing for you to do. This settlement, it wouldn't be the cheque that your husband was shouting about this morning, would it?' he asked me.

'Yes … it was about that. He's keen to get his hands on it because he wants to buy premises to start a business.'

'With the money from *your* family?'

I hesitated. He seemed genuinely interested and concerned. Should I ask him for help? Maybe that was a step too far. He didn't know me at all. There was no harm in saying what I wanted though.

'Yes, and that's the problem. I don't want that. I want Marty to have his dream, but I want some of the money to return to England.' I looked at the man and said, 'I'm sorry, I shouldn't be telling you all this. It's nothing to do with you.'

'It's not a problem. You must feel quite alone with your memory loss and no family around. Any time you want to talk, my door's always open for you. My name's Matthew by the way, although most people call me Matt. Your name's Libby, isn't it?'

'Yes, how did you know?'

'From hearing your husband shouting at you. The walls aren't very thick in this block.'

'Oh, yes, sorry.'

'Would you like to come in for a cup of coffee or something?'

'I was just on my way to the bank, so I'll take a rain check on the coffee if you don't mind. I have to try and sort something out about the money. They said if I want English pounds or traveller's cheques, I have to order them a week in advance. I have to have the money in the bank in the first place to pay for them, and if I bank a cheque, that's going to take time to clear, and then I'd have to wait another week for the cash. It's hopeless. I don't know what I am going to do,' I said close to tears. I took a deep breath before charging on. 'By the time the cheque clears, which Marty wants to go into a joint account we opened, he'll have probably spent most of it on a property. It just seems hopeless, I'm never going to be able to go and I really, really need to!' I blurted out, tears beginning to spill from my eyes. I looked up at Matt, ready to apologise for my outburst, but hesitated again. He looked like he was deep in thought.

'Hmm. You could always pay for a special clearance on the cheque which would speed things up,' he said.

I hadn't known about special clearances. That might be the answer. 'Really? How much would that cost, and how long would it take?'

'About twenty or twenty-five dollars I think and it would probably be cleared in a day or two. What bank are you with?'

'The National.'

'I know they have a branch in London. I was over there last year and used it to transfer money back to Australia. You can have money transferred directly to London. And you can exchange dollars at the airport to obtain English pounds. So, you don't have to wait around for traveller's cheques or cash from the bank. Would you be going to London first?'

'Yes, that's where my cousin lives. I'd arranged to stay with her when I arrived. That might be the answer. Oh, thank you Matt! I'd better rush off and make enquiries at the bank. Thanks again.'

I turned and moved towards the steps.

'Let me know if you need any help,' he offered.

'I will,' I said, 'thanks again.'

At the bank I was informed that I *could* transfer money to their UK branch. Special clearance on the cheque would take twenty-four hours and I had to pay for that when I deposited the cheque. That was going to be the sticking block. I needed the money to pay for it. I only ever had a small amount of money in my purse, Marty insisting on holding on to most of our money, and it was more than likely that Marty would come to the bank with me when I deposited the cheque anyway. So near, yet so far! I had the possibility of overcoming some difficulties with Matt's knowledge, but there were still what seemed like insurmountable problems to face. I could only pray for a miracle.

23

The miracle appeared at my door the following morning. Angry that the cheque hadn't arrived again, Marty and Brett had not long left on their property search when there was a knock on the door. I opened the door to find Matt, our neighbour, standing there.

'Morning Libby, I wonder if you would come into my flat for that coffee. I have something for you.'

'For me? Yes, of course, just let me grab my bag and keys.'

I followed Matt into his kitchen where he also had a small table and two chairs.

'So how do you like your coffee?'

'Well, I've discovered, after trial and error, that I like it with milk and one sugar.'

Matt laughed. 'That's just crazy, isn't it?'

'I'm getting used to it; learning new things about myself each day.'

Matt placed my coffee on the table, together with a large white envelope. 'I believe that might be what you've been waiting for,' he said.

I picked up the envelope and saw it was from a law

firm.

'But how …?'

'I hope you're not going to be angry with me, but when I returned from my shift this morning, I found this sticking out of your letterbox. The postman had just delivered it. It looked like official documents so I grabbed it, reasoning I could always shove it back in if it didn't look like it was from your lawyer. I could see it was. It was a close call; your husband came down the stairs as I was heading up. Luckily, I'd stuffed it under my jacket.'

I was speechless for a moment.

'I'm not angry with you at all, Matt. You might have just saved my life.' I meant that literally, but was not going to tell him that.

'I thought it might help you given what you told me yesterday.'

I nodded.

'You said you pulled it out after coming off shift. What do you do Matt?'

'I'm a radiologist at Vinnies. Doing the night shift for the next few weeks.'

'Vinnies?'

'St. Vincent's Hospital.'

'Oh, I think I might have heard of that.'

My hand trembled as I opened the envelope. There were several pages of documents: a bill accounting for revenue raised and outgoing costs for the estate, a page that I had to sign and return confirming I've received the money and attached to the pages was a cheque for $148,480.63 made out to me; Elizabeth Miller.

'Oh my God!' I cried, 'this is it!'

'And your opportunity to bank it and escape before that husband of yours discovers you have it, young lady,' Matt said.

'Listen to you, calling me a young lady as though you're old enough to be my father.'

'I am probably old enough to be your father. I'm thirty-nine.'

At my age I thought thirty-nine *was* old. Although Matt didn't look it. His wrinkle free face made him look youthful. He kept his brown hair short in a smart style, he was also slim and fit looking. His skin was fair and a little freckly, the type that could burn easily. Overall, he was quite an attractive man I noticed as I looked at him.

'How old are you, Libby?' he asked me.

'I turned twenty-one last January according to my passport.'

'There you are then. How about you drink your coffee and then scoot around to the bank. No time to waste. Have you got enough money to pay for the cheque clearance?'

'No.'

Matt reached for his wallet on the worktop and pulled out two twenty-dollar notes.

'I don't need that much,' I protested.

'Take it,' Matt said. 'You can pay me back when you can withdraw some of the cheque money.'

'Thank you so much Matt,' I said standing. 'Is it alright if I leave the papers here in your flat? I have to sign one of them and return it to the lawyer to say I've received the money. I'm worried if I take them into our flat Marty will find them. He was livid this morning when there was nothing from the lawyer again.'

'I'll just bet he was,' Matt said. 'Look Libby, I'd like to help you further if you'll let me. After you've been to the bank late tomorrow morning, and sorted all your business out, I can drive you straight to the airport. You are bound to find a seat on a flight to London. I've noticed that your husband has been going out every morning this week with his mate. Do you think he'll go out again tomorrow?'

'I hope so. He's getting fed up with it though, so I can't guarantee it, they might decide not to go tomorrow, unless he knows the money is in the bank.'

'You'll have to persuade him somehow if he decides not to.'

'Okay, let's hope it doesn't come to that. I can't thank you enough Matt. Why are you helping me? Most people wouldn't want to get involved.'

'I was shocked at what you told me had happened to you and your family,' he said. 'And I don't like what I see and hear of your husband. I am not surprised that you were thinking of leaving him before the accident. I'm just surprised that you married him in the first place.'

'So am I,' I sighed. 'Look, I'd better head off to the bank. I'll sort out some clothes ready to pack after Marty leaves in the morning and then knock on your door when they've gone. Is that okay?'

'Yes, for sure. I'll see you in the morning. Good luck Libby.'

Luck. I was undoubtedly going to need luck if this plan was to work.

I woke on the couch Thursday morning huddled under some blankets feeling sick and sore. My whole body was racked with pain from sleeping on the uncomfortable lumpy thing. Not only that, despite having a soothing bath the night before, I felt very sore. I whimpered at the memory of what had occurred with Marty.

He had come to bed late after consuming his usual round of drinks with Brett and instead of crawling into bed as he normally did, he'd pulled the sheet and blankets off me and declared it was time he resumed his marital rights. Only he hadn't verbalised it so politely.

I'd been dozing, remaining on half alert for his footsteps when I must have dozed off again. I was horrified to see a naked Marty climbing onto the bed and hear what he was saying.

'I've waited long enough Libby. A man can only stand so much, you know, of sleepin' with a woman beside him in bed night after night and not touchin' them. I need a root.'

'No Marty, I'm not ready!' I pleaded.

He ignored my protests, and before I could move, he yanked my nightdress up exposing my pants.

'Bloody hell, whatcha wearing these for!' He ripped my pants off me, and climbed on top of me.

'No, Marty, No!' I cried in shock. He grabbed my hands and pinned my arms above my head with one of his. I couldn't believe how strong he was. I opened my mouth to scream and he placed his other hand across my mouth.

'Shut up Libby and don't struggle, it'll all be over soon. You don't want me to hurt you, do you?'

I was too shocked to answer him and lay rigid beneath him.

Marty forced my legs open and thrust himself into

me. My body was dry and unreceptive and I felt like he was ripping me apart. It seemed to go on forever. His thrusts increased in speed until he reached his climax and collapsed onto me.

'See that wasn't so bad was it,' he whispered into my ear before rolling off me, removing a sheath, which he threw on the floor, and then turned over to lapse into a drunken sleep.

I remained frozen for a few minutes and then as I felt my stomach heaving, I charged to the bathroom and retched into the toilet. I felt blood trickling down my leg and was horrified. I wasn't sure if the bleeding was because I was about to lose the baby or because he'd hurt me so much. After a short while the bleeding seemed to stop. I then ran a hot bath, scrubbed all over and remained soaking in it, replenishing the hot water until it ran cold. Throughout this process I couldn't stop sobbing, worried about losing the baby. Having Marty's baby was the last thing I wanted really, but I was beginning to get used to the idea and the baby had become hugely important to me. I couldn't remember my family, but I would know this baby; providing I was able to carry it to full term.

After drying myself off, I tiptoed into the bedroom to grab a fresh nightie and another pair of pants from my drawer, and returned to the bathroom to dress. Marty was still out cold. I grabbed some sheets, blankets and the eiderdown from the linen cupboard and retreated to the living room. The room stank of beer and cigarettes. Marty didn't smoke; it was Brett who filled the overflowing ashtray. There were beer bottles strewn around the room. I picked up the bottles and the ashtray, dumping them in the kitchen before returning to the lounge and opening the windows in the hope of clearing the air a little, despite the freezing temperature of the room. I made a makeshift bed up for myself and huddled under the covers.

I'd continued to sob and couldn't stop shivering. I had been tempted to knock on Matt's door, asking if I could stay there, until I remembered he was on night shifts and wouldn't be home. I also didn't want Marty to know I had any contact with him. The thought of Marty snoring in bed down the corridor made me feel angry; how dare he do that to me when I'd said no! The morning was going to be hell, but with any luck I'd be on a plane to England tomorrow and *never* have to see him again.

When I'd deposited the cheque, the bank had said it would be cleared by late the following morning, so fingers crossed I'd be on my way to England by the evening. It seemed like hours before I drifted off into a troubled sleep.

On Thursday morning I crawled up from the couch, stretched to iron out the creaks in my back, folded the bed-clothing and shoved them back into the hall cupboard. I wouldn't have to think about them ever again with any luck.

I could hear Marty showering in the bathroom and wondered if he had any guilt about his attack on me. I suspected he didn't. Rape. That's what it had been. Although I doubted he would see it that way. I just hoped that he was going out today. I dressed in the bedroom and retreated to the kitchen before he came out of the bathroom. I was sitting at the table munching on some toast when he made his appearance.

'Right Libby, we're goin' down to the post boxes in the

lobby and gunna just sit there and wait for the postie to come today. I wanna word with him. That lyin' bastard of a lawyer either hasn't sent the cheque yet or there's a problem with the post.'

Marty said all this without making any eye contact with me.

'But it could be hours before the post comes Marty. It's only a little after eight. They won't come this early.'

'I don't care. I am gunna wait down there all mornin' if I have to. And you too.'

'No. I'm not standing down there all morning,' I told him. 'You go down if you want and I'll bring you some tea and toast.'

'I want you there ready for us to go off to the bank.'

'I absolutely refuse to do that. If the cheque arrives this morning we can go to the bank once they open. There's no need whatsoever for both of us to be down there all morning.'

I said all this with an assertiveness stemmed from anger over his actions the night before and in the safe knowledge that there'd be no cheque today.

There was silence for a few seconds before Marty said, 'Alright, you win, I'll go on me own. Bring down some toast and tea for me then.'

With that Marty walked out the door. Then I started to panic. What if the postman told Marty he'd put the envelope in our letterbox yesterday? If Marty discovered that he'd think I'd somehow managed to get hold of it, even though he had the only keys, and then he'd want to go to the bank. The money wasn't in the joint account, but one of the staff might say something about my large deposit yesterday. There'd been raised eyebrows when I'd banked it asking for a special clearance and I'd felt obliged to explain how I'd acquired such a large sum of money. The bank had asked me to bring my passport and driving licence in this morning as further proof of identification. As if I greatly resembled the picture in the passport anyway. I just hoped there would be no trouble about it.

When I took Marty's toast and tea down to the entrance lobby, I found him sitting on the floor reading a newspaper. *And he wouldn't let me buy any papers!*

'I popped to the corner shop to get a paper so I'd have somethin' to do to pass the time,' he said; a sheepish expression on his face.

'Good thinking, otherwise you might nod off in boredom,' I said drily.

I handed him his food and drink and turned to walk up the stairs.

'I'm sorry about last night Libby,' he called after me. 'I just couldn't hold out any longer. A man has needs you know.'

I had no desire to discuss last night with him but wanted to know one thing.

'Did we always use contraception when ... you know?' I felt embarrassed about having this conversation, but was curious as to why he'd used a sheath.

'Yeah, of course, neither of us wanted any kids. You have that cap thing and I always carry a spare Frenchie in case,' he said with a nod and a wink, tapping his top pocket. *Ugh!*

I didn't respond to that, but turned and headed back up the stairs. At least he'd apologised. He knew what he'd done was wrong. So how come I was pregnant then? I knew that sheaths and the cap didn't always provide full protection. I'd asked the doctor about the cap on Monday before he'd tested me, and he'd told me they weren't fool-proof. Had I been seeing someone else after I decided to leave Marty?

Two hours later I was walking downstairs with a cup of coffee for Marty when I heard voices. *The postman!* I paused on the stairs to listen.

'Sorry mate, I'm just a relief postie. Can't help you. There's nuthin' here for you today. The regular's off on sick leave.'

'How long has he been off sick?'

'Four days mate. A few of us have been coverin' his round.'

'Were you on duty yesterday?'

'No mate, it was one of my colleagues back at the depot.'

'I'm waitin' for an important letter to come from near Newcastle. How long would it take for a letter to get here?'

'Depends whether it was sent from Newcastle or outside Newcastle. From Newcastle itself I would say two days probably at the most. From other places it could take a few days longer.'

'It's from outside Newcastle, so that could explain it. Okay, thanks mate. I'll see you tomorrow. Maybe I'll be lucky then.'

I was *so* relieved. Luck was with me again! The regular postman was off sick and different people had been covering his shift. I continued down the stairs as though I'd heard nothing. Marty was gathering up his paper, plate and cup.

'Oh, I just brought you a cup of coffee,' I said innocently.

'The postie's been. Nothing again today, but he said it could take quite a few days for post to come from outside Newcastle. I reckon it'll come tomorrow.'

'Well, you'd better get out there looking again today,' I emphasised.

'Yeah, I'll walk around to give Brett a shout. Can't park at his place. You can take this lot up,' he said handing me his used cup and plate.

Marty returned to the flat with Brett a short time later and after Brett had a quick cigarette (because Marty wouldn't let him smoke in the car, but it was okay to pollute our flat), Marty told me that they would probably be out until late.

'Okay, bye and good luck,' I called after them.

I watched the car pull out of the drive, and impatient to get out of there, I raced into the bedroom and took a small amount of clothing from the drawers. Just as I was about to pull the small suitcase from the wardrobe, I heard the sound of a key in the door and froze in fear.

24

Shoving the case back into the wardrobe I held my breath. The door seemed to open with exaggerated slowness; the squeak of its hinges echoing down the hall. At first no-one appeared which freaked me out. My heart was beating wildly. I was expecting to see Marty walk in, angry because he'd somehow uncovered my plot. Or perhaps he was thinking of implementing his plan to get rid of me sooner, now he knew the cheque was on its way. I glanced around the room, looking for a handy weapon. A bedside lamp would have done, but there wasn't one. There was no bedtime reading in this household. The only thing I could spot was my comb nestling in my hairbrush on top of the chest of drawers. My hair still wasn't long enough to use anything on it, but the comb's long steel point would surely cause some injuries. I reached across to grab it in preparation.

Instead of Marty walking through the door, it was Brett. I breathed a sigh of relief. Brett was harmless enough – unless Marty had sent him to do his dirty work. Was I becoming too paranoid?

'Brett? What's going on?' I asked walking out into the

hall with the comb hidden in my hand.

'Forgot my smokes, didn't I? Sorry if I startled you opening the door like that. I was just double checking my pockets, to make sure they weren't squashed in there somewhere.'

'Oh, okay.'

I waited until Brett re-emerged from the lounge clutching his cigarette pack which he shoved into his jacket pocket.

'Okay, see ya Libby,' he called, leaving once again.

I breathed a sigh of relief and returned to the bedroom. I checked that they'd driven off once more, and waited a further ten minutes before I grabbed the suitcase again and began packing. I planned on buying some new clothing when I arrived in London, but until then I would still need a few things. I went to the hall cupboard, pulled out all the bags and boxes where I retrieved my passport, Helen's letter and my birth certificate which I placed carefully into my handbag and then replaced all the items I'd removed from the cupboard. Last, I gathered my toothbrush and some toiletries from the bathroom. Satisfied I had all I needed, I locked up the flat and knocked on Matt's door.

I was nervous as hell, constantly glancing over my shoulder to the staircase, afraid that Marty or Brett would re-appear at any moment. After what seemed like an age, Matt opened the door.

'Sorry you caught me in the bathroom. Come in before anyone sees you.'

I explained what had happened with the postman this morning and then the close call I'd had with Brett returning to the flat.

'We'd better get going then,' Matt said with concern. 'Here's your documents. Did you say you had to sign something? You'll need to do it now as we won't be coming back here.'

'Oh, yes. And I have to post it back to the lawyer. Do you have any envelopes and a pen?'

Matt opened the bottom drawer in his kitchen and pulled out an envelope. He took a pen from a jar on the counter top and passed both to me. I picked up the pen and paused over the envelope. My hand started to shake.

'What's the matter?' asked Matt.

'I don't know if I can write,' I told him. 'You know, since the accident. The only writing I've done since the accident is signing my name. I had to ask the receptionist at the doctor's surgery to fill in the registration form for me. At the unemployment office, Marty filled their forms in for me.'

'Just sign the document and let me address the envelope for you then.'

After I signed the required page, Matt addressed the envelope, placed the document in it and sealed it. I folded the rest of the documents and put them into my handbag in case I had to show them to anyone at the bank.

'I'll post this for you on my way back from the airport,' Matt said. 'You walk around to the bank now and I'll follow in my car with your suitcase shortly. You might be a while in there. I'll park in the side street around the corner. We don't want anyone in the block seeing us leave together – just in case. Okay?'

'Right. Very clandestine. Thanks Matt.'

At the bank I asked at the enquiry counter if my cheque had cleared. The assistant asked me to wait a moment, then informed me that the manager wished to see me. I followed her into an office near the rear of the bank.

'Hello, Mrs. Miller, I'm the manager Andrew McDonald. I would like a quick word with you.'

He invited me to take a seat where I remained silent, waiting for him to speak. Clearing his throat first he said, 'It seems that you banked a very large cheque yesterday and asked for a special clearance on it?'

'That's correct,' I replied.

'May I ask what this money pertains to?'

'It was the settlement of my parent's estate. They died in a fire at my childhood home last October. I have all the documents here from the family lawyer if you would like to see them.'

'Oh, I'm sorry to hear about your family Mrs. Miller, and yes, I would like to see them. Is that where you sustained your injuries?' he asked pointing to my face.

'No, I was in a car accident almost seven weeks ago. My face was badly cut as you can see from the scars.'

I passed him the documents.

'Oh dear, you have been through it haven't you?' McDonald said perusing the documents. 'And I understand that you wish to transfer a large sum of this money to our London branch today?'

'That's right, I'm flying out to London today. I was born in England and all my family still live there.'

'I see. And Mr. Miller, is he going with you?'

'No, we've separated.'

'Did you wish to transfer all the money to London?

And do you wish to close your account?'

I hesitated. I *did* want to transfer *all* the money, but I'd decided that I would transfer half to the joint account instead for Marty. It was set up so we could draw money individually without the other person's signature. He didn't really deserve the money but I wanted to be free and clear of him, so that he'd have no excuse to try and contact me again.

'Yes, I want you to close my personal account and no, I don't want you to transfer all the money. I would like you to transfer half of the money, after your costs, to the joint account I still hold with my ex-husband. With the other half I would like two thousand dollars in cash and the rest transferred to London.'

'I see. I notice that you and your husband only opened the joint account a few weeks ago. So, your split must be very recent.'

'Yes, after the accident we thought we could make a fresh start of things, but it hasn't worked out. I'm returning to England.'

'Well, all this will take a little time to prepare. If you would care to return to the bank later this afternoon, say about three, I can have all these matters dealt with for you.'

I hesitated. I knew it must be close to eleven-thirty by now. Returning this afternoon was not an option for me. Matt would probably need to grab some sleep and later had to go to work.

'No, Mr. McDonald. I have no intention of returning this afternoon. As I told you a few minutes ago, I'm flying out to London today and still have a lot to do. I'll wait here while you deal with this. And I expect you to expedite my requests immediately.'

McDonald was silent for a minute before eventually saying, 'Yes, alright. Do you have your passport?'

I passed it over to him remarking, 'The picture was taken prior to my accident of course, and before I lost all my hair.'

McDonald examined the photo and turning to me said, 'well I can still see it's you, so everything is in order.'

The Manager finally left the office and I relaxed. The bloody cheek of him. Talking to me in such a condescending way. Who did he think he was? It was *my* money! And there was no way I was going to allow him to jeopardise my chances of escape.

Twenty-five minutes later, McDonald returned with a number of papers and slips for me to sign.

'If you can just sign all these, then that's everything taken care of. Are you sure that you want to be withdrawing such a large sum of money in cash?'

'I'm quite sure, thank you.' I signed all the necessary paperwork and he handed me first the cash and then two A4 sheets.

'That's for you to take to the bank in London,' he said pointing to the top A4 sheet. 'The other sheet details the transfer of money to both accounts and our fees. It will be approximately four days before the funds are available to draw on in London. The address of the London branch is on there. The bank is in Threadneedle St.'

'I'm sure I'll find it,' I said standing.

'Well good luck Mrs. Miller, and I hope all goes well with your journey.'

'Thank you, Mr. McDonald.'

I walked slowly out of his office and through the bank. My real inclination was to run, feeling as though I had just committed a massive robbery, but for decorum's sake I continued walking with dignity until I exited the bank, turned the corner and looked about in panic. I didn't know what Matt's car looked like. All the parking places were taken and the first few cars were empty. Down the hill I finally saw a man climbing out of his car waving.

'Matt!' I cried with relief, and broke into a run.

'Everything go okay?' Matt asked as I almost threw myself into his car.

'Yes, eventually. The manager wanted to see me and there was a moment when I thought the pompous fool wasn't going to process my transfer. He told me to return at three this afternoon, but I held my ground and insisted he do it immediately.'

'Well done, let's get moving then.'

Matt started the car, pulled out and at the top of the street turned into the main road that he said would take us towards the airport.

'So, you were living in London last year?' I asked him.

'I was over there for nine years, working as a radiologist. The plan, when I first went over, was to spend just a year there, but I met someone and we ended up living together.'

'You didn't marry and have a family?'

Matt hesitated for a moment before answering. 'My partner was a man, so a family wasn't an option.'

'Oh,' I said feeling very foolish. 'Sorry, I just assumed. What happened, why did you return to Australia?'

'He died of cancer.'

I didn't know what to say to this. I was curious as to what kind of cancer his partner had suffered with, but it somehow felt too insensitive to ask him. Eventually I said, 'That must have been tough for you.'

'Yes, it was. It was very sudden. One moment he was fine, then he received the diagnosis and was gone in less than a fortnight. It was a rare form of aggressive stomach cancer. I remained in our house for a few months after his death, and then his family decided to sell the place. I had no claim on Pete's property as a male partner and Pete hadn't written a will, so the family inherited everything. We were so shocked with the news of his illness and busy dealing with the repercussions of it, that it probably never even crossed Pete's mind about his lack of will. He would've no doubt assumed his family would do the right thing anyway, but they wanted me out. I decided to return to Australia and settled in Canberra initially, working on a short-term contract, then obtained the position at St. Vincent's and returned to Sydney, which is where I am from originally.'

'I'm so sorry Matt. It must be hard to lose someone you're so close to. Although I feel very sad at the loss of my family, it is more theoretical for me. I can't even remember much about them you see, so it's not like you.'

'Nevertheless, it meant that you were alone, with no support, and all your family in a country many thousands of miles away.'

'Like you were.'

'Yes – although I did have some very good friends there, who put me up when I had to leave Pete's house. I couldn't have managed without the support of my friends.'

I was still feeling sore and uncomfortable from last night's events and edged back hoping to alleviate my discomfort. To my acute embarrassment, Matt noticed and thought it was because of what he'd just told me.

'Are you okay Libby, you're not upset about me telling you I'm gay, are you?' he asked.

'No Matt, I'm in discomfort because …'

I blurted out what happened without thinking and then felt really awkward. He asked me to tell him a bit more and, although I felt uncomfortable with such an intimate topic, I filled him in on how things had been between Marty and I since returning to Sydney.

'You told Marty you didn't want him to touch you last night?'

'Yes, but he threatened to hurt me, so I did nothing. From shock mainly.'

I noticed Matt's hands clench tightly around the steering wheel.

'*The bastard!* You don't want to report him to the police?'

I laughed. 'You have to be kidding! To start with it's his word against mine, although I'm sure there is plenty of evidence to show non-consenting intercourse. But the police would no doubt inform me that there is no such thing as rape in a marriage. Besides, anything that would delay my departure is a no-no as far as I am concerned.'

Matt sighed, 'Yes, you're probably right about the police and I agree you shouldn't delay your departure.'

'I'll just have to buy a cushion to for the plane or something,' I laughed.

'You seem very relaxed about it all Libby, for something that must have been very unpleasant for you.'

'It was, and last night I was in a terrible state, upset and angry, but this morning I'm excited, nervous and just bloody relieved to be leaving. I won't ever have to see him again.'

'You don't think he'll come after you for the money?'

'No, I left him half of it and he hasn't a clue as to where I'll be. I doubt it would even occur to him that I'd be travelling to England, and I can't see him going there. I don't think he has a passport. I searched every square inch of that flat looking for clues about myself, which is how I found my cousin's letter and *my* passport, but I didn't see one for him. He was in Vietnam some years back, so I don't know if the army issued him a passport. He had his army papers, but there was no sign of a passport. Besides he has half the money. I'm sure he can use it to achieve his dream of owning a used car lot. I don't think Marty has any real feelings for me. From what I gathered in my cousin's letter, our marriage was over anyway.'

'It was very generous of you to leave him half of the money. You could have taken it all.'

'I could have – I don't know what the legal position is on a marriage split and what happens when the wife has been left a pile of money from *her* family, but I'm sure he would have been entitled to some anyway. Besides, he'll have no excuse to look for me now.'

'Yes, I suppose so, but I still think you've been generous considering what he did to you. Most women wouldn't be so thoughtful. So, changing the subject, what are your dreams, Libby?'

'I don't really have any at this very moment, except to escape to London.'

'A smart, educated girl like you though could really do something with her life. Especially now you have a little money behind you.'

'I'm not educated. According to Marty, I left school at fifteen and just worked in dead end jobs.'

'Well, I think it's an absolute waste. You're clearly very intelligent, you should think about doing some studying when you return to England and then either go to university or consider starting a business.'

'Hmm. Maybe. I haven't given it any thought really. I'd have to go back to school first. I have no qualifications that would get me into a university.' *And with a baby that would be difficult.*

We were both quiet for the last few minutes of the journey. Matt pulled into the car park, collected a parking ticket and then announced he was coming into the terminal with me to ensure there was no difficulty in purchasing my plane ticket.

'You don't have to do that Matt. You've done more than enough for me.'

'No, I insist. What if there are no seats available on a flight today? You'll have to go to a hotel. I can take you if that's the case. Also, no offence intended, but the airlines might be suspicious of a young woman with so many scars and a short back and sides' haircut attempting to buy a ticket with cash. If I am with you, I think matters will go smoother.'

'You're probably right. Once again, you're here to help the damsel in distress.'

'I've told you it's no problem. I just want to make sure you're safe. Come on, let's go.'

Matt retrieved my small suitcase from the boot and we entered the terminal.

'I've never bought a ticket from the airport itself; I think we'll have to go to an enquiry desk of the airline. Do you have a particular preference? Qantas perhaps?'

'Qantas would be fine,' I said. 'I've heard of them, but I'm totally ignorant when it comes to flying.'

'Economy or business class?'

'Economy, if that's the cheapest. I'm not sure I have enough money on me for a business class seat.'

We looked around, noticed a customer service desk for Qantas and walked over to it.

'How can I help you sir?' the Qantas attendant asked, automatically addressing Matt.

'We'd like a single economy ticket to London, today if it's available. Can we purchase that here?'

'Yes sir, you can. Just let me see if there are any seats available. We have a flight departing at four pm today.'

The woman lifted the phone and spoke to someone for a few minutes before confirming there was a seat.

'Yes, we have a seat available in economy. Are you looking for a one ticket way or return?'

'One way,' both Matt and I chorused.

'Is it for you sir?'

'No, it's for Libby here.' Matt pointed to me and the woman seemed to do a double take when she caught sight of my scars.

'It *is* as bad as it looks,' I said. 'I went through the windscreen of a car in an accident.'

The woman blushed and cast her eyes down.

'Can I see your passport?' she asked.

I produced my passport and repeated what I'd told the bank manager that the picture had been taken prior to my accident. The woman scrutinised the passport and me before deciding everything was fine. She informed me that the ticket would cost seven-hundred and twenty-dollars including airport taxes. I handed over the cash and the woman hand wrote a ticket for the flight before passing it and my passport back to me.

'I hope you enjoy the flight. You'll need to check your luggage in at our check-in desks when they open in … approximately forty minutes,' she said looking at her watch. 'Boarding will commence approximately sixty minutes before departure.'

'Thank you,' I replied tucking the ticket and passport into my bag.

After moving away from the counter, I turned to Matt, 'We've done it Matt. We've done it!' I exclaimed excitedly and threw my arms around him.

'Yes, we have,' he replied happily, 'but now we need to exchange some dollars for pounds. These exchange places at the airport never give you a very good rate, so don't change all your money here, just enough to see to your needs when you arrive in London.'

'How much do you think I'll need?'

'I'd say just about a hundred and fifty pounds would be more than enough. If you decide you want to catch a taxi from the airport, you'll need a hefty amount. And you might need to buy some things when you arrive. You can change the rest of your dollars at a bank in London.'

After completing the exchange, I asked Matt if he had time for lunch – my treat. I had noticed there were a couple of cafés on the public side of the departure gate.

'I'd like that very much Libby, but no alcohol mind, as I'm working later.'

We ordered toasted ham and cheese sandwiches with coffee and found a table to sit at. I handed Matt the forty dollars I owed him from the day before.

'Thank you, for the money and the sandwich,' Matt smiled at me. 'You're all set to go once you check your suitcase in.'

'Not quite yet,' I replied. 'I have to buy some books to read on the plane. I've been craving a book to read and Marty refused to let me spend any money on one. We had so little. So now I'm going to treat myself to a couple to take on the journey. It'll pass the time while I wait for my flight anyway. And I want to see if I can buy a small bag to put the books in. Would they sell anything like that in the departure area? There's nothing out here.'

'Yes, there'll be places that sell books – and bags, in the duty-free shops. The bags they sell won't be cheap though. And you need to see if you can get a cushion,' Matt said with a serious face, 'although they will provide you with one on the plane. You could ask them to give you an extra one. Are you sure you're okay Libby?'

'Yes, I'm fine,' I assured him.

'Well make sure you take it easy in London for a few days. Are you going straight to your cousin's place?'

'Yes, she was expecting me to join her before the accident but she doesn't know that I'll be turning up in a day or so. I haven't been able to let her know.'

'I hope it goes well for you Libby. As much as I hate to leave you, I need to get moving and grab a few hours' sleep before work tonight,' Matt said standing and pushing his chair under the table. 'I'd really like to say keep in touch and let me know how you're getting on, but I don't think that would be wise, in case Marty somehow discovers. We don't want him to know where you are.'

'No,' I said, standing to join him, 'Oh Matt, I can't thank you enough for all you've done. Give me a big hug.'

Matt folded his arms around me. 'It's been a pleasure knowing you. If I'd had ever had a daughter, I would want her to be just like you. Goodbye Libby, and the best of luck with everything.'

'Thanks, Matt, that's the best compliment anyone could give me, especially looking like this.'

Matt slowly released me and said, 'you still look beautiful, you silly girl, and don't let anyone tell you otherwise.' He turned and began walking out of the terminal, but with a half turn, and not breaking his stride shouted over his shoulder, 'and get yourself an education young lady.'

'I will,' I whispered to his retreating back.

25

Bristol June 2000

Beth Carey stops at this point and says, 'So that's how I managed to escape to England. I hope that's all you need to know. I'm feeling totally exhausted after telling you all that.'

Frank could empathise with her but he wanted to move on and hear what happened next.

'I would like to hear how things went after moving to London,' Frank said.

'Why? And how would that be relevant to your investigation?'

'I believe it might well be and would allow me to connect all the dots,' Franks tells her. 'I would greatly appreciate it if you could take us through it. Look if you're feeling exhausted, perhaps we could come back again tomorrow?'

'*Again?*'

'Yes, as I said, we need to go over events once you arrived in London.'

'Is that absolutely necessary? Is this an official Newcastle

Police enquiry? You haven't said.'

'It's semi-official,' DI Radcliffe, who had been sitting in silence up to this point says. 'His boss contacted my boss, asking us to work informally with Detective Inspector Bailey.'

'My boss has put the case of the unidentified remains into an unsolved case file,' Frank adds. 'He prevented me from investigating any further. However, after the second crime came to light, I felt I had to take it further. My boss wouldn't cover the cost of me coming to the UK officially, so I've taken long service leave and I'm covering the costs myself, with his knowledge and agreement. It would be very helpful if you could continue with your story. And I assure you I'll tell you more about our investigation following that.'

'I'm curious as to what this is all about. I thought all that part of my life was over. To be honest, it's not been easy going through it all again.'

'Yes, I can see that. And I appreciate you doing this. I can promise you there is a very valid reason.' *One that he hasn't even disclosed to DI Radcliff.*

Frank looks at Beth Carey and he can see that she is in two minds about the whole matter. He really needs to hear the end of her story to see if his theories are correct. Besides, he doesn't want this to be the last time he meets with her. And he still has to persuade her to give him a DNA sample. He hasn't decided how he's going to approach that yet.

When she'd told them about the rape, he'd found himself clenching his right fist in anger. If Martin Miller had been in the room with them, he would have taken a swing at him. She was so fortunate to have a neighbour who was willing to help her. Without him, things could have been very difficult. It was a good thing Mrs. Carey had been brave enough to open up to him.

'We could come later in the day if that would be more convenient,' Frank says.

'No, that won't work. Alison, my daughter, might walk in on our discussions in the afternoon. And my son often pops in after work. I would rather neither of them were around. Morning is better. Same time.'

Frank drops DI Radcliff off at his station and returns to his hotel. He is now convinced of one thing; Beth Carey was not involved in the murder of his mystery victim – nor does he believe she played any part in covering up the crime. His liking for the woman might be clouding his judgement, but after listening to her he is sure she is telling the truth. That's one potential suspect eliminated. He opens his brief case, takes out the case files and spends the rest of the afternoon and evening going over them.

The following day after settling in with refreshments, Beth resumes her story.

26

Libby's Story
London Late May 1975

I found the flight exhausting, with stops in Singapore, Bombay and then Bahrain. I had very little sleep and half an hour before landing the bathroom mirror in the aeroplane toilets presented a ghastlier reflection than normal with dark circles under my eyes.

The plane landed at Heathrow, London at four-thirty pm on Friday. Departure from Sydney had been at four pm on Thursday and I'd spent thirty-three and a half hours travelling and yet in principle I arrived just over twenty-four hours later. Weird. That meant London was nine hours behind Sydney.

It was a great relief when I finally passed through passport control – I was worried whether they were going to let me in. Once again, I'd had to explain what happened to my face to serious custom officials staring intently at me.

After collecting my suitcase, I searched around arrivals for a public telephone, then realised I had no British coins.

I wanted to phone Helen to warn her of my arrival, but couldn't see where I could change some of my notes to do this. It was Friday evening by the time I exited the terminal. I just hoped that Helen would be home, otherwise I'd have to go to a hotel for the night.

I staggered out of the terminal building into glaring evening sunshine and a heat that shocked me. I'd always believed England was cold. Peeling off the new coat I'd bought at Sydney airport, I climbed into a cab and recited the address of my destination, having learnt it off by heart on the flight.

Despite my extreme exhaustion, I found a new lease of life as the streets whizzed by. This was London and I'd arrived.

Helen lived in a suburb called West Hampstead and the cab eventually pulled up at what looked like a huge house. I paid the cab driver, giving him a generous tip and asked if he would wait to see if Helen was home, explaining that I would need to find a hotel if she wasn't. I walked up the path to the entrance and marvelled at the large wooden front door, which had ornate half-glass panels either side of it. I'd never seen such an enormous door. I knew Helen lived in flat 1, so that would probably be on the ground floor I surmised and there was a bell there with the name 'Fallon' on it which I rang.

A young fair headed woman with short bouncing curly hair and startling blue eyes opened the door. She looked similar to me in my wedding photo. Family!

'Helen?' I asked.

'Yes?'

'I'm Libby. I'm sorry I couldn't phone you before

leaving Australia, there was no opportunity and I had no English coins to ring you from Heathrow airport. I hope it's alright that I've just turned up.'

'Oh my God! Libby. Of course it's alright, come in.'

She rushed forward and gave me a big hug. 'I'm so glad you've finally come. We've been so worried about you.'

I waved to the cab driver who drove off. Helen was still chatting away to me. 'You look exhausted. Long flight? Yes of course it was. Our uncle Jimmy did it in the sixties and he said it was a nightmare and he would never do it again. You remember Uncle Jimmy, don't you? You would have been about eight or nine at the time when he came to stay with you.'

Helen chatted on incessantly all the way into the flat. I found it hard to keep up with everything she was saying.

'Just dump your bags down there,' Helen said indicating a place just inside the entrance door to her flat. 'I imagine you could do with a nice cup of tea.'

'Oh yes please.'

I followed her into the front living room where she invited me to sit down. She then walked back and turned right into a small kitchen. The kitchen opened on to the lounge with a large cut out opening and half wall, so I could still just about see her. There was no window in there which I found strange. As she prepared the tea she said, 'So you received my letter then? Gosh, I only sent it last week. That was fast!'

'You sent me a letter last week?' I said panicking.

'Yes, what's wrong?'

'I didn't receive it before I left Helen. Oh no, Marty will have it. Did you put your address on it?'

'Yes, of course I did. Is that going to be a problem?'

'I'm afraid it might be. I need to explain.'

I described my hospital recovery and what life was like living with Marty once we returned home – including the rape on my last night in Sydney and also how I overheard snatches of a conversation between Marty and his friend talking about getting rid of me.

'My God Libby, why didn't you go to the police?'

'The police? No, Marty would have denied everything. They would probably have put it down to paranoia on my part, following a severe head trauma. No, going to the police wasn't an option. I just had to get out of there.'

I explained how my neighbour Matt helped me with the lawyer's documents.

'You were lucky to have his help. So, you got all the money. That's great. Marty didn't deserve a penny of it.'

'No, he didn't really, but I thought he might be legally entitled to it. I was worried he'd come looking for me, or find a lawyer to track me down if I took it all, so I left him half of it. He should be happy with that.'

'Half of it? God, I wouldn't have left him a penny after what he did to you and what he was planning if you heard him right.'

'Yes, but if I had taken all of it, he would have had a reason to come looking for me. Now he won't. It does worry me though that he'll have your address. He wanted *all* the money to buy a property and set up a used car business. He might not have enough now to do exactly that, but he could do plenty with what I left him. What did you say in the letter?'

'I said how sorry I was about your accident, asked

how you were and whether you were still planning to come over here. Oh cripes, that means he'll figure out that you've come here!'

Helen looked at me with concern.

'Exactly. Look I know I've only just arrived Helen, but would you consider moving just to be safe? I might be completely wrong, but I believe Marty is dangerous. He might come after me to vent his anger. If he did that and I wasn't here, he could take it out on you.'

Helen sat in silence for a few minutes. I knew it was a big ask. I'd only been there five minutes and I was asking her to move. She was probably wondering what on earth she'd let herself in for.

'I don't have any particular attachment to this flat,' she finally said. 'So yes, Libby we could look at moving. It's not easy to get places just like that in London though,' she said snapping her fingers.

'There's something else I need to tell you Helen. I'm pregnant. I only discovered this last Monday when I went to see my new doctor.'

'But I thought you and Marty had stopped having sex,' Helen said, looking embarrassed. 'That's what you told me in one of your letters anyway.'

'Did I mention that I was seeing someone else?'

'No.'

'Then I don't know Helen. Marty claimed we always used contraception. Perhaps I had a fling with someone else or Marty and I had a night of passion for old time's sake. It must have been before the accident.'

'Did you tell Marty about the pregnancy, because that may well make him come after you?'

'No, he has no idea. From what he said, neither of us were interested in having children, so I doubt very much that he'd be interested in this child anyway – even if it was his.'

'God Libby, what are you going to do? Are you going to have it?'

'What do you mean?' I asked her.

'I mean are you going to have an abortion, or see the pregnancy through? You're still quite young. Do you want to have a baby?'

'I hadn't even considered an abortion. I didn't plan this, but no, I wouldn't have an abortion.'

'And you'll keep the baby?'

'Of course I'll keep it. I couldn't give my child away; even though it could be fathered by a man I can't stand.'

'Just checking. You've been through so much and to find out you're pregnant on top of it all. Will you ever tell Marty about the baby?'

'Never, I can't … I don't want to have contact with him Helen. If it somehow comes out, and I doubt it ever will, I'll lie and say that I had a one-night stand with someone else and that that person is the father of the baby. You never know I might have.'

Helen said nothing in response to this and sat looking at her lap.

'Do you think that's unfair of me?' I asked her.

'No,' she said raising her head to look at me. 'Not after what he's done to you Libby, but what about the child? What will you tell him or her?'

'I'll cross that bridge when I have to. At some point I'll have to change our names as well. I don't want my son or daughter to carry Marty's name. I don't want his name either. But that's for another day. I'll have to obtain some advice about doing that. Changing the subject, I desperately need some new clothes, Helen. I only brought a few of my old ones and there wasn't much choice there. Apparently, I lost many of my belongings ... in the fire at Mum and Dad's.'

I'd hesitated, not feeling comfortable with bringing up the fire, but I'd have to face telling Helen that I couldn't remember anything about it or my parents sooner or later.

'God that was so awful Libby,' Helen said. 'To lose everyone like that. I know you and Gary didn't get on, but still. You must have felt devastated!'

I waited for a few seconds before saying, 'Helen I need to tell you that since the accident I can't remember *anything* much about my previous life, just little snapshots that spring into my head now and then. I didn't even know about you until I found a letter from you dated from March, that I'd hidden along with my passport and birth certificate. Your letter and the documents represented a real lifeline when I came across them. Are we the same age? Did we write to each other often?'

Helen looked at me with a shocked expression on her face before answering.

'I'm eighteen months older than you. You and I were pen-pals for a few years when we were younger, then neither of us wrote to each other for some time until the year before I moved to London and I heard you were getting married. I wrote to congratulate you and since then we have written to each other every few months. At the beginning of March, you wrote telling me your marriage was a big mistake and that you wanted to come home to England, so I invited to you to come and stay with me.'

'That must have been the letter I found. It was the only one that was in the flat.'

'Strange. Would you have thrown my other letters away?'

'I doubt it. Perhaps I left them at work, to hide them from Marty. Some of your earlier ones might have been lost in the fire.'

'Hmm.'

'So, are there any shops around here? I desperately need some underwear and other bits.'

'The only decent place around here is John Barnes which is a department store. It's nearby, up on Finchley Road.'

'Are you free to come with me to this John Barnes place tomorrow?'

'You bet; I love shopping! They have a supermarket in the basement called Waitrose. That's where I do all my shopping. They're only open a half day tomorrow though, being Saturday. We can do John Barnes then and maybe the West End next week, although I was about to suggest we go down to Bristol next weekend for you to be re-united with the rest of the family.'

'I'd love to, but maybe we should leave that for a few weeks. We have to start looking for a new place for you.'

'And you. We can share. That would be the sensible thing to do.'

'I'd love that, but Helen when the baby comes, you won't want to be sharing a flat with a squalling new-born.'

'Who says, anyway we'll deal with that when the time

comes. Now do you want to freshen up, have a shower or bath?'

'I'd love to, I feel very grubby from the flight.'

Helen showed me the bathroom, handing me a towel she took from a shelving unit just behind the bathroom door.

'You freshen yourself up, while I cook some dinner. I was planning on making spaghetti bolognaise, is that okay for you?' Helen called back down the hall.

'Home-made?'

'Of course, how else could you have it?'

'You can bet Marty would have found a tinned or frozen version!'

After eating every scrap of the meal Helen cooked, I licked the last of the sauce off my fork and said, 'Oh Helen that was absolutely scrumptious. Apart from some occasional fresh fruit and cheese, I've been eating ghastly frozen meals for weeks, and before that I was eating hospital food which although it was better than the frozen rubbish, it was not all that great either.'

'Weren't you up to cooking meals when you went home?'

'Marty claimed about the only thing I cooked was fresh chicken and he wouldn't let me cook any meals anyway, saying it was too risky until I was better. He had the freezer stuffed with ready frozen meals that I just popped into the oven. They were disgusting.'

'Don't worry, I'll teach you to cook. Being the eldest at home, in a family of five kids, I had to do a lot of the cooking from a young age. I like food anyway so I was keen to learn. Don't think I'm going to be making meals for you every night though, so you'll have to learn to cook and about the only frozen food I'd have in the house is ice-cream and frozen peas.'

I laughed. 'I'd love to learn to cook. Apparently, my mother was a prizewinning baker, so hopefully I might have picked up some of her skills.'

'I remember eating her fabulous cakes and scones around at your house before you all went to Australia. I used to love going there for tea.'

We sat in silence for a moment and I could see that Helen was staring at the scars on my face.

'Are you feeling okay now Libby with your injuries? Do you need to see a doctor over here?'

'I'm okay thanks … but yes, I should see a doctor. I had some minor fractures to my skull both front and rear, as well as the gashes all over my face – this large one here on my forehead and down my cheek,' I said pointing to the obvious scars. 'The smaller ones were minor glass cuts. The hospital in Maitland said everything's healed well, but I was supposed to have some follow up visits at a Sydney hospital. That won't happen now of course, so I should do something about it here. One of the things I remember my new doctor in Sydney saying was that I shouldn't have any further x-rays, now that I'm pregnant.'

'I'm registered with a good surgery not far from here where they have several doctors. They won't be open at the weekend, but we can walk down there so I can show you where to go and you can register with them on Monday and ask for an appointment. See if you can register with the female doctor. She's the nicest one there.

Your hair will soon grow and cover the scar on the back of your head, your forehead and to some extent on your face. The scars will fade, I had a horrible scar on my knee from an accident when I was young, but you barely see it now. See?' Helen said pulling up her skirt to expose a knee that showed little trace of a scar.

'I hope they will fade; I stand out like a sore thumb at the moment, don't I? People keep giving me funny looks. I had some delays at passport control, both in Sydney and here, until I explained what had happened to me.'

'Understandable I suppose, but when we go shopping tomorrow if anyone looks strangely at you, we'll just say, 'car accident', and that should shut them up. Another cup of tea?'

'Yes, let me do it. I'll just wash the dishes first, after all, you cooked dinner.'

While I made the tea, I asked Helen what she did for work. She explained that she'd trained as a Secretary in Bristol after leaving school and had several years' experience of working in a law firm before coming to London. She now worked in a law firm in the city.

'Legal secretaries earn a bit more money than other secretaries,' Helen told me. 'You should train as a secretary, learning shorthand and typing. I've suggested this in letters to you in the past. I know you left school without any qualifications, so it might be good to study some subjects and take exams as well. Many firms are snobbish about employing staff if they don't have 'O' levels.'

'O Levels?'

'That's the first set of exams you take here at sixteen. Or CSEs if you can't manage 'O' levels, but most employers want 'O' levels, unless you want to work in Woolworths. If you're going to bring up a child, you'll need to earn better money than Woolworths would pay, so I suggest you start looking at options to gain some qualifications.'

'We have shops called Woolworths in Australia as well. I don't think I'd like to work there, although Marty told me most of the jobs I've had have been in shops. Matt, the neighbour who helped me, told me I should take up some study over here, but Helen, I don't even know if I can write yet. I couldn't even talk when I first regained consciousness. I struggled to read anything at first as the words were just a jumble to me. That's alright now, but I haven't even attempted to write anything. The only time I've had to put pen to paper since the accident has been signing my name.'

'Well, you can start tomorrow,' Helen said emphatically. 'You were always a good writer. Your letters were very funny. I'll dig one out and show you. We'll buy a notebook tomorrow and you can start practising. I think I'll phone work on Monday morning and tell them I won't be in for a few days. I'll need to take you around with me to show you the ropes and, as you said, we need to be looking for a flat.'

'Will your firm be okay about that?'

'Sure, I'll just explain the situation, they'll be fine. I'll take the days as leave I'm owed.'

'Thanks Helen. I'm very tired, do you mind if I go to bed now? I think I could sleep solidly for the next week.'

Helen had explained she only had one bedroom and that I would be sharing a king size bed with her.

'The side of the bed nearest the door is mine. I'm sorry

there is no lamp on your side at the moment, but we could buy one for you tomorrow. Come on, I'll show you to the bedroom, grab your bags.'

I followed Helen past the bathroom to the end of the flat which opened into a spacious bedroom. 'Oh fantastic, a doona!' I exclaimed with delight.

'Doona?'

'Yes, this,' I said touching the bedcovering, 'I haven't slept with one of these for ages. Hang on, where have I slept with one of these? Not with Marty, that's for sure. Maybe at home on the farm? Oh Helen, I wish I could remember things.'

'I'm sure things will come back to you in time. Doona? What a funny word! We call it a 'duvet' here, a 'quilt' or it sometimes referred to as a 'continental quilt'.

'Doona, duvet, who cares. I'm looking forward to sleeping under it.'

27

I woke the next morning feeling thoroughly refreshed. I don't think I moved an inch all night. Helen was not in the bed. After washing in the bathroom, I dressed and strolled down to the kitchen where I found Helen.

'Morning. Are you a tea or coffee person in the morning?' she asked.

'Tea thanks, I like coffee later in the morning or at lunch time. But tea I can drink anytime.'

'Me too. What would you like for breakfast? I only have cereal or toast at the moment.'

'I normally only have some toast for breakfast, but I've been feeling queasy and struggling to keep food down some days.'

'That'll be the pregnancy. One or two slices of toast?'

'One thanks. You wouldn't have some Vegemite, would you?'

'Vegemite? Is that Australian or something? We have something called Marmite here and I have a jar of it somewhere. It sounds as though it might be the same. I don't have it very often.'

'Okay. I'll try some of that on my toast.'

My verdict was that Marmite was a little too sharp for me. 'I'll have to see if I can buy some Vegemite somewhere. I might get withdrawal symptoms otherwise. I wish I'd known; I would've brought some with me. They were selling it at the airport in Sydney. I didn't think.'

'I doubt you'll find anyone selling Vegemite here. I've never heard of it.'

'By the way,' Helen said as we headed back to her place in a taxi with all our shopping from John Barnes and Waitrose, 'I phoned home last night after you went to bed and told the family about your arrival and the circumstances. They knew you were supposed to be coming before the accident, but we weren't sure if you'd still be coming. Dad was very concerned and he agrees that we should move. In fact, he tried to persuade me to come back to Bristol with you instead of looking for another place in London. I said I didn't want to do that, but that we'd go down in a few weeks.'

'Did you tell your father everything, including the rape and Marty's talk about getting rid of me?'

'I told mum about the rape, and when she passed me to Dad, I mentioned everything else to him. That's why he was concerned. Mum and Dad send their love and are all looking forward to seeing you.'

The weekend passed with us relaxing, chatting, cooking and eating. Helen gave me my first cooking lesson and I was delighted with the result. 'You're a natural,' Helen declared.

Helen did most of the talking that weekend, providing

details of all the family and showing me pictures she had in an album. I couldn't wait to meet them all.

I also practised writing in a new notebook I'd bought. I was clumsy and awkward with the pen to begin with and although I tried to copy the style from an old hand-written letter of mine Helen showed me, the end results were nowhere near as neat.

On Monday morning, after phoning work, Helen took me to the doctor's surgery to register. I completed the forms and obtained an appointment for Thursday. Helen then realised I would have to acquire a National Insurance number and so that was another thing we had to do that morning. We also completed a Housing application for me at the council offices.

It had been an exhausting morning but I was keen to start looking at alternative accommodation, worried that Marty might come after us.

In the afternoon Helen took me down to a Housing Association where we were interviewed by a friendly Australian. 'Don't mention the money you have,' Helen whispered on the way into the little office.

The Australian woman was sympathetic to my situation. 'I know what some Aussie men are like,' she sniffed after Helen mentioned that I had fled to England – where I was born, she added – to escape a violent husband. Helen asked if there was any hope of us acquiring a flat through the Association, reminding the woman that she'd been on their list for a year already.

'We have nothing at the moment,' the woman told us, 'But if something comes up, we'll be in touch. We do house single people as well as people with children, but those with children are usually council referrals.'

Disappointed, we trekked back to Helen's. 'I can't do anything else today, Helen, I'm shattered.'

'Me too. We've achieved a lot today mind you. Tomorrow we can go out looking at flats through estate agents.'

'Why didn't you want me to mention my financial situation to the woman? Would that exclude me from getting a place?'

'More than likely.'

'Do you think I have enough money to buy a place in London?'

'How much do you have?'

'Not sure, probably a little over thirty-five thousand pounds judging by the exchange rate I received in Australia.'

'Bloody hell Libby! You could buy several houses in Bristol for that money. But London – probably a decent flat, or a small house, depending on where you looked at buying.'

Helen went to explain how expensive various areas of London were.

'It would make sense to invest some of the money, otherwise I might just fritter it away. I'd hate to do that after all Mum and Dad's hard work.'

'Yes, you're right but don't rush into anything yet. Okay? You can talk to dad about it. Being in the building trade, he's experienced at buying properties.'

Tuesday, we spent traipsing from one agency to another without success. I was keen to offer my pot of money to find a decent place, but Helen insisted that we must stay within the bounds of what we could afford, based on two salaries similar to hers.

'You'll be living off your money anyway until you find a job,' Helen reminded me. 'You won't be eligible to sign on the dole. If there's nothing suitable in this area, we might have to look elsewhere.'

We viewed a two-bedroom flat, but it was a dark, damp smelling basement that both of us rejected.

Before we returned home, Helen dragged me into a Secretarial College where I enrolled and paid for the next full-time course which started the following week and ran through to late July. Helen also took me into Lloyd's bank, to open an account.

On Wednesday Helen returned to work and I accompanied her into the city armed with an A – Z of London so that I could find the National Bank of Australia and withdraw some money. I discovered I had an hour to kill before they opened, so I began to explore parts of the city and its wonderful old buildings. When I finally returned to the bank, there were some delays while I presented my documents and discussed my business with the deputy manager.

I spent the rest of the day exploring my new city. In a café near the Barbican one of the men serving there was an Australian. I asked him if he knew where I could buy some Vegemite, and he directed me to the Australian Gift shop, near Australia House in the Strand, close to Aldwych. I checked in my A-Z and set off. The Australian Gift shop did sell small jars of Vegemite, although at an extortionate price, and I purchased four jars to keep me supplied for several months.

I attended the doctor's surgery on Thursday morning, where I was seen by a lovely female doctor. I summarised everything I'd experienced over the past year – including events I couldn't remember like the fire at my parents. The doctor nodded sympathetically and said she'd make a referral to the Royal Free Hospital in Hampstead as she wrote notes. I also mentioned my pregnancy, saying I wasn't absolutely sure how far advanced I was.

'Close to eight weeks would be the least time, but perhaps I'm further along,' I said, 'I just don't know'.

The doctor suggested an internal examination to help clarify matters, and asked me to remove my underwear and pop up on the bed. I was nervous about her touching me and was choking back tears as she approached me.

'Hmm', said the doctor after examining me, 'there is evidence of vaginal tearing that is healing here, have you had some rough intercourse recently?' she asked.

'Yes … my um, estranged husband raped me the night before I left Sydney,' I told her, tears beginning to slide down my face.

'You certainly have been through the mill, haven't you?' she said sympathetically. 'No wonder you left him. I'm afraid women don't have it easy, even in these enlightened times. I'd say you're about nine weeks along. I'll do a referral to the hospital for you to have a scan when you're further along. All finished now, you can re-dress.'

The doctor spent some time making notes and then finally said, 'I'd like to see you in another few weeks. Can you make another appointment on your way out?'

As I turned the key in the internal door leading into Helen's flat, the phone rang and I hurried to answer it.

It was Coleen Pringle from the Housing Association informing me that she had a place that had become available.

'It's not self-contained I'm afraid, and you'd have to share a bathroom and toilet with one other person,' she said *'but there are three rooms plus a kitchen. Would you and your cousin be interested in viewing it?'*

'Yes, when could we do that? Helen won't be back from work until shortly after six pm.'

'Would six-thirty this evening be suitable for you?'

'Yes, that'd be great,' I said, trying not to sound too eager. I noted down the address that woman gave me which I looked up in the A – Z. It was probably only a fifteen-minute walk away. I rang Helen with the good news. She sounded just as excited as me.

At six-thirty promptly we were waiting outside the house. Colleen arrived a few minutes later and opened the door.

'It's the ground floor of the house that's available,' she said, repeating details of the shared facilities on the first floor.

'I'll let you look around on your own,' she said and wandered back outside to have a cigarette.

There were two double rooms at the front of the house; the front one having a gas fire. Along a hallway was another large room with a bay window like the front room and another gas fire. It led onto a small kitchen with a lino floor.

The only cupboard in the kitchen was under the sink and there was an old-fashioned freestanding dresser that the previous tenants had left behind which I found charming.

'This is so cute,' I declared.

'My grandmother – I mean *our* grandmother had one of these in her house,' Helen said.

'There's no cooker, so we'd have to get one and look that's a gas point, isn't it? It looks like the one at your place. Much better than electric. I could buy us a new gas cooker. Oh Helen, we could use the room off the kitchen here as our living and dining-room, and then have a bedroom each. I know the rooms are smaller; not as nice as your current place, and they look a bit grotty at present, but we could paint them and put nice things in them. Our *own* things. There's a garden as well. Shall we have a look?'

We opened the back door and walked out into a disappointingly small yard. 'Oh well it's somewhere to hang the washing and put a small table and chairs,' I said. 'Let's look at the bathroom.'

Upstairs we inspected the separate toilet and huge bathroom, which was surprisingly clean. The bath had seen better days though and was covered with unattractive blueish/green streak marks and the enamel coating was chipped in places. It didn't look very enticing.

'We could always install a new bath,' I suggested.

We walked downstairs and out of the house to join the housing officer.

'What do you think?' Colleen asked us.

'What would the rent be?' Helen asked.

'It's ten pounds a week,' she answered, 'you'd have to sort out the utility bills between you and the tenant upstairs, there's only one supply.'

'We'll take it, thank you,' Helen said, 'that alright with you Libby?'

'Yes, definitely,' I said nodding enthusiastically.

'When would you be able to come in to do the paper work? I know you work during the day. Would ten on Saturday morning suit you?'

'Yes, thank you, that'd be great,' Helen said.

After the housing officer left, Helen and I were literally jumping for joy. 'It's so fantastic Libby, so cheap! I pay almost double that for my place now. We'll be able to save so much. Only five pounds a week each.'

'It's exciting isn't it, we'll have to go furniture shopping at the weekend, forget about clothes for now. I can start looking at things tomorrow. I'll pay for it all,' I added. Helen had told me she didn't own any of the furniture in her flat.

'We don't need to buy all new things Libby,' she said – 'including the cooker. You can pick up very good second-hand furniture and appliances all over London. There are several places up the top end of West Hampstead past the station. The only furniture items I think we should buy new are mattresses. Second-hand bed bases are fine but not second-hand mattresses.'

'Okay, I'll look at the shops up there tomorrow. John Barnes does some furniture I noticed. I'll look in there tomorrow for mattresses as well as a heater for the middle room.'

The following day I was busy visiting second-hand

shops and where I put down deposits on furniture, a fridge and cooker for us. Helen could check them out before they were delivered.

Saturday morning Helen and I called into the Housing Association Offices to sign the paperwork which we learned was a licence, rather than a lease.

Helen gave notice on her flat and we had a month to decorate the new place, organise a cooker and all the furniture.

Every night through the following week we trekked down to the new place, loaded with some of our belongings to leave at the new flat and painted for a few hours.

We hired a cab to move the last of our things. 'I'm going to buy a second-hand car next week,' I declared. 'We can't keep catching cabs everywhere. Do you have a licence?'

'Yes, I've had one for a few years. I've never driven in London though, only family vehicles in Bristol,' Helen said.

'If I find a car in the week, would you feel up to driving down to Bristol next week? I'd be willing to share the driving with you.'

I didn't add that I'd share the driving if I was able to work up the courage to get behind the wheel. I would need to practise around the local streets where we lived, which were pretty quiet. There weren't so many cars on the road back then.

'You don't have a British licence.'

'I'm allowed to drive on my Australian one, until I obtain one. I checked the other day at the post office.'

'Okay, it would be wonderful to have a car to use, if

you're sure.'

I took the following Monday morning off from my college course to wait in for the telephone company to come and install a phone in our new flat. Once the engineer had been, I decided to spend time looking for a car and after discovering an ad in a newsagent window near West Hampstead station, I purchased a mini-traveller estate. I thought I'd be really nervous climbing into the driver's seat, but I wasn't, and drove back to our flat without any difficulty.

'Where did you find this?' Helen asked in astonishment that evening as she walked around examining the car. 'It's in such good condition as well! I thought it'd be weeks before you found anything.'

I explained how I found it from an ad that had only been placed in the newsagent window that morning.

'Very resourceful.'

'We can definitely drive down to Bristol now. Although we'll have to arrange insurance. I took a chance driving it back here because it wasn't very far,' I said.

'I can do that tomorrow at work. Can we put both our names on the policy?'

'Of course, it's for both of us to use.'

On Friday evening Helen and I set off for Bristol. I'd been practising my driving around streets close to our flat, building up my confidence, but this was a whole new ball game. Negotiating our way out of London was time consuming and the traffic was very heavy. It took us almost an hour to reach the outskirts of London and by then I was becoming agitated. I didn't want to drive on the motorway, so we took an 'A' road instead.

At the halfway point Helen took over the driving and joined the motorway which didn't faze her.

'We're nearly there,' Helen announced a few minutes after turning off the motorway that led into Bristol. 'I can't wait to see everyone. This is Gloucester Rd and we live in a street that runs off this in a suburb called Bishopston.'

It was all meaningless to me. In a side road Helen pulled up outside a three-storey house. It had taken us three and a half hours to arrive at Helen's family home and we were famished; despite munching on supplies we'd brought with us.

'Mum should have something for us to eat,' Helen assured me as she dragged me into the house. I was suddenly feeling very shy and nervous.

'Hello everyone, we've finally arrived,' Helen shouted as she used her key to enter the house.

A body of people emerged from all directions, swamping Helen with hugs and kisses in the entrance hall.

'Hello, my lovely,' said a woman who wrapped her arms around me. She had a broader accent than Helen which was somehow familiar. She released me and stepped back. 'The last time I saw you, you were only this high,' she said, indicating a low-level height. 'Come in, come in, we've all been waiting for you. I'm your Aunt Ginny,' she added.

'Anything to eat mum, we're really hungry?' Helen asked after greeting everyone.

'Yes, come into the kitchen. We've all eaten, it's late, but I've saved something for you, which I hid from the greedy mob earlier.'

We walked through the house entering a large kitchen/ dining room at the rear. Aunt Ginny pulled out a small set of steps, opened a cupboard and climbed up to retrieve a round tray with what looked like a home-made pizza.

'Oh, yummy! Pizza. Are there any anchovies on it mum, only Libby is allergic to all kinds of fish and seafood?'

'No, just salami, tomato and cheese, it's part cooked so it won't take long,' she said popping the pizza into the oven.

'Since when has Libby been allergic to seafood?' asked a fair- headed man walking into the kitchen.

'Dad!'

'I'm only asking, because I don't remember that.'

'Yes,' interrupted Ginny, 'don't you remember when we used to have fish and chips on Friday night little Libby wouldn't eat it. Only the chips.'

'As far as I know, that was only because she was *afraid* of fish, not because she was allergic to it. You used to be terrified of fresh fish shops,' he said turning to me. 'Anyway, I'm Helen's Dad, your Uncle Kenny and this is my brother, your Uncle Jimmy,' he added turning to introduce another fair-headed man who had followed him into the kitchen. Again, Kenny had a familiar accent – one where the words sounded like they were curling around his tongue.

'Hello, it's lovely to meet you all finally,' I said, looking around the room where a large crowd had gathered.

'Oh, I haven't introduced the rest of them,' said Helen. 'These are my brothers, Harry who's twenty, Danny who's fourteen, and my sisters Julie, she's eighteen and Sherry, she's sixteen. And these are our cousins, Uncle Jimmy's kids, Billy who's ten and Joey, he's seven. They're all your cousins,' said Helen sweeping her arm across the group of young people standing watching me.

'Hello everyone, it's great to have so many cousins,' I said. I noticed that most of Helen's siblings, apart from her and Sherry, who took after their father, had their mother's dark brown hair. Jimmy's kids were fair like Helen and Sherry.

'When did you acquire the posh Australian accent?' Uncle Jimmy asked. 'When I was in Australia, I didn't hear many of them, except from rich toffs your father was building houses for.'

I turned to Jimmy and said, 'according to my ex-husband, I wanted a job in David Jones, so I improved my accent and the way I spoke.'

'David Jones, I remember that shop, Maggie took me in there once, it's a bit like John Lewis over here,' he explained to everyone.

'Maggie?' I asked.

'Your mother, we knew her as Maggie, not Margaret,' Aunt Ginny said.

'Oh okay. Anyway, when I was finally able to speak,' I continued, 'because I couldn't when I first regained consciousness after the car accident, this is how I sounded. That's all I know.'

'I spent about six months with you and your family back in the sixties. Nineteen sixty-three it was. You were about nine at the time. A real little tomboy.'

'Sorry, I don't remember that,' I said blushing, although there *was* something familiar about him. Perhaps being around them would help jog my memory. It was so frustrating not being able to recall significant events in my life. Everything in my past was so fuzzy.

'We heard about your memory loss,' Ginny said. 'It must be so terrible for you, not remembering things. Can't you remember anything?'

'Just fragments of my life as a child on the farm, being on a beach, and learning to swim in the sea. Did we go to the sea-side at all when you stayed with us?' I asked Uncle Jimmy.

'Yeah, a couple of times. We spent Boxing Day on the beach, in sweltering heat which seemed so weird.'

'The doctor from the hospital I was in after the accident said my memory will probably return gradually, but so far very little has returned,' I added. 'I vaguely remembered my husband, what he looked like and how he sounded, but nothing about being married to him or the life we led.'

'Sounds like a good thing too. You won't be wanting scum like that in your life,' Kenny said. 'He won't want to come sniffing around here, or he'll get a seeing to.'

'Dad!'

'Come on you lot, out of here.' Ginny waved at everyone, indicating she wanted them to leave. 'The girls' pizza is ready. Let them eat in peace and quiet.'

Helen and I spent the night in Helen's old room while Julie bunked in with Sherry. The family had exhausted me with old family photo albums, many which included me and my family before we emigrated. I was shown pictures of my parent's wedding and photos of my father at different ages growing up. The pictures brought tears to my eyes. My parents seemed familiar to me but I just couldn't remember my life with them.

When I finally went to bed, I was really feeling the loss of my immediate family. All those memories erased. Aunt Ginny said it was normal to forget events from when I was young, like some of the outings the family had had before we moved to Australia. But what about the memories from when I was older? Would I ever be able to connect with them again?

We woke to a cacophony of sounds in the house on Saturday morning. 'Home sweet home,' Helen murmured dragging herself out of bed.

After breakfast we helped with clearing up before Helen dragged me out of the house to catch a bus into town to go to John Lewis to select curtain fabric for my bedroom and the living room in our London flat.

While we were waiting for a bus home I said to Helen, 'Do you realise that everyone in our family has a name that ends with 'ee' sounds, apart from you? I know my name is Elizabeth but I'm called Libby. My mother who was Margaret was called Maggie.'

'My mother's name is Gina really, but she has always been called Ginny. It's a family tradition. I have it too, don't worry, I haven't been left out. They mostly call me Hellie.'

I had noticed that.

We both burst into fits of giggles.

28

We settled comfortably into life in our new flat. The only
'fly in the ointment' was the bath. The surface was porous
and difficult to clean. With the water stains it never *looked*
clean. We never *felt* clean after using it. We realised this
was all psychological; we knew it was clean because we
scrubbed it every time we had a bath. We didn't linger in
it for one second longer than necessary. We were in and
out of it in lightning speed. Washing our hair took a few
minutes longer and required keeping the water running
repeatedly to fill a jug which we tipped over our heads.

'I'm sure we have the fastest baths in the west,'
I remarked one day when Helen returned from the
bathroom after a very brief stint. Helen wouldn't hear of
me buying a new one, but I did find a replacement.

As I was walking up towards Kilburn High Road late
one afternoon, I noticed builders filling a skip with rubble
from a house they were working on. There was a rather
smart looking enamelled steel bath with handles sitting
just inside the front wall. I paused, watching the builders
for a few minutes and then approached one.

When I learned that the bath was being thrown away,

I asked if we could have it. He told me that it needed to be collected that night or it was going on the skip that was being collected in the morning.

When Helen returned home that evening, I took her down to look at the bath. 'He said we can have it.'

Helen decided that we couldn't carry it up the hill on our own. She said that we'd have to wait for Gerry – our upstairs neighbour to return home and ask him to help us. Knowing how late Gerry returned I could see Helen was wavering about it.

'Look how immaculate the bath is Helen. I don't understand why they're throwing it out. It would be such a waste if we don't take it, and those handles would come in very handy as my pregnancy advances. It would help me to climb out of the bath with ease.'

'Yes, I can see that. Okay, we'll wait up for him. I just hope he isn't going for a drink tonight, otherwise he might not be up for it,' Helen said.

Gerry, the upstairs neighbour we shared the house with, either traipsed up to his ex-wife's house to look after their little ones while she attended night school, or he went out for drinks with his mates.

We hadn't experienced any conflict of use with the bathroom. Gerry worked on the other side of London and rose early most mornings, bathed and left the house before we needed the bathroom. We bathed in the evenings when we had the house to ourselves. We usually only bumped into him at weekends.

It was almost midnight before Gerry returned. Eventually we heard the key in the door and rushed out to greet him. We explained about the bath and he was keen to help collect it, although we could smell he'd been drinking. We hurried down to the building site and I was relieved to find that the bath was still there. We lifted it out with Gerry on one end and us on the other, and started walking back to our house.

At the next intersection we encountered a couple coming along from the left carrying a couch. Crossing the road from the other side were two women carrying a table. We all stopped momentarily and laughed at our midnight escapades.

The next day I approached the Housing Association to ask if they could provide a plumber and an electrician to install the new bath and an electric shower I'd purchased, saying I was willing to pay for the labour. It was another couple of weeks before the work was finally completed. It was a messy job, as some tiling work was needed, but we were all delighted with the result.

'Now we can have either a leisurely bath or a quick shower,' Helen concluded.

After graduation from the secretarial course Helen organised for me to do some relief holiday cover at her firm so I could then use them as a reference. With my pregnancy advancing I didn't look for a full-time position, but I found long term temp work through an employment agency. The office, a legal firm, was in Finchley Road, not far from John Barnes, so I was pleased I didn't have far to travel to work.

After two follow up trips to the Royal Free Hospital, I was given the all clear on the injuries I'd sustained in

Australia. They were surprised to hear that little of my long-term memory had returned though. I also attended the hospital for scans and all was progressing well with the pregnancy.

I enrolled in a college to study a range of 'O' levels in September that year but these were part-time evening courses and I had to do most of my studying at home. I set up a desk in my bedroom, so that Helen could watch TV in the living room.

According to calculations made, the baby was due in early January, but on the night of December the twelfth my waters broke. Although I'd read some things about giving birth, I remained ignorant about many details. I was under the misguided view that it took several days for the baby to come after breaking waters.

In a panic Helen rang the hospital; they asked her to monitor the timing of any pains and to bring me in as soon as possible. She found me in the kitchen calmly making toast and tea.

'What are you doing Libby, we have to go to the hospital now.'

'There's no rush is there? I'm hungry and they probably won't give me anything to eat for *hours*.'

I was completely relaxed as I ate my food. Unlike Helen, who was hovering around me like an old mother hen. Every few minutes a pain interrupted my meal.

'Come on Libby, we have to get going.'

Helen looked like she was on the verge of a nervous breakdown, so with some reluctance I rose from the table, grabbed the last piece of toast, stuffed it in my mouth and picked up my bag (where I'd thrown in a jar of vegemite).

After a lengthy and painful labour, I delivered a six-pound ten-ounce boy on the morning of thirteenth December. 'Premature', the doctor who delivered him announced, 'but there are no respiratory issues and he seems fine.'

Some hours later I was nursing him in bed and Helen asked, 'So have you decided on a name for him.'

'Yes, I'm going to call him Matthew after the lovely neighbour who helped me in Sydney.'

'You know what the family will call him don't you?'

'Mattie,' we both chorused.

29

Bristol June 2000

'It's time for a break,' Beth Carey says stopping at what seems like a natural point on the third morning.

All Frank had really wanted was a summary of events, but once Beth started, he didn't like to interrupt her. At the same time, he's found all her recounting useful in gauging her strength of character. He's found himself sinking more and more into her life, as though he was with her. If only. He loves the sound of her voice with its slight Aussie twang and he finds her looks mesmerising. He suspects today's long ramblings are all about avoiding what's coming next. When he'd discussed the lengthy recounting sessions with George Radcliffe the afternoon before, Radcliffe said, 'Don't worry about it. It beats having to deal with some scumbag. I'm finding it quite relaxing.'

That'd be right. Radcliffe looks like he nods off regularly, during the sessions. Frank inserts another tape in the machine thinking it was lucky he'd bought a number of spares.

When Beth returns with fresh coffees, a large plate of

assorted sandwiches and some side plates, Frank says, 'I'd like to move forward to events in August nineteen seventy-six now and what followed after that if you don't mind.'

Beth shudders.

This is going to be quite emotional for her.

'Okay. Let me just have something to eat and drink first. Help yourselves. I made these before you arrived this morning, knowing today would be a long session. I'm not going into work today.'

'Don't mind if I do. Thank you,' DI Radcliffe says leaning forward to select several sandwich quarters, placing them a plate before settling back to eat.

They make small talk about the sights in London that Frank visited when he first arrived in the UK, until she is ready to start again.

30

Libby's Story
London August 1976

It was ten pm on a Friday night and I was waiting outside
a Tandoori House on Finchley Road for the cab I'd ordered
to take me home. The air was thick with humidity and I
could feel perspiration running down my neck and back.
London had been unbearably hot that summer (worse than
I remember it being in Australia!) and, given the weather,
I thought an Indian meal had not been the wisest choice,
but it was my colleague's favourite restaurant and being
her birthday, it was her decision. The food *was* very tasty.

It was the first night I'd ever been away from Mattie,
who was now eight months old. I thought perhaps I
should get the taxi to take me to Helen's place instead of
going home, so I could collect him, or crash out there for
the night. The bed I'd bought was still in my old room and
I'd left Mattie's old cot there as we sometimes stayed over
with Helen. They would both be fast asleep though. I was
confident that Mattie would be fine under Helen's care,
but I wasn't sure about how *I* would feel to wake to an

empty flat without him.

The Housing Association had offered me my own flat three months prior and so I'd reluctantly left the cosy place I'd been sharing with Helen to move into a two-bedroom flat in South Hampstead that backed onto an over-ground railway line. It was a spacious, self-contained flat that meant Mattie could have his own room and Helen could also have some privacy in her relationship.

Helen had met a trainee solicitor, Chris, ('the family won't dare call him Chrissie, will they?' I'd asked Helen) who was working in another city firm. Chris still lived at home with his parents in Chalk Farm, but would often come over to spend the night with Helen. Chris had been keen to move into our place, but Helen had baulked at this.

'Dad would kill me,' she'd claimed.

I still worked part-time in the local legal firm where I'd been working as a temp before Mattie's birth. They'd offered me full time permanent work after Mattie was born, but I'd wanted to spend time at home with him while I was breast feeding. I also had to finish my 'O' levels, which I switched to studying by a correspondence course so that I could be home with him. I'd taken the exams at my old college just a few months before, working hard to complete the courses over one academic year.

When Mattie was four months old, and was eagerly eating solids, I switched him to bottles and returned to work two days a week while he attended a nursery. I thought it would be good for Mattie to interact with other young children and I certainly needed more brain stimulus. The extra income was also handy, although I'd invested in several properties in Bristol, guided by Uncle Kenny, and I received an income from the rents of these.

The cab eventually turned up and I jumped in hoping it might have air-conditioning. No such luck. It was sweltering and even with the windows down there was little in the way of relief from the humid air. Just as it pulled up outside my house, I spotted a man entering the shared front door. I thought it must be the elusive downstairs neighbour I hadn't met.

There were only two flats once you entered the front door, one that opened into a small ground floor flat and another door that opened on to the staircase leading to my flat which was over two levels. There was also a basement flat with a separate entrance. All the flats had use of the garden at the rear, but neither flat from the raised ground floor entrance had direct access to it. We had to enter the garden by exiting the front door, going through a side gate and along a passage.

Off my living room to the rear there were double doors opening onto a small balcony on the garden side. The balcony railings were closely spaced and Mattie couldn't fit through them, but once he started climbing, they could be a problem. My living room, kitchen and dining room were open-plan with windows fronting the street off the living room as well as the doors leading to the balcony. There was also a window to the rear in the kitchen which I left open day and night. 'No one is going to be able to climb in there!' I exclaimed to Helen's concern about security. 'It's too high.'

I opened the door to the living room and immediately went over to open the balcony doors. I hadn't bothered with lights as with the front curtains open, light was streaming in from the street. I was just about to turn towards the kitchen when I heard the humming of a familiar tune that made all the hairs on my body stand up. I froze. *Surely, I must have imagined it?* I listened. There was silence. *I had imagined it.*

As I began to move again the humming resumed. I took a few more steps and reached out turning on the kitchen light. I swivelled around and scanned the room. Sitting in the single couch chair on the far side of the living room was a man. I could only see the outline of his shape but I knew who it was. He must have been the man I'd seen entering the front door.

'G'day Libby, you're lookin' good,' he said.

I remained silent, my mind whirling with questions. How did he know where I lived? How did he get in? Had he been to Helen's? She wouldn't have told him where I lived. Helen! Mattie! Were they okay? Did he know Mattie was my child?

'Well, aren't you gunna greet your o' hubby Libby?' Marty drawled.

'What are you doing here Marty?' I asked him.

'I could ask the same of you.'

'You know why I'm here.'

'And why is that?'

I remained silent. I noticed a small screwdriver I'd left on the worktop and, turning around slightly to hide my actions from Marty, I carefully slipped it into the pocket of my skirt. I began to move out of the kitchen towards the door to the landing and stairs when Marty came flying across the room and grabbed me.

'I asked you a question Libby.'

'Our marriage was a sham and you know it. You had no feelings for me, the way you raped me proved it. And I certainly had none for you. I could barely remember you. Let me go!'

I squirmed out of his grip and stepped back. He was blocking the way to the door leaving me no escape option.

'I also heard you telling Brett how you were going to get rid of me, so I wasn't going to hang around after hearing that.'

'Well, well, well, little Miss Nosey heard something she shouldn't've. But. You. Took. The. Money. Libby,' he said, emphasising and dragging out each word.

'Only half of it. I could have taken all of it, but I left you half so you had plenty to do something with.'

'But it was my money, Libby. I *earned* it!'

'Earned it? What do you mean, you *earned* it? It was money from *my* parents anyway.'

'What?'

Marty looked confused for a moment as though gathering his thoughts.

'No,' he finally said, 'I said I *deserved* it.'

'You said earned, not deserved. What did you mean? And why would you deserve it anyway?'

'I said *deserved*! I deserved it because of the shit life I had growin' up. The injury I got servin' my country in some godforsaken bloody war. The long hours I put in workin' for your father over the years, for bugger all payment. All those bucks he made buildin' houses, he squirreled away. Your brother was gettin' the farm. We shoulda had the money to start the business I wanted.'

'But you said my father was *giving* us some money and was going to lend us more money for the business, only the fire caused that to go on hold. I'm sure the money I left you was far more than he'd have lent us anyway.'

'Yeah, but you took half of it, Libby. I needed all of it to buy somethin' in Sydney.'

'I left you more than enough to get started. What did you do with it anyway? Did you start a business with Brett?'

'Yeah, I did, only we couldn't do it in Sydney could we? Not without borrowin'. It's doin' very well thank you. I've left Brett runnin' the show so we could do a little catch up.'

'So why have you come Marty? If you're doing well, there's no reason for you to be here.'

'Oh, but there is you see. A little matter of the rest of the money. I want it. I have a new woman now and I've made plans.'

I laughed. The whole thing seemed so preposterous.

'Then why don't you divorce me?' I said. 'The courts would say that you've had your fair share of any marriage settlement.'

'I wasn't thinkin' along the lines of divorce. Where's the money Libby?'

'I don't have it in the bank anymore. I invested it.'

'Clever girl. So, if somethin' was to happen to you, then seein' as I'm still your husband, I'd get it all wouldn't I?'

I'd made a will that left everything to Mattie, with Helen as guardian. Helen and I had discussed the possibility of anything happening to me and we'd created a file verifying that Marty had had his share of the money with proof I'd brought with me, but I suddenly panicked thinking Marty might be right. As he was still legally my husband, he might be able to get his hands on the money. I didn't know if Marty knew about Mattie, and if he did, then Mattie's life might be in danger.

'How did you find out where I live Marty? Did you track down Helen? And how did you get into my flat?'

I could tell from the smirk on his face that this was exactly what'd happened. He jangled a set of keys in front of me with a readily identifiable Australian key ring I'd bought at Sydney airport and that I'd given Helen. It was Helen's set of keys to my place.

'If anything happens to me, then Helen will call the police. If you've been to her place, she'll have already phoned the police. She knows you are dangerous.'

'Dangerous eh. I like that. Has a nice ring to it. No, I don't think she'll be speakin' to anyone at all.'

'What have you done to her Marty? You haven't hurt her, have you?' I asked becoming slightly hysterical, 'and what about—'

'Her kid? Nah, I didn't touch the kid. He's an innocent. Mind you, he might be in trouble if someone doesn't go around there soon. But I'm sure it'll be alright. Seems like someone lives upstairs.'

He thought Mattie was Helen's child so he couldn't have been upstairs in my flat. What had he done to Helen? I had visions of her lying injured or dying, and Mattie crying out for her, only for no-one to come. I knew Gerry was away on holiday so no-one would be entering the house who might find Helen or Mattie. The thought made me desperate. I *had* to get help to them, but I had to play it carefully with Marty.

'We didn't give anyone the new address, but presumably someone found out. You must have spoken to them, to get Helen's details. If anything happens to Helen and then me, they would soon know you ...' I realised I'd probably said the wrong thing and clammed up.

'Don't worry I'll be tyin' up all loose ends.'

'You're out of you mind if you think you'll get away with—.'

'I know I'll get away with it. I'm not here, am I? Never been to England.'

Puzzled by what Marty meant by that, I backed up to the balcony and looked down, contemplating a jump. The drop to the ground was at least eighteen feet, possibly more. *"These ceilings must be at least twelve feet high,"* I remembered Helen saying when we first walked into the flat. There was a floor below me which probably had the same ceiling height and then part of the basement. The garden was several steps up from the basement, but the garden level didn't reach anywhere near the basement ceiling height. So that was at least eighteen feet, I surmised. And that was if I landed on the grass. If I fell short of the garden landing on the concrete outside the basement flat, it would mean either death or debilitating injuries. If I jumped though, I might be able to clear it. The trouble was I couldn't see anything much out there. The sky was cloudy and there was very little moonlight.

'What are you planning on doing to me Marty?' I asked stalling for time.

'Oh, I thought a swan dive off this balcony might do the trick. It's a long way down there to the basement area. I checked it out just before you came in. I'd thought about that as a possible solution at the flat in Sydney, once the money came through. Makin' out like you'd jumped from the balcony there. You know, "poor scarred accident girl, devastated followin' the death of her family and now after losin' her looks and memory, can't take it anymore and commits suicide." That's what the papers'd say. It was just one of the options I was considerin'. The scars have healed nicely by the way.'

'Why are you doing this?'

'Because I can,' he sighed. 'I'm no longer the eager kid tryin' to please everyone that grew up in that home. Vietnam changed all that. You sheilas have no idea what it was like fightin' over there. The heat, the insects, the *invisible enemy* pickin' us off. Clever buggers those Vietnamese were. It was their territory; they knew the lay of the land. Not like us. Bloody sittin' ducks we were most of the time when we went out on patrol. Mind you, I managed to kill quite a few of them as well.'

'So, you killed some Vietnamese fighters?' *He's used to killing!*

'Course I bloody did! What do you think people do in a war? I killed their soldiers, and men from villages who were supposed to be on our side – women as well. The Vietkong'd use men and women from the southern villages to trick us into thinkin' it was safe territory, layin' booby traps for us. I saw some of me mates blown to bits like that. It bloody drove me near mad. It was kill or be killed. You couldn't trust *anybody*. If it wasn't for the drugs, I don't think I would've survived more than a few months.'

'The drugs?'

'Yeah, a steady supply of all sorts was always available, comin' over from the Yanks. The drugs messed with our heads a bit, but made life more bearable. We took whatever we could get our hands on. After I was shot, all the drugs cleared out of me system in rehab.'

'I'm sorry you had a hard time in Vietnam Marty. You're right, I can't imagine what it was like. But that doesn't justify what you might have done to Helen, or what you're planning to do to me now.'

'Listen to you, Miss Goody Two Shoes, Miss Moral High Ground who took off with the money. It was *mine*. I made a decision a few years ago that I was gunna do *whatever it takes* to better my life, instead of always bein' the loser. I'm the one with the power now. *I'm* in control. I'd like to say it was nice knowin' you, but … on the other hand I do have a lot of respect for the connivin' way you got hold of the money though. How did you do that?'

'The postman gave me the letter from the lawyer when you weren't there one morning. He came late,' I lied, worried that mentioning Matt's involvement might place him in danger.

He was silent for a moment as though trying to remember a time when that could have happened. I took the opportunity to edge closer to the balcony.

'Right,' he said, not looking entirely convinced. 'And how did you get away so quickly?'

'I discovered that I had a passport and other things I'd hidden from you in the flat. Clearly, I'd planned on leaving you before the accident.'

'That so? My mistake for not checkin' everythin' carefully then.'

Making my move, I turned and quickly climbed the balcony close to the wall, using it for balance. I was preparing to move forward for a huge leap when Marty grabbed one of my legs. My balance became precarious and the basement concrete was directly below me.

'No, I want the privilege of doing this. Straight down by the head I think would be best.'

Marty reached up with his other hand to grab me but I kicked out hard with my free leg, freeing myself from his grasp, edged forward, bent my knees and took flight before I overbalanced, circling my arms up in the air like I'd seen long jumpers do.

I landed with a heavy thud on the grass hearing a crack in my right foot. I dragged myself up and started limping towards the side passage, but suddenly Marty was rolling on the grass in front of me. I turned and looked into the basement. No lights were on there. I knew Jill and Mark, who lived there, were regularly out until late and if they were home, lights would have been on. It was Friday night. No lights were showing on the first floor either.

The boundary on one side was a tall neglected hedge. The other boundary had a high brick wall which I stood no chance of scaling. That left the back fence that bordered the railway line which was a fairly low metal fence, less than my height anyway. I quickly hopped over to the back fence before Marty was back on his feet. I stood more of a chance that way. I knew I'd never make it to the side passage as he was closer to it.

It was agony putting my right foot on the ground. I could climb over the back fence, but where to after that? Was there room to edge along to another property and climb any of their fences? I wasn't sure how high they were as I'd only seen them from my balcony. I did know that they were higher than the back fence on our place. The drop to the railway line was probably another twenty feet and I didn't think I would survive that with one dodgy foot. What if I broke the other one? The railway line was too dangerous to even consider.

I pulled up my long skirt (a bloody inconvenient thing to be wearing at this moment) and painfully climbed the fence. My skirt caught on a piece of jutting wire. I turned and attempted to free it. As I finally ripped it free, Marty was over the fence and grabbed me. In the struggle to free myself from him we edged towards the drop to the railway line. I slipped and began slithering down the railway embankment.

31

Bristol June 2000

Frank watches as Beth Carey takes a deep breath, places a hand over her mouth, stands and rushes out of the room. She had turned deathly white a moment before and looked like she was going to be sick. She'd been shaking in the last few minutes of speaking; perhaps asking her to recount this event was proving too much for her.

'What do you think DI Radcliffe?' Frank asks turning the tape off. 'Should we stop at this point? Mrs. Carey seems quite upset.'

'Leave it a minute. She might come back. It can't be easy for her.'

'I think I'd better check on her.'

Frank leaves the room and almost bumps headlong into Beth just outside the door. He puts his arms up to prevent them from colliding, making physical contact with her. It's like a jolt of electricity passes between them and, looking into her startled eyes, he can imagine his look much the same.

'Sorry,' he says stepping back from her.

Beth clears her throat.

'Apologies for my hasty exit. It was proving too much for me, thinking back to that night. I'm ready to start again now.'

'We understand,' Frank says. 'Are you sure you want to continue?'

'Absolutely. I'd like to get this over and done with.'

32

Libby's story
London August 1976

As I dropped, branches of bushes snapped with the weight of my body, cutting and slicing into my skin. I screamed and blindly grabbed hold of some deeply rooted thick buddleia bushes near the top of the bank, managing to halt my fall.

Marty was standing right above me though and stomped on my right hand. My arm fell to my side and I howled with pain, clinging on with every ounce of strength with my left arm and scrabbling my left foot around attempting to gain a foothold. Something dug into my side as I swung into the bank. *The screwdriver!* With my shaky damaged right hand, I managed to pull the screwdriver out of my pocket. I had to stop him from stomping on my other hand. If he did, I would fall and was likely to die. Then no one would know about Helen and Mattie. I couldn't let that happen. Anger was driving me and I blanked out the searing pain in my hand and body. Marty was laughing and looking towards South Hampstead station just down to the right of the property.

I heard the toot of the train as it began to pull out of the station. As he lifted his right foot to stomp down on my left hand, I raised my right arm and with all the strength I could muster I screamed out a deep throaty 'NO!' and thrust the screwdriver savagely into his left leg. Marty screamed, overbalanced and tumbled down the embankment into the path of the approaching train.

I grabbed hold of the bushes with my damaged right hand to gain a better grip and tucked my head down, praying that I could hold on. I knew I couldn't climb up the embankment with my dodgy foot. I could still hear Marty screaming, so he hadn't fallen in front the train, which would have surely killed him, but he was clearly very hurt. The train stopped and I heard carriage doors open. When the sound of people's voices reached me, I called out to them for help. Someone must have had a torch as I saw a light illuminating the bushes I was clinging to.

'Hang on love,' a man called out, 'we'll get you down soon.'

Sirens sounded in the distance and after what seemed like an eternity, I felt someone grasp me around the waist.

'Let go love, we've got you,' a man, whose voice I recognised from earlier, told me.

I was passed down to waiting hands and collapsed into a stranger's arms. Looking up I realised they had formed a human tower to reach me.

'Thank you,' I sobbed to the small group who'd gathered around me. 'Can someone call an ambulance and the police and send them around to my cousin's place immediately? I think my ex-husband might have hurt her very badly.

My baby son is there too. Her name is Helen Fallon. My son's name is Matthew. They're address is two-hundred and sixty-five Messina Avenue, West Hampstead.'

A couple of people rushed off towards the station. I wanted to go as well, but I simply wasn't capable and remained half-sitting, half-lying in a woman's arms beside the tracks. A jacket was placed around my shoulders. Despite the intense heat of the night, I was shivering and blood was dripping from my face, arms, chest and legs from my encounter with the sharp edges of the bushes. It seemed a long time before ambulances arrived near the station and the stretcher bearers made their way down the line to collect Marty. I learned the train had run over both of his legs. A nurse who'd been on the train had helped to stem his blood loss, but his life was still in danger. He was sedated and his screams finally ceased as they carried him off to the ambulance.

'Can you take me to my cousin's house first, I want to get my son,' I asked one of the men who'd brought a stretcher for me.

'Just lay on the stretcher miss, they'll bring your son to the hospital. We'll make sure of that. You need to have those wounds seen to. Looks like you'll need quite a lot of stitches.'

It was funny how my brain considered practicalities as they were about to close the doors on the ambulance. I called out, 'Can you please ask them to bring my son's pushchair that's at Messina Avenue, otherwise I'll have nothing for him at the hospital. I don't think I could manage to carry him with my injuries.'

I was optimistically hoping that Mattie and Helen

would be alright.

At Accident and Emergency, I was parked in a cubicle sitting in a wheelchair. The ambulance men had staunched the flow of blood and temporarily dressed the worst areas. Frustrated with the delay I wheeled myself out to a desk to speak to a member of staff. She was typing as I approached her but then stopped to attach a sheet to a clip board. Surrounding her was a mountain of files.

'Hello, I wonder if you could tell me if my cousin Helen Fallon has been brought in yet, and my baby son; Matthew Miller is his name.'

The woman didn't reply immediately. She took some time to check through a list before saying, 'Yes, they have – your son has been taken up to the Children's ward and your cousin is having emergency surgery.'

'Is Mattie alright? Has he been hurt? And what's happened to Helen?'

'Your son seems fine; they're just checking him over. I don't know what your cousin's injuries are – all I know is she's in surgery. Can you give me their details to complete the paper work? I only have their names.'

'Yes, of course. But I need to let my aunt and uncle know what's happened to their daughter. They live in Bristol. Can I phone them from here?'

'Do you know their number?'

'No, Helen always phoned them. I've never had to. I'll have to ring Directory Enquiries, if I can use your phone. What's the name of this street? I've forgotten.'

The woman gave me the address and passed me the phone together with a pen and some paper. Being right-handed, it was very difficult for me to hold the pen with my damaged fingers. The receptionist could see this but didn't offer to help. After obtaining the number, I managed to dial the house in Bristol. Uncle Kenny answered it after four rings.

'*Hello,*' he said in a sleepy voice.

'Uncle Kenny, it's Libby. I'm ringing from the Royal Free Hospital in Hampstead. I'm afraid Helen has been injured. She's having emergency surgery right now. Can you and Aunt Ginny come up here?'

'*Christ, what's happened to her Libby? Was she hit by a car or something?*'

'No. It was my ex-husband who hurt her. Somehow, he managed to track her down. I don't know the extent of her injuries or how she is; they're unable to tell me anything. All I know is that she's having emergency surgery at present. I think you need to get up here as soon as possible. The hospital is the Royal Free in Pond St, Hampstead in North West London.'

'*Fucking hell Libby, what have you done? We're on our way.*'

With that I heard the phone being slammed down in my ear. He blamed me. And it *was* my fault. If Helen should die … I couldn't bear thinking about it. After providing the woman on reception with Helen and Mattie's details I turned to her and said, 'Can I go up to the Children's ward? I'd like to see my son.'

'You need to have your injuries seen to first. You can't go up there in that state. You're still bleeding.' I looked down and could see blood was coming through the temporary dressings.

'Well could someone hurry up and see to me, because

I really want to see my son. I'm sorry, I know it's not your fault, but I've been sitting in there for what seems like hours.'

A doctor and nurse finally attended to me after a further lengthy wait. I had to have stitches to my face (again!), legs and breasts. Other cuts were not too deep and were cleaned up. Two fingers on my right hand were broken and were bandaged. They gave me a hospital nightie and dressing gown when they removed my ruined blood-stained clothes which were bagged up, as the police would want to examine them, I was told. After taking an x-ray of my foot they decided to put a plaster cast around it. I had cracked some bones and torn the ligaments in my right foot.

When I explained that I had a young son to look after and that I would find things impossibly difficult to manage in the house with crutches, they inserted a heavy plastic base in the plaster which meant I could bear weight on it without the need for crutches. After some hours I was finally able to visit Mattie in the Children's ward.

'Is Mattie okay?' I asked one of the nurses on duty when I entered the ward. 'He said he didn't hurt him.'

'Your son was very wet, distressed and a little dehydrated when he was brought in, but otherwise okay. We've changed him, fed him and given him a drink. He's sleeping peacefully now. Who is the 'he' you are referring to?'

'My ex-husband. He attacked my cousin in her home, where Mattie was. And just left her for dead and Mattie alone. Then he came after me.'

'Are you alright, you look like you have been in the wars a bit.'

'It was a bit like a war, but I'm fine. The 'ex' isn't though. Can I see Mattie now?'

The nurse took me to see Mattie, who was sleeping in a cot in a room with several other babies. I could see that he was unmarked (*thank God*) and wore a strange set of pyjamas. I really wanted to hold him and let him know I was here. Carefully I picked him up, wincing with the pain in my hand, and hugged him to my chest. He woke and looked at me with sleepy eyes.

'Hello cheeky chops, Mummy's here now.'

He gave me a huge smile, put his arms around my neck and immediately nodded off again. I sat with him for some time before placing him back in the cot. I told the nurse that I had to go and find out what had happened to my cousin.

'Can I take Mattie home in the morning though?' I asked.

'If by morning you mean today, I'm sure once the doctor comes in for his rounds, he'll discharge him.'

She must have noticed my puzzled expression so added, 'It's just coming up to quarter to eight now.'

'I knew I'd been down in Accident and Emergency for *hours*.' I looked towards the windows and could see glimpses of daylight through the slats in the vertical blinds.

'Okay, I'll be back as soon as I can.'

After going back down to Accident and Emergency admissions, I discovered that Helen was in intensive care up on the fourth floor. I eventually found my way into the right room without any intervention. Helen looked so fragile lying there attached to breathing equipment. Uncle Kenny and Aunt Ginny had arrived and were sitting by her bed, their faces pale and drawn. It must have been about six hours since I'd made the call to him and it probably took them about three hours to drive to the hospital in London. Kenny rose from his chair when he saw me and shouted, 'You! You're responsible for this. You've brought this on our family. Get out, I don't want you in here.'

'I would never do anything to hurt Helen,' I cried with tears streaming down my face. 'You know that. I'm very sorry. I don't know how Marty found out where she lived. We took care not to give our address to *anyone* at the old place.'

'Well, someone knew and told the bastard. You should've come to Bristol after you both knew he had Helen's old address. I *told* her. He would never have found you there.'

Aunt Ginny rose from her chair, took Kenny by the arm and said, 'Kenny please. Stop it. It's not Libby's fault. You know Hellie was the one who wanted to stay in London. And you can see Libby has been injured as well.' She released her hold on Kenny and walked over to me. 'Come on my lovely, let's take a walk.'

'He doesn't really mean it Libby,' she said once we were outside the room. 'He's just very upset. We still don't know if Hellie will survive.'

'What did he do to her? What were her injuries?'

'He ruptured her spleen and they have had to remove that. She had to have one of her kidneys removed and she had internal bleeding from the severe kicks he gave her. She also has some head injuries, although they're not serious. They've managed to stop the internal bleeding, but we don't know if she is going to pull through Libby. Hellie is strong, but she seems so weak and vulnerable lying there.'

Ginny and I held each other and let the tears flow. 'I'm sorry Aunt Ginny. I'm so sorry this has happened,' I said.

'So, tell me what happened to you?' Aunt Ginny eventually said.

I recounted the events, from finding Marty in my flat to the final scene that played out on the railway embankment.

'You must've been absolutely terrified!' Aunt Ginny said aghast.

'I was, but I think it was pure rage that drove me at the end knowing he'd left Helen with injuries and Mattie all alone. I just had to get help to them.'

'I can tell you, your actions definitely saved Hellie's life. The doctor said if she'd laid there until morning she would've died. I'll let Kenny know and make sure he understands what happened. Did they bring that man Marty into this hospital, because it might cause problems if Kenny finds out he's here?'

'I don't know. To be honest I haven't given him a thought since they took him off. I haven't asked about him. I will though. They're going to release Mattie later this morning. I'll go home then, get some clothes and come back. Oh … I've just realised. I haven't got any keys to get into my place – or my handbag. And I'm sure the police will want to talk to me at some point. I haven't seen anyone yet, so I don't know when that will be.'

I told Aunt Ginny I'd return as soon as I could and

walked out to the lift lobby. I was just about to step into the lift when a nurse from the Intensive Care Unit called out to me, 'Elizabeth Miller? Are you Elizabeth Miller?'

'Yes,' I replied.

'You're to wait here, there's a police inspector wishes to talk to you.'

Here it comes. I waited by the lifts until an overweight, short, middle aged, slightly balding man in a suit puffed up the stairwell followed by a taller and slimmer younger man similarly dressed.

'Elizabeth Miller?'

'Yes, are you the policeman I was asked to wait for?'

'About bloody time! Do you realise the running around we've had to do trying to find you? First A & E, then to the children's ward, back to A & E, back to the children's ward, now up here.'

'I'm sorry no one told me you were looking for me until just now.' I wondered why he hadn't used the lifts.

'I'm Detective Inspector Moore, and this is Detective Constable Cooper. The doctor in A & E said you were fine to take down to the station for some questioning.'

'To the station? The Police station? In these hospital garments? What about my son?'

'I've informed them that you'll be coming with us, and they'll keep your son here until you return. We'll drop by your house on the way to collect some clothes. It's currently being examined for evidence. Someone will find clean things for you and we'll take them down to the station for you to change,' he said.

'Can't you ask me any questions you want here at the hospital?'

'I'm afraid not.'

'Can you bring me my handbag and keys as well, otherwise I won't be able to get back into my flat.'

'We'll collect them for you, but you won't be able to have your keys back until we've examined everything.'

It seemed like I was being treated as a criminal. Reluctantly I followed detective Cooper into the lift. Inspector Moore took the stairs, suggesting he had some kind of issue with lifts.

When we arrived at my place, I saw several police vehicles parked outside. The young detective constable jumped out of the car and talked to a female uniformed officer who entered my building. She returned with a bag and opened the door. 'I've packed a few things here for you. I hope they're okay.'

'Thank you,' I said gratefully.

It was more difficult than I imagined attempting to dress with two bandaged fingers that I couldn't bend. I was clumsy and it took several attempts to button the blouse I found in the bag. I thought it was a bloody stupid thing to pack, but then realised I was being unfair, the police constable wouldn't have known I had broken fingers.

Once dressed in a blouse and skirt and my one sandal, I was shown into a room that reeked of cigarettes and body odour.

'For the record we are interviewing Elizabeth Miller. This is an informal interview, but we will be taping it for our records. I have to warn you though, anything you do say, will be taken down and may later be used in evidence against you ...'

33

I was so astounded at the detective's statement I was only able to stare at him open-mouthed, at a loss for words. They *were* questioning me as though I was a suspect in a crime.

'Why are you cautioning *me*?' I eventually asked him.

Ignoring me, Detective Moore said, 'Can you take me through the events of last night.'

I swallowed back my anger and began. 'When I returned home from an outing with colleagues, I discovered my ex-husband sitting in my flat.'

'What's your husband's name?'

'Ex-husband. Marty Miller. Martin is his full name, but he goes by the name of Marty.'

DC Cooper made notes.

'And is this the man you are talking about?' He showed me a Polaroid photograph of Marty taken from what looked like a hospital bed. He looked a bit drugged up.

'Yes, that's him.'

'You say he was *inside* your flat? You didn't meet him outside and invite him in?'

'No, he was inside my flat.'

I then told them about the conversation that took place between Marty and I in the flat before I attempted to escape.

'He thought as he was still legally my husband, he would inherit any money or investments I had. He'd planned to kill me in Australia, once the money from my parent's estate came through. But I managed to get my hands on the money before him and escaped.'

'Taking all the money I assume,' DC Cooper interjected with a hint of sarcasm.

'No, I left him half of it. I could have taken it all, but I didn't want him to have any excuse to come looking for me.'

'I see,' said DI Moore. 'And how did you come to believe that he was planning to kill you in Australia?'

'I overheard him talking to his friend when he thought I wasn't listening. He confirmed that tonight and told me one of the methods he had considered using to get rid of me.'

'Which was?'

'In Sydney he planned to throw me off the balcony of our second floor flat, to make it look like I had committed suicide. His plan last night was to drop me off the balcony in my flat here.'

'Have you at any time contemplated suicide?'

'No, why would I? Especially now I have a son. No mother would do that to their young child!'

'Oh, you'd be surprised. So how did you end up on the railway embankment?' DI Moore asked.

I explained in detail the sequence of events that led to my eventual rescue.

'So, you're saying that Mr. Miller was attempting to cause *you* to fall on the railway line and you stabbed him with a screwdriver to prevent him from doing that?'

'Yes, that's what happened.'

'He wasn't trying to pull you up from where you had fallen to prevent you landing on the line?'

'No! Definitely not. He had stomped on my right hand with his boot, which is why I have two broken fingers,' I said holding my bandaged hand up for them to see. 'And he was about to stomp on my other hand to cause me to let go when I stabbed him with the screwdriver.'

'We've recovered the screwdriver and managed to speak to Mr. Miller briefly, and he tells us a different story.'

'I bet he does.'

'He told us about the car accident you had in Australia and how suicidal you were after you began to recover, being badly scarred, losing your memory and discovering all your family were dead.'

'Yes, he told me that's what he was intending the story to be if he'd killed me with his balcony method back in Sydney. Another method he considered was to feed me with seafood as he knows I am allergic to it. I was expecting a baby at the time. That is something special anyone would want to live for.'

'So, you knew you were pregnant before you left Australia?'

'Yes.'

'And is your ex-husband the father of this child?'

'No. Well actually I don't really know. When I asked him about children, he said neither of us were interested in having kids and that we'd always used a contraceptive device, so I don't believe my son is his. He doesn't look anything like him. Or me either. From what I'd told my cousin in letters, we were no longer intimate, so it's quite likely that I had an affair of some sort. I can't remember.'

I looked up to see DC Cooper had a sceptical look on his face.

'I have very little memory of what happened in my life before the accident. I only know I must have become pregnant before it. After the accident it was clear we weren't a loving couple by any stretch of the imagination. There was no *real* affection for me at all either in the hospital or after we returned to Sydney. In Sydney he just attempted to control everything I did and made demands on me.'

'Lots of men aren't demonstrative when it comes to women in their lives,' DC Cooper suggested. 'They prefer the company of men and to talk about things like football.'

'I wouldn't really know, but how many of them would rape their wives? That's what he did to me the night before I left Sydney. Ask my doctor here if you don't believe me. I still had internal damage over a week later,' I said.

'Rape?' DC Cooper asked, 'but he was your husband.'

'Yes, and of course, husbands can't rape wives, can they?'

'Hrrmph.' DI Moore cleared his throat. 'Blood tests could ascertain whether he is the father.'

'I don't really care if he is the biological father or not. He's never going to be a father to my child, and I doubt he would ever want to be either. How is he anyway? I was told that his injuries would lead to the loss of both legs?'

'Yes, that's right. Doctors were able to stop the blood

loss, but he *has* lost both legs, one above the knee and one below the knee.'

'He's a silly, silly man. I can't make sense of his actions. He had half the money my parents left me and from what he said he put it into the business he wanted and it's doing well.'

DI Moore continued as though I hadn't spoken. 'We will of course, have to interview him more extensively; his doctor only gave us a brief amount of time with him. Your husband claims he came to London to make sure you were alright as he was worried about you and wanted to discuss a divorce because he has met someone else. He said that you were deeply distressed about the suggestion of a divorce which is why you jumped, first over the balcony, and then tried to jump down onto the railway line in front of a train.'

'Sure. He's bound to come up with plausible excuses for his actions towards me. If I was supposedly so distressed over the idea of a divorce how come I'm in London and not with him in Australia? And what hasn't been brought up in this interview so far, is my cousin Helen. How does he explain her injuries if he just came to see I was alright?'

'He claims to know nothing about her injuries. He said when he went to her house the door was open and when he went in, he found her lying on the floor already unconscious. He thought she was dead. He claimed he was then worried about you so he looked around, found your address and left to wait outside your place for you to come home when no one answered to his knocking.'

'He's lying. I'm sure he thought she was dead, or very close to it. But he's the one who hurt her. No one else.'

'We don't have any evidence of that as yet. Until, and if, your cousin regains consciousness, we won't really know. We're examining the scene at her house, but of course we're going to find evidence of him being there, as he admits it.'

'Why didn't he call the police or an ambulance if he found her like that? There's a phone in the house. And what about my son? Marty thought he was Helen's son. He told me he left him there thinking he would be okay as he could see someone lived upstairs.'

'Mr. Miller said he went to phone the emergency services, but the phone had been broken and was unusable, that whoever attacked Miss Fallon broke the phone.'

'It's all lies. If the phone is broken, then it was him who did it.'

At that point someone knocked on the door and asked DI Moore to leave the room. He returned a few minutes later with a passport in his hand.

'Do you know a man by the name of Mark Russell?' he asked.

'No, never heard of him,' I replied puzzled.

'The man in this photograph,' he said placing the open passport in front of me, only allowing me to see the photograph, 'can you identify him?'

'Yes, that's Marty, the same man you showed me a photograph of earlier.'

'And you've never heard of the name Mark Russell?'

'No, is that a passport with that name on it?' I asked pointing to the passport DI Moore had just placed in a file. 'That would explain what he said to me. Remember earlier I told you that when I told him that he wouldn't get away with killing me, he said "I'm not here." That explains what he meant. He came over here on a false passport. Let him try and explain that.'

'Yes, that might be difficult,' DI Moore sighed. 'I think we've finished with questions for today,' he said. 'But we may need to interview you again. You're free to go. We can give you a lift back to the hospital if you'd like.'

'Yes, I would like that, thank you. When will I be able to go home and have you damaged any of the doors to gain entry to my flat? How did you know which flat was mine?'

'We could see the balcony doors were open and a light on. After we spoke to your husband this morning and he explained his version of what happened, we knew which flat to enter. Your neighbour on the ground floor let us in the main door and we forced entry to your flat. You'll have to have your door repaired I'm afraid. We should be finished with it by late afternoon. You'll be able to return home then.'

'Okay, thank you. Can I just ask one thing though? Is my ex-husband at the Royal Free Hospital? My aunt was concerned that if he was there and my uncle discovers it, there might be trouble.'

'No, he was taken to a different hospital due to the nature of his injuries.'

I was relieved to finally leave the police station and return to the hospital. They returned my handbag and keys which had been brought to the station from my flat. Before I left, the inspector asked me for the name of my doctor. Perhaps he believed me. I was incensed at the pack of lies Marty had fed to the police. Everything he'd said sounded feasible on the one hand, but I'd like to see him explain that false passport.

When I returned to the hospital, I spent a few hours playing with Mattie, who seemed unfazed by his new surroundings, until he fell asleep. The nurses assured me they'd give him his lunch so I could go and see how Helen was.

I entered the ICU with trepidation. I didn't want another scene with Uncle Kenny. I found a nurse who told me that Helen had regained consciousness for a few minutes about an hour before, but that she was heavily sedated and sleeping again.

'Are my aunt and uncle still in her room?'

'Your aunt is, your uncle left about ten minutes ago.'

I thanked the nurse and popped my head around Helen's door. I saw Aunt Ginny sitting beside Helen and hobbled quietly over to her whispering, 'Hi Aunt Ginny. I heard that Helen woke up a little while ago.'

'Hello Libby love, yes, she did. She recognised us, spoke for just a few minutes and then drifted off again. The first thing she asked was whether you and Mattie were alright.'

'Typical Helen; thinking of others first. What are the doctors saying?'

'They're hopeful that she'll recover, but it won't be a quick recovery.'

'How long do they think she'll have to remain in hospital?'

'We don't really know. I'll stay on in London, until she's discharged. Kenny might return home in a day or two. The kids can look after themselves, but it'd be better if one of us was there.'

'Do you want to stay at my place? I can bunk in with Mattie.'

'No … but thanks for the offer. We'll stay at Hellie's while Kenny's still up here, then I'll probably stay on there.'

'I don't know if you can go there yet. I've been interviewed by the police and they're examining both places. They say mine will be released this afternoon. I don't know about Helen's.'

'I'll get Kenny to check with them. Have you got keys to Hellie's place?

'Yes,' I said, digging around in my bag for them. 'But I don't know if the police will have forced her front door.'

'Kenny can sort all that, don't worry.'

'What can I sort?' asked Kenny as he walked in the door.

'Hellie's front door, if the police have had to break it in,' Ginny replied.

'Can I see you outside a minute Libby?' Kenny said in a stern voice. *Oh God, he's going to ban me from coming here.*

I followed my uncle out of the room and into the lift lobby. He apologised for his behaviour earlier. We spoke for about five minutes before I left him to go in search of a canteen or café, feeling quite bereft. Helen was showing signs of improvement but she wasn't out of the woods yet. And, although Kenny had apologised and was speaking to me civilly, both he and Aunt Ginny seemed a little distant. I wondered if the warmth that had previously existed in our relationship would ever return.

34

Helen made a gradual recovery, with Aunt Ginny beside her much of the time. Kenny travelled up at weekends. After several weeks the hospital announced she was well enough to be discharged. Her parents insisted that she return home with them to Bristol and give up her flat in London. Helen was so weak, she agreed to this without argument. Her boyfriend, Chris, was no longer on the scene after receiving a pasting from Kenny.

Once the police were able to complete a formal interview with Helen, Marty was charged while still in his hospital bed; with two counts of attempted murder and, after confirmation from Australia House, travelling on a false passport.

I was distressed at the idea of Helen leaving London permanently, but she needed to be surrounded by her close family through her recovery.

When I visited Helen, the friendship between us was as warm as ever. On her final day at the hospital, we parted tearfully before she set off for Bristol.

'I'll come back to London Libby – when I'm well enough,' Helen said, 'or you could always come to live in

Bristol. I don't want to lose you or Mattie.'

'I don't think your family would welcome me there.'

'Nonsense. I've spoken to them about what happened. I know Dad went off on one at you, but he regrets that now. Besides the person who caused the trouble is now incarcerated and will remain there until the trial. The police told us that when he completes his sentence he'll be deported to Australia. He's no longer a threat. Even if he wanted to, I doubt he'd be able to do anything to either of us ever again without his legs. He wouldn't dare approach us if he knew there were some big strapping men in the background.'

'Yes, I suppose you're right about Marty,' I replied. But I wasn't sure she was right about her family wanting me in Bristol.

Marty's trial took place approximately ten months after the charges were laid against him. It was a harrowing experience for Helen and me, giving evidence in a court.

I filed divorce papers against Marty, wanting to be completely free of him and changed Mattie's and my name to Fallon. Helen stayed with me throughout the trial, with her parents in a nearby hotel. On the final day of the trial Helen raised the subject of me moving to Bristol again.

'Won't you re-consider moving to Bristol Libby please, I miss you and Mattie so much,' she pleaded. 'I hate living at home again. Everything was fine while I was recovering and spent lots of time in my bedroom, but now I'm working again, I hate it. I miss having someone I can confide in and talk to. Julie's resentful about not having her own room anymore and sometimes I can't stand the noise. I long for a bit of peace and quiet. We could share a place again.'

'You wouldn't get much peace and quiet now Mattie is charging around the place. I have to constantly keep an eye on what he's up to.'

'Yes, but he's such a good kid. Not like my brothers were at his age. He'll sit contentedly and listen to us read to him and he plays quietly, he doesn't demand constant attention like my brothers used to.'

'No, he does often seem content with his own company, but he likes to know I'm around. There is one possibility,' I told her. 'The tenants on the ground floor flat in Montpelier have given notice. We could move in there and see how it goes. Mattie could share with me again. The upstairs tenants will also be leaving soon. They told your father they were hoping to move to Canada. I don't know when that will happen, they're waiting for their immigration papers. You could have that flat when it becomes available and then you'd have your full independence again.'

'Oh Libby, that sounds wonderful. Let's do it, please!'

'Okay, you talk to your parents though. I don't want to be the cause of a rift between you.'

'It will be fine,' Helen reassured me.

35

Bristol June 2000

'That's how I ended up moving to Bristol,' Beth says when she finishes relating everything. 'I didn't really want to remain in London after Helen left anyway. And although Marty was in prison, I didn't like the idea of him knowing where I lived. It seemed safer to move away.'

'I can understand that,' Frank says. 'Everything you've told me has been very illuminating. I don't want you to be alarmed by what I'm about to ask you next, but I wondered if you would be prepared to give me a DNA sample?'

'Why on earth would you want DNA from me?'

'Well as I said when we first met, there were items belonging to the driver of the other vehicle involved in your accident back in nineteen seventy-five that were found with the skeletal remains. The other crime we've been investigating is a hit and run accident which occurred last year. We believe the victim had some connection to, or knowledge about, the remains we found, and in her dying words left me a message to come and see you.'

'Goodness, how dreadful for her to die like that. And

how strange. Why would she suggest you come and see me?'

'I'm not sure and I have further enquiries to make as yet. Another person linked to your accident also suggested I should talk to you. Would you be willing to give me a DNA sample?'

Frank looks at Beth Carey who has gone silent and still with her head down frowning, considering his request. Finally, she looks up and smiles.

'I don't really understand why you would need it, but okay, I trust you know what you're doing. I'll do it, as long as the sample is destroyed if it doesn't give you the answers you're seeking.'

'Agreed. Thank you,' Frank says.

36

Following his lengthy sessions with Beth Carey, Frank decides he's more than a little in love with her. He can't believe he only met her a few days ago, he feels like he's known her for years. He loves her striking blue eyes and the way her hair, almost a pinkish blonde with odd silver streaks, bounces in waves as she turns her head. He's fascinated by the faint scars that criss-cross her face. Clearly, she's not self-conscious of them as she wears her hair swept back off her forehead where the largest scar splices almost across the width of it. At first glance a person might think they were wrinkles, frown marks (like the ones he knows he frequently wears across his forehead) or smile lines. It's only when you look closer that you can see they're scars. He finds they make her even more beautiful.

Despite his feelings, Frank knows he needs to remain completely professional with her and not overstep any boundaries.

Back at his hotel Frank makes a call to Australia before turning in for the night, hoping to catch DS Lowry. He's in luck, Lowry tells him he has just arrived at his desk.

He asks him whether when he checked Susan Kennedy's tax file, he ascertained what companies she'd worked for during those years as there were no notes on it in his file copy. Lowry confirms that he had only checked the last few years she was employed and at Frank's request, agrees to check her full history.

The next morning Frank takes the DNA samples he has to a company on the outskirts of Bristol. He pays for private testing and is informed that it will be three days before he receives the results. After dropping the samples, he returns to his hotel and makes another call to Australia, where it will be evening there. When the phone is answered by Charles Farrell he says, 'Hello Mr. Farrell, Frank Bailey here. I'm calling from the UK so can't talk for long. I just have a couple of further questions I'd like to ask you if that's okay?'

He asks his questions and jots down Charles Farrell's answers.

Having done as much as he can, Frank decides that he'll spend the next few days as a tourist while waiting for the DNA results.

He travels to the city of Bath to see the Roman Baths, impressed that they have survived after such a long period of time. He visits the Wookey Hole caves down in Somerset. He finds them comparable to Jenolan caves in New South Wales.

Frank also makes an appointment with a private psychiatrist in Bristol. When he meets the doctor in person, he explains that he's making enquiries about a case he is investigating, but stresses that he needs their conversation to remain confidential as it concerns complicated legal issues. Frank provides the psychiatrist with full details and is more than happy with the psychiatrist's response.

A text alert on the British mobile phone he'd purchased tells Frank the results of the DNA tests are ready for collection. He drives out to the clinic, collects them and as soon as he's comfortably seated back in his hire car, tears open the envelope. The results are as he expected.

Early this morning he'd received confirmation from DS Lowry that Susan Kennedy worked at Miller's Motors from nineteen seventy-five until she married in nineteen-eighty. The final connection. Questioning Miller and his partner will have to wait until he returns to Australia with the evidence. But first he must tackle the delicate situation of Beth Carey. He phones her at her office, telling he has the DNA results and would like to arrange a meeting with her.

'*Why don't you come and join us for dinner tonight,*' she says.

'Us?' he queries.

'*Yes, both my children will be eating at home tonight. Matt and Ali. Come and join us. It won't be anything too fancy though. It's just a typical Thursday night meal.*'

'I really don't want to put you to any trouble,' he says.

'*No trouble at all. You'd be very welcome, except you have to stop calling me Mrs. Carey. I insist you call me Beth. Say about seven pm?*'

Frank considers his situation after Beth hangs up. He's thrilled to have the opportunity to spend some time in Beth Carey's company. He's just not sure how appropriate it is for him to be having dinner with her and her family though. Perhaps a meal first will help to break the ice a little. He purchases a bottle of both white and red wines to take, unsure what she'll be serving.

Frank Bailey has featured considerably in Beth's thoughts over the past week. She's found herself increasingly attracted to him during the time he spent in her house. His thick dark hair with greying streaks is very becoming and her stomach tingled with butterflies each time she looked into his large brown eyes. He's a little overweight, but somehow it suits him. She really likes Frank; he seems thoughtful and sincere for a policeman – not like those she's encountered in the past. She thinks how lonely it must feel to be in a strange city so far from home. And that moment between them at their last session where they'd had physical contact; that was *really* weird. She's looking forward to his company this evening. Over the past few days, she's been trying to work out why he wanted all that information from her and the only answer she could come up with was it was something to do with her ex-husband Marty. Has he committed some other crimes that have only recently come to light? She doesn't see how it could involve her, but maybe Frank just wanted to know more about Marty's character.

37

'I hope you're not a vegetarian or anything?' Beth says as Frank follows her into the kitchen/diner later that evening. 'I forgot to ask.'

'No, like most Australian men of my age group, I'm rather partial to meat – although I can happily eat vegetarian meals. I've brought a bottle of both white and red wine, not knowing what you were cooking. I hope that's okay?'

'Thank you, they're both very welcome. Ali likes a glass of white. I'm more partial to red myself. Can you open the red for me? I think there's already an open bottle of white in the fridge. We're having chicken and leek pie with sautéed potatoes and salad. I hope that's fine with you? The pie is home cooked.'

'Any home cooked food sounds delicious to me. It becomes tiresome always having to eat out when you're travelling.'

'I know exactly what you mean. When we travel to Europe for our holidays, I always prefer self-catering, so that if we want to eat a home cooked meal we can. Especially when we're staying near the sea. I become fed up with the restaurants mainly catering to sea-food lovers. Being allergic to it, I find when I eat in a restaurant that has predominantly sea-food on the menu, I often feel quite sick after as though there has been some mild cross-contamination with the food.'

At that point a young man and woman enter the dining room.

'This is my son Matt and my daughter Alison,' Beth says.

'Ali,' the daughter says, correcting her mother. 'Are you going to tell us what the mystery concerning Mum is about?' she asks cheekily.

'Ali,' Beth admonishes her. 'You're being rude.'

'Well, that's what he's come here for isn't?' Ali asks innocently.

'Yes, okay but let's enjoy dinner first.'

Frank tells Beth that the meal tastes like heaven to him. Pleasant banter is exchanged amongst the group with Frank adding a number of Australian anecdotes that have them all laughing. From the conversations Frank gleans that Matt's role in the family is of the sensible, responsible eldest child. With Beth being a widow for the past twelve years, Matt would have been just entering his teens then, Alison a young girl of about seven. He can see who Matt takes after. He suspects Alison or Ali, full of cheeky grins and banter, takes after her father with her straight brown hair and hazel eyes. She has some of Beth's beauty though, especially the shape of her eyes, nose and mouth.

He helps them all clear the table. There is a moment where his hand brushes Beth's as they reach for the empty glasses. There's no electric current this time, only a comfortable warmth. He's sure Beth has noticed it as well. She turns away quickly and insists they should all retire to the living room.

The meal that Frank enjoyed so much is sitting heavily in his stomach as he chooses one of the individual lounge chairs. He feels queasy with nerves. Beth sits on the large couch, her children either side of her.

'So – the DNA results. Were they as you hoped?' Beth asks.

Frank clears his throat. 'Yes, although I wouldn't say it's what I *hoped* for. What I am about to tell you is quite shocking news.'

He pauses and notices the three Carey bodies lean forward, alert. Frank winces, knowing what he is about to say will have a devastating impact on their lives.

38

Frank returns to his hotel at midnight and places a call to his boss in Newcastle, explaining the evidence that has come to light. He asks the Chief Super to organise search warrants and to wait for him to make the arrests on Monday morning when he'll be back in Newcastle. He stresses that they need to keep the information quiet so that there are no leaks to the press. CS Palmer agrees to all this.

Frank busies himself packing before crashing out with exhaustion, grabbing a few hours' sleep.

At six-thirty his alarm wakes him and he drags himself out of bed, showers then orders a continental breakfast. At seven-forty, checking he has packed everything, he places another call to Australia. After hanging up he feels emotionally drained but he needs to move on. He phones the hire car firm, arranges to leave the car at Heathrow airport, settles his hotel bill and heads off to the Carey house.

At nine promptly he knocks on her door. Ali opens the door and beckons him in.

'Mum's out in the kitchen. She's made us sandwiches

for the journey and she's waiting for you to call the airline.'

Frank walks into the dining area and watches Beth wiping down the kitchen worktop. She has a worried look on her face.

'Morning Beth,' he says. 'I hope you managed to catch a few hours' sleep.'

'Not much, as you can imagine. I've been to work and everything is sorted there.'

'Good.'

'You phone the airline first Frank, to see if they can change your ticket,' Beth says handing him the phone.

Last night Beth and her children agreed to fly out to Australia on the first available flight. Frank's hoping they can travel together.

Frank pulls out his documents on which he has written the contact number for Singapore Airlines. 'I splashed out on Business Class for this trip. They didn't have any economy seats left when I booked anyway. If they can change my ticket, I'll ask them what they have available for the three of you. I can tell you, when I looked into economy it didn't look very comfortable. You'd be better off in Business Class. If they don't have any seats available, we'll have to check out flights with other airlines leaving today.'

'I remember when I came over in seventy-five, it wasn't very comfortable, but on one leg of the journey I had three seats to myself and was able to spread out. I doubt that would be available these days, long distance travel being more common. I'd like to travel business class if possible.'

'Ali and I will travel economy, if you can get seats. You go business class Mum. You need to arrive as fresh as possible,' Matt says coming into the kitchen.

'Oh, hi Matt, everything sorted with work?'

'They weren't too happy, but what could they do? Only sack me. Which they haven't done as yet. Because I couldn't give them a date when I'll be returning to work, they've said they can't guarantee my job will still be available.'

'Are you okay with that?' Beth asks,

'It's fine Mum. All this is more important.'

Frank indicates that he's through to the airline and they remain quiet while he talks to them. He manages to change his flight, but has to pay an additional fee. He then asks about the availability of further seats in both in business class and economy. He listens for a moment and then placing his hand over the phone says, 'They only have one economy seat remaining on this evening's flight and two available in business class. Shall I reserve them?'

'I'll travel in the economy seat Mum; you and Ali take the business class. Don't worry about the money. I can pay you back for the cost of my ticket.'

'Okay, let's do it. Pass me the phone Frank. I'll settle this.'

Frank steps back and passes the phone to Beth. She pays for the tickets, arranges to collect a printed copy at the airport, and as she hangs up, her face lights up with excitement.

'It's done!' she shrieks. 'Never in a million years would I have thought I'd be excited about returning to Australia. I thought I'd never step foot in the place again.'

'You managed to get us seats then?' Ali asks entering the kitchen.

'Yes, and you'll be travelling business class with me.

Matt has kindly volunteered to sit in the one economy seat they had left,' Beth says. 'Perhaps you could swap with him halfway through the journey.'

Ali's delighted smile at the news fades with this suggestion. 'Okay, I guess it's only fair,' she says. 'Wait until Karen hears I'm travelling business class.'

'Ali!' Matt and Beth chorus.

'What? You said I can tell her we're going to Australia. I've already told her that. I didn't tell her *why* we were going. Now I will tell her *how* I'm going.'

'We'll have to leave here soon,' Frank says checking his watch.

'Ali and I are all packed and ready. What about you Matt?'

'Yep. All set.'

'Right. Go and amuse yourselves elsewhere you two, I want to talk to Frank.'

Matt and Ali discreetly leave the room. Beth waits until the door closes behind them. 'Have you spoken to—'

'Yes, I have. As you can imagine it was a difficult call. Everything's arranged as we discussed.'

Beth nods and turns her head away. Frank's sure that he caught a glimpse of tears welling in her eyes.

'Anyway,' she says. 'We're all packed and ready Frank, shall we load the car? Hope we can fit it all in, we seem to have quite a bit of luggage.'

39

Newcastle June 2000

The force swoops on Martin Miller's house and two business premises on Monday morning. They catch Miller showering in his home and pick up his partner, Brett Saunders, at the Charlestown premises. The two men are placed in separately guarded rooms, waiting to be interviewed.

Frank decides to tackle Martin Miller first. With DS Rachel Sharp accompanying him he enters the room. He sets the recording, introduces himself and Rachel, reads Miller his rights again, sits down and looks up at him. Miller has that look of cocky arrogance he remembers from his recent visit. He thinks back to when he first met Miller with Sergeant Pryce in nineteen-seventy-five. At that interview Miller played the worried husband, concerned about his wife and anxious to get back to her at the hospital. Sergeant Pryce had dismissed the concerns Frank had raised. His gut instinct had been right then and Miller was not going to escape justice this time.

'What's this all about?' Miller demands. 'I didn't even

get to finish me shower! All that nonsense you lot were spoutin'. And where's me lawyer?'

'Your lawyer will be here shortly Mr. Miller. You were cautioned when we arrested you, and again now. You have been arrested for the murder of your wife Elizabeth Miller, on or about the eleventh of April nineteen seventy-five.'

'Nah, you got that all wrong,' Miller interrupts. 'She's livin' in the UK. I should know, I served twelve years for her attempted murder in nineteen seventy-six.'

'The woman you attempted to murder was not Elizabeth Miller, but Elizabeth Farrell as you well know.'

'Wha ... whadya you mean? That's the sheila that caused the accident. She died. Went into the river.'

'No, Mr. Miller,' Frank says, 'only her car went into the river. We have established through DNA testing that the woman you took to Maitland Hospital, claiming that she was your wife, was in fact Elizabeth Farrell.'

'What? Are you tellin' me that I took the wrong woman to the hospital? You know it was a bit confusin' that day and I was in a lot of pain. No wonder she had trouble rememberin' me. You know with all those injuries she had; how could I tell?'

'Nice try Miller. But that won't wash. You hid your wife's body somewhere and then later removed it to a place you knew up in Blackbutt Reserve, where she lay undiscovered for the next twenty-four plus years until last December. You made the mistake of leaving evidence linking the remains to Elizabeth Farrell. I'm sure it's your DNA we found all over the evidence at the scene and—'

'You came to see me about this,' Miller interrupts. 'I

told you I know nuthin' about that body.'

'We're also charging you with four counts of deception and fraud,' Frank continues.

'They are:
- Intention to defraud by a false and misleading statement.
- Obtaining a financial advantage by deception.
- Intention to deceive, and …
- Obtaining property belonging to another.'

'I don't know what you're talkin' about. I never deceived no one. I thought that woman was my wife, Libby.'

'You're further being charged with abduction of Elizabeth Farrell and her false imprisonment in Sydney after she was discharged from hospital.'

'No way. She was free to come and go as she wanted.'

'So, you're admitting that you took Elizabeth Farrell back to your Sydney flat?'

'I'm admittin' nuthin'. I'm not sayin' another word until my lawyer's here.'

Frank has an impulse to laugh at Miller's weak defence. He feels jubilant as he and Rachel leave the room and head towards Brett Saunders.

Saunders looks up at them nervously as they enter the room. 'Why am I here?' he asks, and Frank can see Saunders' leg jigging up and down under the table. He hopes the man won't continue doing that as he finds it irritating.

'Are you charging me with something?' Saunders asks. 'Because I can tell you now that I keep everything legal and above board in the business.'

'You're here to answer some questions Mr. Saunders. At the present time you're not being charged with anything, only helping us with our enquiries. But I have to tell you that we will be recording this interview.'

Saunders relaxes a little and the leg stops moving. *Thank God.*

Frank switches on the recording device, introducing himself and Rachel.

'Can you tell us when you last saw Elizabeth Miller – the woman known to you as Libby Miller?' he asks.

Saunders looks confused for a moment, before answering.

'In Sydney, at her and Marty's flat just before she took off to the UK. Why are you asking me that?'

'I have to tell you that was not Libby Miller.'

'What? What do you mean? Course it was her. Who else would it have been?'

'The person Martin Miller took to the hospital in Maitland following his car accident was a woman called Elizabeth Farrell.'

Saunders looks even more confused.

'What?' he says shaking his head. 'I don't know who that is. How can it have been a different woman? I knew Libby and I'm telling you it was her I saw in the flat after the accident.'

'You didn't notice that she looked different?' Rachel asks.

'Well of course she looked different. She'd had all her hair removed and so only had a short stubble of growth. Her face was still a bit swollen and she also had scars and marks all over it.'

'Was there anything else different about her?' Rachel asks him.

Saunders pauses for a minute before saying, 'She spoke differently. More refined. Marty said that when she first woke up, she made sounds like someone with brain damage, unable to form proper words. Once she began to talk normally her voice was all posh. He said she imitated the doctor's speech and put it down to her brain injuries.'

'He would've liked her to have brain damage wouldn't he, so he could have shoved her in a home?' Frank says.

Saunders shifts uncomfortably in his seat. 'Well yes, he did mention that, but that's not what happened.'

'Did he discuss other ways of getting rid of her with you?' Frank asks. Saunders remains silent for a second or two. Frank thinks he's deciding how much to reveal.

'Yes, he did talk about a few ways to get rid of her. She was driving him mad he said. But it was just Marty raving on, usually when he'd had a lot to drink. I didn't think he'd do anything about it. Anyway, she took off, so it wasn't an issue.'

'But he did do something about it the following year didn't he? He travelled to England and attempted to kill the woman who believed she was his wife.'

'Yeah, well that really surprised me. He just disappeared one day leaving me a note saying he'd be away for a while. He didn't say where he was going. Bloody idiot he was for doing that. Look how he ended up. What do you mean by "the woman who believed she was his wife"? She *was* his wife.'

'No, Mr Saunders, as I told you earlier, the woman Martin Miller took to the flat in Sydney, and whom he attempted to kill in London the following year was a woman called Elizabeth Farrell. She was the other victim in the car accident that happened on April eleventh, nineteen seventy-five on Nelson's Plain, next to the Hunter River. Miller took her to the hospital claiming she was his wife and fabricated a false history for this severely injured woman.'

'But how could he do that? And what happened to Libby?'

'We believe she was murdered on the day of the accident. Her remains were found in an old mine entrance on Blackbutt Reserve last December.'

'That skeleton you found?' Saunders asks.

From the look of astonishment on Saunders' face, Frank can see his reaction is genuine. *So, Saunders wasn't working with Miller; Miller had acted alone.*

'Are you familiar with the Blackbutt Hill Reserve, Mr Saunders?'

Saunders now looks very uncomfortable. *He knows something.*

'I er … I went there a few times as a teenager, exploring the area. My family moved from Maitland to New Lambton when I was in my final two years of high school. It's very close to where we lived.'

'And did you ever explore Blackbutt Reserve with Martin Miller?'

'A few times,' Saunders says in a quiet voice.

'Can you tell us the last time you saw Libby Miller prior to the car accident she and Martin Miller were involved in on April eleventh?' Franks asks.

Saunders sits thinking for a moment before answering.

'I saw Marty and Libby the night before they went off to Newcastle. We shared a meal together and couple of beers.'

'Were you aware of any marital problems between them?'

'They seemed alright to me, but Marty told me they weren't getting on too well.'

'And where were you during the time they were in Newcastle and later at the Maitland Hospital?'

'I was working in Sydney. I didn't come back to Newcastle until we moved up here after Libby took off and Marty had the money she left him. He wanted to have the car yard in Sydney, thinking it would be a better investment, but we didn't have enough money, so I persuaded him to come back to Newcastle.'

'We'll require details of the company you worked for in Sydney in nineteen seventy-five so that we can verify what you've told us,' Frank says. 'What did Martin Miller tell you when you first saw him in Sydney following the accident?'

Saunders remains silent. Frank is sure he knows something but is reluctant to say anything that might incriminate his friend – or himself.

'If you know something Mr. Saunders you should tell us now. Otherwise, you might find yourself being charged with offences related to withholding evidence and obstructing justice.'

Frank can see that he's considering his options. Finally, he says, 'Marty told me that Libby caused the accident. That they'd been arguing and she attacked him or something while he was trying to drive. She'd told him she was going to leave him. When she woke up after the accident and didn't remember anything he was really pleased. He'd hoped that they would be able to pick up where they'd left off before any problems had started between them.'

'And you went along with this?'

'Why wouldn't I? It's not my business what happens between a man and his wife. Anyway, Libby seemed fine about all the plans. I told him he should be careful and be nice to her, so there wouldn't be any problems. He was a bit impatient with her at times and I was worried he'd upset her so much she'd walk out. Which is what she did. At least she had the decency to leave him some of the money.'

'I have to inform you Mr. Saunders, that Martin Miller was not legally entitled to any of that money. In the event of Libby Miller's death, if it occurred prior to the settlement of the estate, the money was to go her father's two brothers. Her death did occur prior to the settlement of the estate. Therefore, it's highly likely that you'll have to forfeit the businesses and repay that money to the Fallon family in the UK.'

'What? You've got to be kidding me! What about all the hard work I've put into the business for the past twenty-five years. And the Charlestown premises was not bought with that money. It came from the profits of the business, the business that *I* built up.'

'It will be for the courts to decide that. No doubt it'll be a complicated case, but money will have to be repaid,' Frank stresses.

Frank can see that Saunders is visibly shaken by this. He has some sympathy for the man, aware that he is largely responsible for the success of Miller's Motors. Beth Carey also panicked when she realised she was not entitled to the Fallon money and would have to make arrangements to pay it back. Both Beth and Saunders (to some extent) were innocent parties in this whole matter. He hopes that the Fallon family will not come down too heavily on both of them.

'Moving on, I'm now showing Mr Saunders a photograph of Susan Kennedy. Could you tell me the last time you saw Mrs. Kennedy, Mr. Saunders?'

'She used to work for us back in the seventies when we started the business. She and Marty became involved, planning to marry. But after Marty was arrested in England, and it was clear he wouldn't be coming back for a while, she left to marry in nineteen-eighty sometime. She came to see Marty one day when he returned from England in eighty-eight. By then I think her husband had died. Marty wasn't interested in having anything to do with her. That was the last time I saw her until back in January this year. She popped into Charlestown one day out of the blue, looking for Marty, but he was on his honeymoon.'

'Did she tell you what she wanted to see Mr. Miller about?'

Saunders nodded. 'She mentioned that she'd seen his wedding pictures in the paper and noticed a likeness in his new wife to how she had looked in the seventies.'

Saunders face has turned bright red and he is looking distinctly uncomfortable again.

'And did she mention anything else?' Frank asks.

'She mumbled stuff about their time together. I don't really remember.'

'Did you tell Martin Miller about her visit?'

'Yes, I did mention it in passing when he returned from his honeymoon.'

'What did he say when you mentioned her visit.'

'Nothing. He wasn't interested. He's been a little preoccupied with his new wife.'

Saunders is wriggling in his seat again. Frank thinks he's not telling the whole truth.

'And so, you didn't see Susan Kennedy again following her visit to Charlestown?'

'No.'

'Were you aware that she was killed in a hit and run accident in late January this year.'

'Yes, my wife Vicky noticed it and told me about it. She knew Susan back in the late seventies when Vicky and I got together. We went to Susan's wedding. Vicky and I talked about it and decided it was probably teenage kids yahooing around in a stolen car, high on something.'

'You didn't think it was anything to do with Martin Miller?'

Saunders's face turns a brighter shade of red at this question.

'Well Vicky did allude to the possibility, but the car that hit Susan was a normal car from what the papers reported. Marty only drives specially adapted cars because of his disability, doesn't he? He couldn't have had anything to do with it.'

'Can you tell me what you were doing on the night in question? It was Friday the twenty-eighth of January.'

'You don't suspect me, do you? I know the following night we had Marty and his new wife Joanie over to dinner. That would have been the Saturday. I remember because Vicky was doing a bit of stirring and mentioned Susan's death. It had been on the front pages of the paper that day. Vicky and I were out with the kids on the Friday night. It was my son's nineteenth birthday. We had a meal at our club, Wests, in Lambton, then returned to our house in Charlestown, about eleven thirty.'

Frank checks that Rachel has made notes of what Brett Saunders has said and then looking up at him says, 'We'll have to speak to your family and check with the club to verify your movements, but thank you for coming in. We have no more questions for you at the moment, but we'll require you to sign a formal printed statement regarding the matters we've discussed. We'll be in touch to let you know when this will happen.' Frank turns the recording machine off.

Saunders stands and shakes his head. 'I don't understand how Marty could have swapped Libby for this other woman. How is that even possible? There must be some mistake. Have you questioned him about it?'

'I can assure you there is no mistake Mr. Saunders. DNA evidence doesn't lie. Martin Miller is currently helping us with enquiries. You may not see him for some time.'

40

Three days later Frank enters the squad room announcing, 'Team meeting in five, thank you everybody. I want you to report back on everything that's come to light so far.' Frank's usual small team has been expanded to speed up evidence gathering.

'DS Lowry, we'll start with you,' Frank says once the group is assembled.

'A search of Martin Miller's house revealed a set of prosthetic legs. When questioned, his wife Joanie told us he practised walking around in them every morning, but seldom left the house in them, preferring his wheelchair. Miller married his present wife Joanie last December, but they'd been living together for over a year before that. She told us Miller already had the prosthetics before she moved in with him. DC Rogers can tell you more.'

Frank nods to Rogers who continues with the findings.

'The prosthetics are those that are made with a shoe attached to help with balance. A trace on the product codes,' he starts 'established that the legs were made for Miller three years ago. It wasn't the first set of legs he'd had either. His hospital records show that he's proficient in the use of them and, although he isn't licenced to do so, the hospital told us that it's likely Miller would have been capable of driving an automatic car using the prosthetic legs. The car that we suspect was used in the hit and run incident was an automatic.

'Forensic testing on clothing from Miller's wardrobe and his prosthetic shoes,' Rogers continues, 'revealed traces of fibres similar to the type of carpet used in the manufacturing of vehicles of the same model and year as the burnt-out vehicle believed to be responsible for Susan Kennedy's death. The techs have confirmed they are a match. They've taken fibres from the vehicle Miller normally drives, but they've said they're different.'

'The man whose vehicle was stolen and found burnt-out following the hit and run,' Lowry interjects, 'identified Miller as the person who came to see him about using his car as a trade-in for a newer vehicle from Miller's Motors. He'd been unaware that Miller had prosthetic legs, although he noticed he walked awkwardly. Another little nugget we have is that a couple of hairs the techs picked up from Susan Kennedy's flat is a match to Miller, so we can place him there,' Lowry adds.

'I suspect Miller went to Mrs. Kennedy's flat and removed any photographs or written notes linking him to her,' Frank says recalling the blank spaces in the photograph album.

Lowry nods and continues, 'When we questioned Miller's wife regarding their movements the night of Susan Kennedy's death, she admitted that she'd fallen asleep during one of the films they watched and was very hazy about the time she woke and they went to bed. Miller's alibi is therefore not secure.'

'Good work. I think we have sufficient evidence to charge Martin Miller with Susan Kennedy's death as well as Elizabeth Miller's. Now we need to prepare a solid case for prosecution on the two murder counts. Miller still denies murdering his wife. Nothing he is saying will stand up in court however. Right, DCs Patel and Tyler what do you have for us?'

'We've traced Martin Miller's neighbour Matthew Gardiner, the man who assisted Elizabeth Farrell in escaping from Miller in Sydney. He's provided us with a statement of events,' says Tyler.

'We've also collected evidence from archive records at Maitland Hospital about Elizabeth Miller's treatment there,' DC Patel, a brand-new member of the detective team adds. 'We've traced and interviewed a couple of staff who were working at the hospital at the time. Unfortunately, Sister Mary O'Connell who had quite a bit of contact with the patient, is now deceased.'

'Okay, Good work team. We've already had Miller before the Magistrates with the other charges. Now we can add the murder of Susan Kennedy.'

Martin Miller is charged with Susan Kennedy's death; he now has two counts of murder to account for. He is also charged with four counts of fraud. Frank had Rachel look into the Fallon Farm fire, and although they both had suspicions that Miller was involved there was no evidence to link him. Much as he would have liked to, Frank is unable to proceed with the charges of abduction and false imprisonment of Elizabeth Farrell. In her statement, Beth

Carey admitted that, although she'd had concerns, she had left the hospital of her own free will with Miller. Frank thinks there should be some charge they can lay against Miller for attempting to pass off Beth as his deceased wife.

'We've got enough on Miller to ensure he'll never be a free man again,' the chief tells Frank to allay his disappointment.

Miller's case has been committed to the Supreme Court for trial and he is to be remanded in custody until then.

Beth Carey visited the station and signed a statement summarised from Frank's recordings in Bristol, although she asked him to make minor amendments. She provided him with copies of the documents she received from the lawyer in Raymond Terrace and bank records of the monies received and paid to Miller in nineteen seventy-five. Frank and his team work long and hard to build up an airtight case for the Crown Prosecutors.

Once charges have been made and a press statement released, Frank places a call to England to speak to DI George Radcliffe.

'Morning George,' he says once he's put through to him. 'We've charged Miller and a statement has been released to the press. You need to visit Kenneth Fallon now and obtain an official DNA sample. As we discussed, you can tell him that I DNA-tested Beth Carey when we suspected her real identity, comparing it to samples I'd managed to obtain from Sydney. Make sure you tell him that Beth Carey was a completely innocent party in all this. I'm sure he knows, but stress that there were huge gaps in her memory and Miller fabricated a web of lies that were believable because the two girls, Libby and Liz, knew each other growing up. You still have a copy of the photograph of the two girls I left with you, don't you? Take that to him. Tell him that due to the seriousness of the investigation, I wouldn't allow Beth to make contact with any of them until after the investigations were completed. I believe Mrs. Carey is now en-route to New Zealand to visit Kenneth Fallon's daughter.'

'Don't worry, I'll explain that I sat in on the interviews with her and her ignorance of Miller's crimes was very clear.'

'Okay, thanks George. Can you get the results of the formal DNA samples to me as soon as possible?'

'Will do.

41

Wellington, New Zealand July 2000

'It's just unbelievable Beth, what that man has done to our families,' Helen cries out in shock after Beth has revealed the extent of Martin Miller's actions and how it all came to light.

'I'm so sorry Helen. I had no idea I wasn't Libby when I came to London.'

'Of course you didn't. It's that man's fault. One good thing though, he was never your husband. You always said you couldn't understand why you'd married him – because you hadn't,' Helen laughs. 'Seriously though Beth, it makes no difference to me that you are not a blood relative. You've been like a sister to me, and I've felt closer to you than to my real sisters. At least I don't have to call you by a different name. It was difficult enough changing from Libby to Beth.'

'I'm so happy to hear you say that. I was afraid you would want to cut me off and have nothing further to do with me.'

Beth had been nervous on the flight to New Zealand,

worried about how Helen would react. Even though Helen had lived on the other side of the world to her for many years now, there'd always been a special bond between them since they'd met up in London in the seventies. They'd maintained contact through the years after Helen married her New Zealand fiancé Paul. They exchanged cards on birthdays, talked on the phone every few months and emailed each other regularly these days. Since Helen moved out to New Zealand in the late seventies, they'd met up in person only twice. Once when Helen had visited family in Bristol with her eldest child who was a ten-month-old baby (now twenty-one) and then on a further visit which Helen made without her family some years ago. Beth just hoped that no unpleasant issues would arise to cause fractures in their friendship when it came to sorting out the Fallon money she had to repay.

'Don't be silly. You're my best friend. And it's not as if you and Libby were complete strangers anyway. In that picture you showed me, you look like sisters.'

Frank Bailey had produced a copy of the photo of the two girls as children while they were on the plane to Australia. Both Matt and Ali had exclaimed that they looked like sisters also. It was no wonder that she'd been mixed up about all the details of her life. She'd had experiences that involved Libby and so were familiar to her.

'What are we going to do about poor Libby's remains?' Helen asks Beth.

It was something Beth had not thought about, being preoccupied with other matters.

'I don't know Helen. What do you think should be done? I don't know when the police might release her.'

'I'm sorry, it's not really your problem. I'll talk to Dad about it.'

Beth nods. It would be best if Kenny made the decisions.

'How's everything going with your family in Sydney?' Helen asks after a pause. 'Did you recognise any of them? Are you remembering anything from your life with them before the accident?'

Before Beth could answer Helen was called out of the room to deal with demands from her children.

While she was gone Beth thought back to when Frank had pulled the hire car out of the parking lot at Sydney Airport. She'd wondered whether she'd recognize her father or either of her brothers, Brian and Rob. Frank had told her that he'd asked only the three immediate family members to be present for this initial meeting. What would her husband Richard have made of it all? Richard, who was such a lovely man. She loved him dearly, but he never set her heart pounding. He was more like a favourite old pair of slippers. Comfortable and relaxing to be with. And above all, safe.

She'd met Richard Carey shortly after moving to Bristol, following Marty's trial in London. After joining his legal firm as a secretary, it was Richard who had first called her 'Beth.' Employed as Elizabeth Fallon, reverting to use of what she believed to be her maiden name, Richard quickly found the name Elizabeth tediously long and so, for expediency, began calling her Beth.

The name Beth felt more 'adult' than her childhood name of Libby and it quickly came into regular use in her life.

Six months into working at the firm Richard asked her

whether she would be interested in training as a legal executive, explaining that she could earn more money this way. He'd told her that although she was a great secretary, she was wasted in this role and really should consider studying to become a solicitor like his sister Catherine had. Beth had explained that she was currently studying 'A' levels and wouldn't have the time.

Female solicitors were rare in the seventies and Catherine, Richard's sister, who had qualified in the sixties, only had assured employment because the company was owned by the family. How likely would it be that she would gain employment if she trained anyway?

A further few months down the line she and Richard were dating. A year later he proposed and they were married within six months. Richard then persuaded her to go to university and study law, as she had successfully passed her 'A' levels by then.

Neither of them knew that his life would be cut short with a debilitating cancer eight years later.

Richard had not baulked at her background, and if he was alive to hear Frank's revelations, she's sure he would have travelled out to Australia with them, supporting her and the kids in this life changing event.

'Beth?'

She hadn't realised Helen had returned. Jolted back from her memories, Beth explains that she recognised her father as soon as she saw him and then instantly passed out.

'When I came around, he was spouting a load of gushy stuff at me and calling me Lizzie. You know I don't handle that kind of thing too well. I think I probably upset him with my reaction of almost pushing him away and saying "I'm called Beth now." It was all I could manage in the moment.'

'You did that instead of crying then,' Helen says.

'Yes, you know me too well.'

'And how are things between you now?'

'Better with my father. We've had some long walks together – just the two of us, and on occasions I recognise places – from before. He's told me quite a bit about my mother; he misses her so much. I think I remember her from photographs hanging around the place, but sometimes I think I'm picking up on my father's memories. He slips into my childhood name of Lizzie at times which irritates me a little. But I'm feeling closer to him now, and we've had physical contact. Hugs, hand-holding, that kind of thing. I managed to call him Dad the other day, which brought tears to his eyes. I'd been avoiding it.'

'Good. It will all take time. You've been apart for more than twenty-five years.'

'I know. Brian and Rob, my brothers, are driving me mad throwing incidents at me – events they expect me to remember. I did have memories of building sandcastles with a younger boy on a beach – which of course was probably my brother Brian. And I can recall holding a young baby which was no doubt Robbie as my father still calls him. He's eight years younger than me. But they don't seem to understand that I have very little memory of them. In some ways it was a relief to board the plane to New Zealand just to have a bit of breathing space. Dad told me that they adored me before … before I disappeared from their lives and really looked up to me because I'm the eldest.'

'I know what that's like – although I couldn't honestly say that my brothers and sisters adored me; maybe when they were little, but not as they got older,' Helen says.

'From what I saw of you all, the boys still adore you, there was just a bit of sibling rivalry from your sisters.'

'That's for sure. What about the rest of your family?'

'I've met them all now and they're a great bunch. My brother Brian is married to a beautiful woman from New Zealand whose father was Maori and whose mother was Yugoslavian, from Dalmatia. Rob's second wife, Mina, is from India and she's beautiful as well. I have a Norwegian uncle on my mother's side. My grandmother is Irish. So, I have an interesting family. But it's been a little overwhelming at times, being around them all. So many cousins plus aunts and uncles I could only vaguely remember. Then there's my cousins' spouses and their children as well. And I have a bunch of nephews and nieces I'd never met. There are new cousins and of course, half siblings for Matt. It's seemed endless.'

What Beth doesn't tell Helen is that the large gathering her father put on to meet the rest of the family was a little like 'déjà vu'. Similar to how she'd felt meeting Helen's family in Bristol all those years ago. Awkward, embarrassed and a little overwhelmed. Only this time she did remember a few of them. This time they were her *real* family.

'You said in an email that you'd met up with Matt's father, Steve. But you didn't say what he's like. So, tell me,' Helen says.

'He looks like an older version of Matt,' Beth replies.

'I now know who Matt looks like. As you know, it was always a mystery to me. Do you remember how Matt's thick straight hair used to flop down over his forehead as a child? His father's hair is exactly the same. The same light brown as well – apart from the odd grey strands. Matt keeps his short now to avoid that, but his father Steve wears his longer, just like Matt's was when he was little. My father showed me a couple of photographs taken at our engagement party and Steve had short hair then. Almost identical to the style Matt has now. It was weird looking at those pictures I can tell you.'

'How was your first meeting with him?'

'It was very strange. He came with his daughter Eliza, named after me he said, who is eighteen, and his son Harry, who is thirteen. According to Steve, we said we'd name our firstborn son Harry, which is what *he* did when his son was born. It would seem his wife went along with the name suggestions.'

'Sounds to me like he had difficulty letting you go. Naming his daughter after you and then the name he gave his son was linked to you.'

'Yes, I thought that as well. He told me why he'd chosen his children's names when we were out on the covered terrace. He seemed keen to get us alone for a good long chat, but the opportunity never really arose. Not for long anyway. There were too many people around the house. I wasn't about to take him into a bedroom and it was pouring with rain the day he came down last Saturday. Steve and Matt got on well though. Matt and Ali also got on well with his Eliza and Harry.'

'It must be a bit strange for all the kids, discovering

they have half-siblings.'

'Yes, I think it's a bit of a novelty at the moment. It's only Matt who is half-brother to Steve's children. Ali is sort of their step-sister. Anyway, Steve had to return to Brisbane for urgent business the following day so we didn't get to speak again. He phoned me yesterday morning though and said he'd like to fly down to see me again next week. I said I wasn't sure if I would be there and would let him know.'

'I've just had a thought,' Helen says. 'Although your name is Elizabeth, you were called Lizzie by your family, so your initials were – in principle, L.F. Libby's initials were L.F. until she married Miller. Do you think you found Miller's story easier to believe because Libby had the same initials as you and somewhere in your subconscious you knew that?'

'I don't know. Perhaps. When I was in Maitland Hospital, Miller gave me Libby's Celtic necklace – you know the one I used to wear in the seventies, which he claimed she received from her parents for her eighteenth birthday. It was hers, not mine, because I saw photographs of them together when they were younger and she was wearing it. I assumed it was me in the photos. She might well have been wearing it when we met as adults. According to my grandmother Libby and I met a few times not that long before the accident. It *was* familiar to me and of course the initials LF would have been familiar to me as well. So, I don't know. I still had the necklace – I passed it on to DI Frank Bailey when I saw him to sign my formal statement as it will be needed for Miller's trial.'

'Once the trial is over, and Libby's remains are released,

we could ask your Frank to give the necklace back so it can be buried with her – unless you want to keep it of course.'

'No,' Beth says shaking her head. 'I think you're right. It should be buried with Libby. And just for the record Detective Bailey is not *my* Frank.'

'Hm. So what about Steve? Do you think there's a chance you might get back together with him? You said he's on his own now.'

'I don't know Helen. I doubt it.'

'Is that because you've fallen for Frank?'

'Why would you even think I've fallen for Frank?' Beth asks with surprise.

'You've mentioned him quite a few times and every time you've said his name, there's a little sparkle in your eye. I think it was more than a professional relationship.'

'I do like him a lot, Helen, and we got on really well, but I can't see how it can be anything other than a professional relationship. I'm just someone in a case he's been dealing with.'

'Are you sure about that?'

'I live on the other side of the world to him anyway, so it's a non-starter.'

Beth, Matt and Ali stay with Helen and her family for a week. Beth finds it relaxing spending time with Helen again. Their children, meeting for the first time as adults, all get along well.

Kenny Fallon phones while Beth is with Helen. They have a long conversation about everything, during which Kenny made clear that he didn't want any 'Fallon' money back from her, but warns her his brother might. He also asks her to assist in sorting out the share of money that Miller took. She says she's only too happy to help, and is relieved that Uncle Kenny is not blaming her for anything. Although she now knows Kenny isn't a blood relative, she will always think of him, Ginny and his children, as family. Matt and Ali tell her they feel the same.

After Helen discusses the subject of Libby's remains with Kenny, he asks Beth if she's prepared to arrange for Libby to be interred with her parents in Maitland. Helen offers to fly over to join her in a 'small ceremony' to do this. Beth knows her father and grandmother would like to be there as well, so she agrees to it without further thought.

At the departure gate at Auckland airport, they all exchange hugs.

'I'll join you in Sydney as soon as you have a date for Libby's burial,' Helen says wiping tears from her eyes.

42

Beth thinks her first time alone with Steve Meredith is turning into a bit of a disaster. She'd agreed to go to a restaurant with him, feeling more comfortable in a public space, but they are tucked away in a corner. Conversation has been stilted from the outset. Beth can see he's choking words back and wonders what he really wants to say. She senses some anger simmering beneath his polite smiles. Directed at whom, she's not sure. When she asks him to tell her more about his children, it transforms his whole demeanour and he chats away happily through the main course and into dessert. As Beth puts down her spoon and wipes her mouth with the serviette, he reaches out, runs his hand down the side of her face and says, 'Your poor beautiful face ruined by what that bastard did.' *Ruined? Is that what you think?*

Most days Beth forgets that her face features a number of scars. She no longer notices them in the mirror. Very few people she meets for the first time mention them. Occasionally a new client might trawl out the standard question, 'What happened to your face?' As if, because they were paying her for her time, they have the right to ask.

Beth's standard repost is, 'Car accident. Glass cuts.' She likes to keep it simple and eye contact with the inquisitive soon makes them drop their eyes and sometimes mumble an apology.

Steve however seems to think it's okay to openly make this statement with no awareness of how derogatory it is. 'You know how to flatter a girl, don't you?' Beth says looking him full in the eye.

'Sorry Liz, I mean Beth, it's just that your face was so beautiful, it makes me almost want to cry to see how much you must have suffered.'

'Careful,' Beth says, 'that hole you're digging is getting deeper by the second.'

'You know what I mean though don't you.'

'You said my face *is* ruined and *was*, past tense, beautiful. Clearly you no longer think my face is beautiful, that's what I think you meant.'

'No, no, I didn't mean that at all. I meant the suffering you must have gone through, all caused by that man, with the car accident and then the attack he made on you in London.'

'Okay, we'll leave it at that shall we? Was there some other burning question you wanted to ask me? Only I sense there is one. Why don't you just spit it out?' Beth says feeling a little irritated by this man.

She's noticed that she's been quick to anger in the past few weeks and found herself reacting sharply to people instead of responding to them as she normally would. What was happening to her? Perhaps it was the hounding of the press, who approached them daily with questions. There'd been some sensational headlines like *'Woman*

Returns from the Dead after Twenty-five Years!' plus countless other articles since the police had released their statement to the press. Marty's attack on her in London had been resurrected and put on the front page of every newspaper, whereas it had only warranted a couple of columns on an inner page after Marty's sentencing back in seventy-seven, according to her father.

The press had tracked the family to the house in Coogee and they constantly hung around on the off chance that she, or someone else, would relent and start answering questions. The neighbours had started complaining about the lack of parking spaces in the street.

'Okay,' Steve says, 'first of all I was wondering what happened to the engagement ring I bought you? Surely seeing that would have helped you to remember us?'

Beth is silent for a minute. *Engagement Ring?* Finally connecting the dots, she says, 'When I regained consciousness in the hospital, I wasn't wearing an engagement ring. There was only a wedding ring in my belongings, but of course they weren't my belongings, were they? Martin Miller told me that he'd sold my engagement ring to pay the rent and bills. He was probably talking about the engagement ring *you* bought me and telling the truth for once. That it was mine. Not his wife Libby's. I'm sorry, I never saw it after the accident.'

Steve mutters under his breath for a moment. Beth can see he's very angry.

'Was that it?' she asks. 'Is that all you wanted to know?'

'What's also been bothering me since we met again, is, well ... I've been wondering how you could forget what we had between us? I've never forgotten. Or ever found the same love and passion with anyone else. Did you really forget everything? Did you really forget me? Matt looks so much like me; did it not trigger any memories of me?'

Now we're getting to the nitty gritty of things!

'The doctors called it amnesia, Steve. Memory loss that, sometimes after severe trauma to the brain, is never regained. I was also subjected to, at a very vulnerable time in my recovery I might add, a load of bullshit brainwashing from a very manipulative man. I knew, as one knows deep in their soul, that this man repulsed me and I could never feel any love for him. At the same time over the years, I sensed that I had been loved. I just couldn't remember by whom. I believed I'd probably had a passionate affair with someone outside my 'marriage' that led to my pregnancy.'

Beth pauses for a moment before continuing. 'I say marriage because I saw the evidence of a marriage certificate, I had a wedding ring, I saw photographs and so I believed from what I was told that I was married to this man I didn't like. Frank Bailey, the detective on the case, visited a psychiatrist going through the details of what I'd told him. The psychiatrist said Miller effectively brainwashed me at a very vulnerable time in my recovery, convincing me I was Libby.'

'Did you sleep with Miller? Have sex with him?'

Beth sighs. Another male ego issue. 'Yes, I slept with him after he took me back to the flat in Sydney. But I prayed each night that he wouldn't touch me and he didn't until the very last night I was there. That night he raped me.'

'Oh God, Liz. That—'

Beth cuts him off, before he can launch into another rant about her suffering or what a bastard Miller was. '*You* haven't forgotten our love,' she says, 'because you didn't experience what I did. I'd even venture to say that perhaps you've placed the memory of the love we shared onto such a high pedestal that neither I, in my present form today, or anyone else, could ever live up to. More fool you Steve, wasting your life these past twenty-five years pining for a young woman you believed was never coming back. And no, Matt's appearance didn't trigger any memories. As he didn't take after me, or Miller, I just thought his father must have been very handsome.'

All the anger Beth had sensed in Steve seems to drain out of his body. He slumps down in his seat and leans slightly forward. *Oh no he's not going to cry, is he? Not here!* Beth signals for the bill, takes cash out of her purse in preparation, stands and tugs at Steve's arm.

'Come on Steve, we have to leave,' she whispers firmly in his ear. '*Now!*'

The waiter brings the bill and after a quick check she thrusts notes into his hands and mumbles, 'Sorry we have to go. Thank you, the meal was lovely, please keep the change.'

She drags Steve out of the restaurant and down the street towards his car. He seems to be in a daze. 'Keys, Steve. Where are your keys?' Steve pats his jacket pocket and she reaches in and removes the keys. She opens the car door and shoves Steve into the passenger seat. 'Put your seat belt on,' she commands before slamming the door and walking around to the driver's side. Beth stands outside the car for a minute making a decision. *Is this a crazy idea?*

Steve had only had one beer with his meal because he'd

been planning to drive. She's only had one glass of wine, wanting to keep her wits about her. Before climbing into the car, she pulls out the new mobile phone her father insists she carries with her every time she leaves the house. Beth hates the bloody silly little thing but it's proved useful in warning each other when the press is on the prowl. She taps out a message to send to her father. An SMS they call it. She doesn't even know what that stands for. Her son Matt has a mobile and he calls messages 'texts'.

> Steve is upset. Taking him up North for the night. Will pop in on Gran tomorrow. Probably back tomorrow night. Please tell the kids. Beth x

She waits for confirmation that the message has been sent, climbs into the car and drives north out of the city. She hopes Steve is insured for other drivers. He's given way to sobbing and is slumped against the passenger window. She turns the radio on, setting it at a low volume, not wishing to be too disturbed by his distress. One part of her feels annoyed and impatient with his emotional display. She wants to shout at him to 'stop the bloody crying' and 'man up!' But she remembers what her father told her about how Steve was in the days following the accident. Immediately after the accident they'd apparently gone to Maitland hospital to make enquiries, having been told that the other accident victims had been taken there. Little did they know that when Steve and her father had come to the hospital, she was in a coma, lying in a bed just a few feet away. Steve had caused a scene right outside her hospital room. If only …

They'd spent days joining in the search for her and then after her father had returned to Sydney, Steve had stayed on and spent another week or so combing both sides of the river bank in search of her, barely stopping to eat or sleep, continuing some nights long after dark using large torches he'd purchased. He'd even hired a boat and trawled up and down the river peering and poking into its depths.

'He returned a broken man, Beth. Just like me,' her father told her. Steve didn't have his family nearby to support him as her father had. Steve was an only child and his mother had re-married after many years as a widow and moved to a country town called Orange.

She remains silent while Steve releases his emotions; his head bent; tears streaking down his face. He quietens, pulls a handkerchief from his pocket, wipes his eyes and blows his nose. A quick glance at him and she can tell that he seems to be in a dazed state again. He's lifted his head and is staring blankly out of the front windscreen.

It's just gone midnight when Beth pulls into a twenty-four-hour motel on the New England Highway on the outskirts of Newcastle. She rings the night bell and requests a double room. The proprietor lets her into the reception and she pays for one night, collects the keys and drives the car around to park outside their room. She'd seen a string of motels on the highway from her recent visit to the area and hoped she'd be able to pick up a room in one tonight.

Steve follows her out of the car like a docile lamb. She pulls him into the room, sits him on the bed while she uses the bathroom and then has a generous drink of water from the kitchenette area. She leaves the bathroom light on with the door slightly open to allow a sliver of light to filter into the room and gently begins to undress Steve. He makes no attempt to speak, but complies with her actions. When he's naked she guides him under the bedclothes before stripping her own clothes off and climbing in beside him. She takes him into her arms and hugs him close to her body. She knows he's dropped off when she hears the rhythmic breathing of sleep. She finally falls into a relaxed sleep herself.

Beth wakes as daylight is emerging and realises their positions have altered. She's now lying in his arms. She turns her head to find an alert Steve smiling at her. He draws her into him and kisses her gently on the forehead. 'Thank you,' he whispers. He removes his arm and begins to caress her body. Beth finds herself responding as though they have been lovers for years. They make love with a passion she cannot remember experiencing before, as though her body remembers him as they unite with a natural ease.

They lie apart without speaking for some time afterwards. Beth thinks it would be handy to be a smoker in moments like these, to diffuse the situation. She decides to make matters light-hearted. 'Okay Mr. Meredith,' she says, 'time for a shower, then you can take me off to Maitland for breakfast. I'd like to call in on Gran this morning. I know she'd love to see you. You alright with that?'

'Yes, absolutely,' he says bouncing out of bed. 'I haven't seen her since the seventies, she must be getting on a bit now.'

'She's ninety next birthday and still has full brain

function and mobility. She has her own place and cooks all her own meals.'

'Wow! Can't wait to see her,' he says walking into the bathroom.

'I'm making myself a tea; would you like one?' she shouts through the bathroom door.

'Coffee for me,' he says, 'with milk and one sugar.'

When Beth's father had first brought her up to see her grandmother Beth instantly recognised her and the lilt of her mellowed Irish accent was achingly familiar. She'd told Gran that there was a nursing sister at Maitland hospital called Sister O'Connell who had a similar accent and that she always felt relaxed in her presence, loving the sound of her voice that seemed so familiar.

'I met Sister O'Connell,' Gran had said, 'she came from County Wexford like me. That's why you recognised the accent. She seemed a lovely woman. Long passed on now, your detective told me. She told me about your recovery at the hospital, only of course we both thought we were talking about Libby Fallon.'

'You went up to the hospital?' Beth asked her. She assumed Gran was talking about Frank Bailey when she said "your detective," as her father had mentioned Frank had been to see Gran.

'Yes, I missed you by only a few days. If only I had realised you were there sooner, we could have put a stop to all the malarkey Libby's husband was up to. I would have known immediately that you were Lizzie, not Libby! And you wouldn't have been lost to us all these years.'

They'd both cried at that point and had a long hug.

Gran had then asked her if she remembered coming up to see her just after the Fallon farm fire. Beth told her she didn't remember it and asked what had happened.

'You drove right past their wreck of a house without noticing and when I asked you whether your father had passed on the tragic news to you, you said you hadn't spoken to him since the beginning of the week as you and Steve had been out on jobs until late and you'd been staying over at his house.'

'I must have been looking at the river when I drove past their gates,' Beth said.

'Yes, that's what you said to me that day. I told you about the fire which had killed Libby's parents and her brother Gary and you were very upset. You'd bumped into Libby and her husband outside the Fallon farm the month before when you came up to see us one weekend. You told me you met up with Libby in Sydney a week or so later, but she had no contact phone number and hadn't given you her address – you only knew she lived not far from King's Cross. You hadn't heard from her since. The fire happened only a few weeks after you'd met so I told you she was probably preoccupied with the loss of her family. As far as I know you never heard from her again.'

'She might have contacted me – I don't remember. All these years I believed it was my family who died in that fire. I sometimes had nightmares about it and had tortuous thoughts about the whole thing following a bad dream. I felt guilty that I'd survived and benefited financially out of it.'

'You don't have to feel that guilt any more as it wasn't anything to do with you,' Gran had said, as though this knowledge could erase years of emotional torment at a stroke.

Beth loves Gran's detached three-bedroom house with a large garage and small garden – all designed by her in a long wide block of six houses, three either side of a shared central driveway.

'I didn't want to be living on my own in a house with huge a yard to look after and not have easy interaction with neighbours,' Gran had explained when they first met up in June. 'So, I had the old house that was here demolished and found a contractor to build these. This small community gives us all independence and yet we are all able to keep an eye on each other and mix socially if we wish.'

When Beth had questioned whether the other house occupiers were elderly pensioners as well, Gran had been indignant. 'No, why would I want a load of old folks around me. Why do you think I didn't want to go into a retirement place? I sold three of the other places when the building work was complete to more mature people – one to a recently retired couple in their 60s, and the other two to single people in their late 50s who were still working. I rent the other two houses, to tenants who are over fifty who can't afford to buy their own place. I had a special document drawn up regarding the age of people who can live here – they have to be over 50. I didn't want young people who might play loud blaring music at all hours of the day and night. The location is ideal. We can walk to the shops if we don't want to drive, or there are buses just outside that will take you to the town or the station.'

Beth agreed. She was so happy that she was able to

spend some time with her gran and hadn't missed the opportunity to do so as she had with her mother and grandfather.

The reunion between Steve and Beth's grandmother today is heart-warming for Beth to see. They chat and drink coffee like old friends. But she finds it difficult to look at Steve for any length of time. It's like looking at an older version of her son Matt. Thinking about Steve being a potential 'partner' seems really weird and somehow wrong. She knows her thinking isn't logical, as Matt is *their* son. They could have, in principle, been together all these years. Then it would have been more natural. But now …

The visit to her grandmother, coupled with the earlier events at the motel, seems to have put Steve into a more relaxed mood. When they leave Maitland to return to Sydney, Steve suggests they divert to Orange to meet up with his mother and stay there for the night. Beth tells him she'd rather return to Coogee, but promises to visit him in Brisbane soon. She doesn't want to meet yet another person she can't remember and have to go through all those explanations.

43

After completing legal issues, overturning her recorded death, Beth applies for British citizenship in her real name, whilst she also claims Australian citizenship. She is unable to legally use the name Carey for her passports, as the correct documents were not provided for her marriage to Richard. She wants to fight that argument, but decides it will keep until she returns to the UK. Obtaining Australian citizenship proves fairly easy as she's simply able to provide her original birth certificate (which her father had kept amongst family documents) and apply to the passport office. The British citizenship proves trickier, but luckily Beth has a two-pronged approach to the British Embassy in Canberra.

Beth's father was born in Liverpool in the UK. His parents had emigrated from Ireland to Liverpool before his birth. Suffering through the depression in the UK, the family decided to immigrate to Australia on an assisted passage scheme in 1933 when Charles Farrell was less than two years old. Beth can claim British citizenship through him. Also, with statements from the police, Beth provided the Embassy with the history of her situation in the UK where she led a life believing she was someone else. The fact that she married a UK citizen, bore two children in the UK, and has lived there for twenty-five years also gives her the right to citizenship through her residency. After some weeks Beth finally receives her citizenship papers and sends off her application for a British passport in the name of Farrell.

'You could probably also obtain Norwegian citizenship,' her father says on the morning Beth receives the British Citizenship papers. He's explained Beth's Norwegian ancestry through her mother in their long talks and taking her through the family photo albums.

'It's been difficult enough coping with two as it is,' Beth replies. 'I think I'll leave it at that.'

44

Bristol, December 2000

'Have you made a decision on what you'd like to do?' Beth asks Ali.

They'd discussed the possibility of moving to Australia and Ali picking up a degree course there. At Beth's urging, Ali switched her study modules when she returned to university in October and is now concentrating on modern history. Having learned that she'd obtained a degree in medieval history at Sydney University back in 1974 and that she'd found it difficult to find work linked to it, Beth convinced Ali that medieval history would restrict her options of employment in the future. Particularly if she wanted to work in Australia. Like Matt, Ali has applied for Australian citizenship so it will be easy for her to travel between the two countries.

Matt received his Australian passport last week after applying for citizenship and is intending to remain in Australia after Miller's trial which is due to take place late next month in the Newcastle Supreme Court.

'Yes. I want to finish my degree here Mum. If you want

to move to Australia to be with Steve, I can stay on here by myself. I've only got another eighteen months to go.'

'That's not an option. That's settled then, I'll come back after the trial. Once you've graduated, we can discuss the matter again then.'

'But Mum—'

'There's nothing else to discuss Ali. Whether Steve and I have a long-term future remains to be seen. He's not willing to budge. He said when he was over here in September, he has no intention of moving to the UK, and he wants to stay in Brisbane. I understand he runs a successful business there but all my family live in Sydney. If I was going to live in Australia, I'd rather be a bit closer to them. Steve and I seem to have reached a stalemate.'

'If you're sure ...'

'I am. I'll be seeing Steve next month and I can talk about things with him then.'

Although their relationship had grown steadily during their time together in Sydney, Brisbane and when Steve visited the UK in September with his son Harry, she's still not sure whether it could work long term with his unwillingness to compromise. He wanted her to fit into his life in Brisbane and couldn't understand why she was hesitant. When she'd raised the question of Ali, he'd said she could do a degree in Brisbane instead, like his daughter Eliza, as though it was that simple. Yes, Ali could do that, and they had discussed the possibility, but it was Ali's decision to make. Not Steve's. And she had no intention of abandoning Ali to join Steve.

Beth doesn't mind remaining in England while Ali finishes her degree. It's the life she's used to. She speaks to her father and grandmother each week and she usually chats to her brothers every couple of weeks, although conversation with them is sometimes awkward and the phone calls briefer.

After some complex legal work, financial matters were settled amicably with the Fallon Family. Her house in Clifton from her marriage to Richard, and the two flats in Montpelier are now registered in the name of Elizabeth Farrell. The house she owned in Southville has been transferred to Joe Fallon and she paid Kenneth money against the Montpelier property for him to give to his children. Beth still goes by the name of Carey at her firm, and is in the process of having the matter resolved legally.

45

Newcastle, New South Wales, January 2001

Beth is re-united with her family at Martin Miller's trial. She's pleased to see them all again, but is nervous about giving evidence. Frank warned her in a telephone call to her father's house a few days before, that he'd heard whispers about Miller's defence trying to make out that she knew all along that she was Elizabeth Farrell, and that her memory loss was not real. That *she* had pretended to be Libby Miller to get her hands on the Fallon money and that Miller was innocent. Apparently, he also claimed that Libby died immediately after the accident, so he couldn't be found guilty on the murder charge. They'd both laughed at these preposterous claims.

Beth meets up with Frank at the court where they are taken into a separate room. The crown prosecutors have decided not to use her father or Steve as witnesses.

'Where are you staying?' Frank asks Beth after warm greetings are exchanged between them.

'Dad and I are staying with my grandmother. We'll be here for the whole trial. My two brothers will come and go. One of our cousins lives in Warner's Bay so they'll stay with him.'

She didn't mention that Steve would be coming down to stay with her for the close of the trial.

'Of course, Miller is still claiming his innocence,' Frank tells Beth.

'He did that in London in nineteen seventy-seven. He didn't fool the jury then. Let's hope he won't fool them now.'

Beth is also re-united with Matt Gardner, her old neighbour, at the trial. He is to be a witness for the prosecution.

'It's lovely to see you again Libby,' Matt says when they meet. Despite not meeting for twenty-five years, they both recognise each other straight away.

'I go by the name of Beth now,' she tells him. 'My husband Richard started calling me that and it stuck.'

He nods. 'Suits you.'

'Where are you living these days?' Beth asks him.

'I live in the Blue Mountains, just outside Katoomba, with my long-term partner Ross. We moved there last year after I retired. We were in Surry Hills before that. Our house is in a really picturesque setting. You must come and visit us while you're in Sydney.'

'I'd like that.'

'So, tell me how life was for you in England? Apart from Miller making an attempt on your life that is. I saw an article in the paper back in seventy-seven about what he'd done and the sentence he received. If I'd have known how to reach you then I would have been in touch. I was sorry to hear you'd gone through all that. But you married again?'

'Yes, after my so-called divorce from Miller.'

She tells him about moving to Bristol after Miller's trial and meeting Richard. How she'd named her son after him and goes on to give him a potted history of her life. They exchange details and promise to remain in touch.

The prosecution calls several expert witnesses who give their opinion about Beth's memory loss and Miller's successful manipulation techniques. Beth follows them into the witness box, and apart from challenging her about the extent of her memory loss, the defence refrains from laying any blame at her door for the crimes Miller committed. Isolated in the witness room while the experts took the stand, Beth's father fills her in on their statements when she completes her testimony.

Beth is surprised that so many witnesses are called for the prosecution, some she hadn't seen for more than twenty-five years, including a reluctant Brett Saunders and a nurse who worked at Maitland hospital while she was there. The defence call their own expert witnesses, but they make little impact on the outcome.

The trial lasts four weeks, including several days of summing up by the lead Justice. The jury finds Martin Miller guilty of all charges in less than twenty-four hours.

Frank and Beth stand and punch the air after hearing the verdict. A jubilant Frank engulfs Beth in a celebratory hug. It's unlikely that Martin Miller will ever see the outside of a prison again. He apologises to her immediately after. 'Sorry, I couldn't help myself Beth.'

'No need to apologise; it's fine Frank,' she assures him,

despite the glares emanating from Steve. And it really is fine, Beth thinks.

46

Cessnock and Newcastle, New South Wales August 2003

Detective Chief Inspector Frank Bailey is on duty at Newcastle Central Police Headquarters when he receives a phone call from the Cessnock Correctional Services. The Prison Governor informs him that Martin Miller wishes to make a full confession regarding his crimes and he wishes to make that statement to him, Frank Bailey.

'Why now?' Frank asks.

'*He's been diagnosed with terminal cancer,*' the Governor tells him. '*I believe he wants to leave a record of everything he's done before he dies. I think he was hoping to be released on his appeal, but when that failed and since his diagnosis, he's been quite depressed. He's not prepared to write anything down. He wants you to take down the statement and he'll sign it.*'

'What kind of cancer does he have and how long has he got?'

'*He has liver cancer which has now gone into his bones. He has been given about two to three months to live.*'

'Okay, I'll discuss it with my Chief Superintendent and

get back to you.'

Frank considers the situation this will place him in. On the one hand he really would like to hear Miller's story, for Beth Carey's sake as well as satisfying his own curiosity. On the other hand, he's just in the embryonic stages of a new relationship and the Chief Super might not allow him to spend all his working hours up at the prison. He has received a promotion to Detective Chief Inspector since Miller's trial and is supposed to be directing investigations at Headquarters. If he uses all his own time visiting the prison, this will impact on his personal life and might lead to a breakdown in his relationship. This relationship is important to him. The most important one of his life. He doesn't want anything to spoil it.

The Chief Super reaches a compromise with him. He is allowed one week off his normal duties to take the statement, with the aid of recording equipment, in both visual and sound form. The spoken word will be transcribed by an administrative assistant back at Headquarters. If the statement is not completed within that time frame, Frank is to use his own time to visit the centre. Could be worse, Miller could be in a prison hundreds of kilometres away instead of Cessnock which is not far from Newcastle.

Frank rings the Governor back and arranges for an interview room to be made available for the following day, one where recording equipment is already in place, so he doesn't have to bring in and set up his own.

Cessnock Correctional Centre is a large maximum-security

prison complex for sentenced and un-sentenced males. It's in the Hunter Valley region and was opened in 1972. According to Frank's brother-in-law, Barry, who works there, it could do with a massive overhaul. From the parts Frank has seen over the years, he agrees. He meets with the Governor and is shown into a spacious internal room with no external windows, but it has glass windows above panelling which look onto a corridor – and blinds that can be closed. There will be no visual distractions from the outside.

Miller comes into the room a short time later. He has been allowed to retain the fancy electronic wheelchair he owned before being charged. A guard checks that everything is okay and closes the door on them.

'Morning Martin,' Frank greets Miller politely. 'I hear you want to get some things off your chest?'

'Yeah, have you heard about me diagnosis?'

'Yes, I'm sorry to hear about that Martin.' And he is sorry. Having watched both his parents die from varying cancers, Frank knows it's not a pleasant death. He would also have preferred that Miller had many more years in prison contemplating his crimes. He can see that Miller has lost a substantial amount of weight and most of his hair. He's not a pretty sight.

'What I plan to do Martin, is record everything you say. It will be typed up and then you can sign it. I might also make a few notes as you are talking and perhaps ask you the odd question. But for the most part I'll just be listening to you. Are you happy with that?'

'Yeah, good-oh.'

'Do you have any questions for me before we start?

'Nah, you're right.'

'Whenever you're ready then Martin,' Frank says pushing the record button.

47

The Confession
Marty's story

I first bumped into that sheila, Elizabeth Farrell in Sydney one Saturday back in August nineteen seventy-four. Libby and I'd just had lunch in a café. Libby was supposed to pay the bill and I'd gone to the dunny. On my way out of the dunny I bumped in Libby – well I thought it was Libby anyway – who was in the corridor on her way to the women's.

'Whatcha doin' here Darl?' I asked stickin' my face right into hers. 'I thought you was gunna pay the bill?' I said to her. I wasn't too happy with her. I thought she was tryin' to avoid payin'. I'd only had a quick leak, so I knew she wouldn't've had time to pay. She had our money on her you see.

Anyway, the girl who I thought was Libby pulled back from me lookin' a bit scared. I then got a good look at her and could see it wasn't Libby, but some other sheila who looked quite a bit like her. Only this woman's hair was a bit longer and I realised she was wearin' different clothes.

Libby and I were in Sydney to look at a flat that me mate Brett set up a viewin' on.

The Farrell sheila must have just arrived or somethin' as I hadn't seen her when we were in the cafe. She didn't say anythin' to me and I mumbled an apology and went back into the café where I could see Libby payin' at the counter. When we left, I noticed a little red Austin Healy Sprite parked around the corner. I stopped to have a gander at it before Libby dragged me off. I knew that car was a special edition because you couldn't normally buy a red one. I didn't know it was the Farrell sheila's car at the time.

A few weeks later we were up at Libby's parents' farm outside Newcastle, on Nobles Rd. Earlier we'd dropped a load of our stuff to store at her parents' place so we didn't have to take so much to Sydney and were out at the gates comin' back from a walk. Anyway, a little red car came around the corner and stopped and the driver beeped the horn. Libby turned around and this sheila smiled and waved at her. Libby went over to talk to her. I recognised the woman – and the car. It was the same one I'd seen in Sydney. Libby called me over and introduced me and I could tell the woman recognised me from the café. She didn't say anything, just nodded at me. I asked Libby about her afterwards and she told me it was someone called Lizzie Farrell. She hadn't seen her for a few years, but they used to play together when they were young in the school holidays as the sheila's grandparents had a dairy farm at the other end of the road. Libby's father and this Lizzie's grandfather had had a fallin' out and the girls hadn't seen each other in a while. She told me how everyone thought they were sisters when they were young as they looked so alike. The Farrell girl lived in Sydney and Libby said she planned to contact her once we'd settled into our new flat. I forgot about her then.

Libby made contact with the Farrell sheila just after we moved to Sydney and they met for coffee – only once as far as I know.

After loads of chats with Libby and me mate Brett, we decided we'd like to start a used car business. Libby suggested we ask her parents for an interest free loan towards our costs as we would never have been able to save enough and we didn't want to have huge borrowin'. I was limited with the work I could do and with my old injury. I don't know if you remember, but I was shot in the back in Vietnam. Anyway, we found a place we wanted to buy and arranged to come up to Newcastle for the weekend.

Libby was goin' out with a couple of her old mates on the Saturday night who were movin' to Melbourne the followin' week. We were due to go to Libby's parents on the Sunday for lunch and were goin' to bring up the borrowin' then. Only after thinkin' about it, I suggested that I go and see them first on the Saturday night while she was out, to talk about our plans and ask them about the money.

Libby was always rowin' with her mother and brother. I was worried she'd say somethin' on the Sunday to wind them up and then it'd have destroyed our chances of gettin' any money you know. I got on well with her mother, who I called Mum. I couldn't bring meself to call Fallon 'Dad', but he'd suggested I call him Terry. In my head he was always 'Fallon' though.

I wanted to ask Fallon to *give* us some money, as well as a loan. I didn't want to have to pay so much back to him. Libby's brother was getting the farm so I thought it was only right that Libby got something. I knew Fallon had a stash of money in the bank. They were plannin' to build a new brick home on the site.

I knew Fallon was tight with his money, even though he made loads. He paid me and the other boys who worked for him lousy wages for all the work we did. Despite what Libby said, I wasn't confident he'd give us a loan.

Libby went off to meet her mates and I drove up to the farm, armed with a bottle of fine whisky, some beers, potato chips and a little extra. Both her parents liked a drop of whiskey, and Gary would have one, pretendin' he liked it as well. Playin' the big man. But Libby's father and Gary liked beer as well. Like me.

They were surprised to see me but I explained I was at a loose end with Libby out with her mates, me mate Brett was in Sydney and the friend we were stayin' with was off to a family do, so I'd decided to come up to see them. I told Libby's father I had some business I wanted to discuss with him.

After softenin' him with a couple of beers I asked to talk to him in private in the kitchen, but he wanted to remain in the livin' room, sittin' on their comfy couch by the fire. So I had no choice but to talk with him about the money there, in front of Mum and Gary. Mum thought the car yard idea was great at first, but then bloody Gary opened his gob and said, 'Libby's a loser who can't pay attention to anythin' for five minutes. She'd be hopeless at runnin' a business.'

What he said wasn't right about Libby. Gary was implyin' she was stupid and couldn't do anythin'. Like me, she'd left school early. She'd wanted to get out and earn her own money so she could get away from her bastard brother and avoid havin' rows with her mother. Libby was smart though. I wanted to punch Gary in the face really, but because I was there askin for money, I bit me tongue and said, 'You're wrong about Libby. Just because she doesn't have any qualifications doesn't mean she's not clever.'

Anyway, I explained that I'd been approved for a veteran's loan, and that we'd be lookin' at buyin' a house where we could also set up the car yard. I told them about the one we'd found that had been a successful yard before. How ideal it was. It would give us a home and an income. That me mate Brett, a qualified mechanic, was very good with cars would be doin' it with us.

But Gary had already put a spanner in the works by then. Mum always took his side – he was her darlin' boy. Gary just didn't want Libby to have any money.

Ol' Man Fallon had a soft spot for Libby and I thought he *might* see that it was only fair that she got somethin'.

He said, 'I plan to give money to Libby, but now is not the right time. I consider her too young, inexperienced and foolish to take on the responsibilities of her own house and running a business.'

I reminded him that it wouldn't be just Libby, it would be me, Libby and Brett. Brett and I were five years older than Libby. Fallon knew I had a lot of knowledge about cars – we'd often talk about them on the building sites. I reminded him Brett was a qualified mechanic and worked with cars every day. I said Libby was excited about the whole thing and could deal with the paper work and run the house.

But Fallon wouldn't budge and said, 'If you and Libby spend a year working in Sydney and show me that you can save some money, I might consider it then.'

Might consider it! This was his daughter and he wasn't willin' to give her a helpin' hand even though he had plenty of dough. As well as the new house they were gunna build, they were talkin' about a trip back to England. I was bloody livid, but had to keep my cool and not show it. I excused myself and went off to the dunny. While there I decided to move to plan B. I'd come prepared just in case, you know. I knew Mum kept some sleepin' tablets in the bathroom cabinet. Libby had pinched the odd one when we stayed over there some nights. I went into the bathroom to wash me hands and took one of her tablets from the cabinet.

When I came back into the kitchen which was just off the livin' room, I offered them all a whisky, sayin' I would prepare it. The men had already had a couple of beers by then. I crushed Mum's pill into her glass, addin' loads of ice and a bit of water. In Gary and old man Fallon's drinks I added a generous portion of pure alcohol from a small bottle I'd brought with me. Hopin' it would well and truly knock them out after a couple of glasses. I knew Mum would only have one glass, she wasn't much of a drinker and would then toddle off to bed. Especially with the sleepin' pill mixed into her drink. I knew she wouldn't be able to stay awake.

Sure enough, as soon as she finished her drink mum

said she needed to go to bed as she was feelin' a little under the weather and had to get up early. She banked the fire up in their solid fuel stove in the kitchen and left. I poured the men another drink, with the same treatment as before, but I also poured some of the whisky down the sink. It was a shame to waste it, but it had to look like they'd had a lot more to drink. Gary dropped off to sleep on the couch when he finished his second one. Old man Fallon said he'd had enough and was headin' to bed. He didn't seem too steady on his feet either. They had a fire goin' in the lounge as it was chilly that night. Fallon put the guard around the fire and decided to leave Gary where he was.

I told him I was leavin' and that I'd see them the next day for lunch as planned with Libby. He wished me goodnight and said he hoped I understood where he was comin' from about the money. I told him I did and left.

I drove off down Nobles Rd, and on to Seaham Road, makin' sure I revved the car. There's a nosey old cow lives on the corner there, whose house faces on to Nobles Road and you can be sure she would've heard me and probably peered out the window as I left. I went along Seaham Road a little way and pulled into a gateway. It was another part of the Fallon farm where they had more paddocks, so I knew nobody would be around and the car would be hidden. I put me gum boots on and crossed over the road enterin' the paddocks that led into the back of Fallon's place. I had a torch, but only used it every now and then in case that nosey cow on the corner saw the light. The back of her house looked out over the paddocks where I was crossin'. I could see fairly well anyway as it was a good-sized moon and no clouds.

I'd taken Libby's keys to the house that day so that I could get in easy if I needed to. I went in by the back door that leads into the kitchen. I checked to see that Gary was still crashed out, dead to the world, in the livin' room. I could hear snorin' comin' from the parents' bedroom, so I knew they were out for the count as well.

Mum always had tea towels draped over the front rails of the old kitchen stove. She also always had washin' hangin' on wooden rails above the stove. I opened the fire door and flicked one of the tea towels into the fire to catch alight. I then left the fire door slightly open to allow the flames to spread onto the rest of the tea towels which I knew would soon flare up and catch the washin'. Luckily, I remembered to grab the money Mum always had stashed in a tin in the kitchen before the fire really took hold.

I got the idea for the fire from an accident that happened at the kiddie's home I grew up in. They had a solid fuel stove with all our sheets hangin' above it durin' the winter months. When I was about twelve, one of the staff hadn't shut the fire door properly and we had this terrible fire. Luckily it happened durin' the day so it only destroyed the washin' and blackened the walls before it was discovered and put out, with no-one bein' hurt. I knew this would be very different.

Once I saw the flames were catchin' the washin', I left in a hurry, locked the door and went back across the paddocks, changed back into my shoes and drove off, without any lights to start with, and headed back to Newcastle. I parked the car a few ks from the house we were stayin' in and pulled a hose out from under the bonnet that I knew would look like the car had broken down. I dumped the bottle of pure alcohol in a bin near where I left the car then I flagged down a cab and went back to the house, gettin' it to drop me a couple of blocks away.

Libby was home by this time, a little drunk from her night out. I roused her and told her the car had broken down and I'd had to walk the last few ks home. I told Libby that her father had agreed to give us some money and a loan and that we needed to speak to him more about it over lunch – by this time it was about twelve-thirty. She just smiled and went back off to sleep. I put the keys I'd taken back in her handbag.

Later that mornin' I dragged Libby up; we showered and trudged the few ks back to the car. Libby was pretty ignorant of anythin' to do with the mechanics of cars so, when I opened the bonnet and told her it was just a pipe that had come loose and was easily fixed, she didn't know any better. We set off for her parents' place. I wasn't sure what we'd discover when we got there but when we arrived, we learned there had been this tragic fire and the whole family had died. The neighbour I mentioned earlier had spotted the flames when they reached the roof as they'd really lit up the night sky, and rang the emergency services. But by then it was too late. The family couldn't be saved.

Libby of course, was gutted. There were still fire trucks, police and reporters there when we arrived. The bodies had been moved by then though so she didn't have to see that. Although she didn't get on with her mother and brother that well, she loved her parents and was in a terrible state. We both were. I was genuinely very upset you know. It needn't have happened. If only Fallon hadn't been such a mean, tight fisted bastard.

Outside of Vietnam they were the first people I'd killed.

The fire was investigated and it was decided it was an accident. Their investigations rightly showed that the fire had started with the stove in the kitchen where the fire door hadn't been properly closed and had dropped open to set alight to the towels hangin' there. They examined the bodies and it was discovered that Libby's mother had taken a sleepin' pill as well as havin' a small amount of alcohol. A large amount of alcohol was discovered in the men and it was thought this was why they hadn't woken up when the fire spread. All this came out at the inquest.

I was questioned and said I'd left just after eleven that night, tellin' them Gary had passed out on the couch, the mother had already gone to bed and Mr. Fallon was just about to go to bed when I left. All true. Of course, the woman on the corner confirmed the time my car passed her place and pulled into Seaham Road. As I knew she would. So, I was never a suspect.

I didn't know the parents' lives were insured as well as the house, so when it was ruled an accident, that meant that there would a big pay out which proved to be a handy bonus for us.

48

Cessnock Prison August 2003.

Miller stops talking at this point saying that going through the events of that night has made him 'feel all emotional' and that he needs to go and lie down. Frank is not surprised by Miller's revelations. He'd always suspected Miller was somehow connected to the fire but when they'd looked into the records there didn't appear to be anything in the reports that would point to his involvement. Miller's confession has also brought to light why he had seemed vaguely familiar to Beth. She had encountered him *twice* before the accident and had met with Libby in Sydney, where photos or other information might have been shared about Miller.

The knowledge that Miller had gone to the Fallon farm with a plan which led to the family's deaths showed a callous premeditation that makes Frank feel sick. He doesn't know why it affects him so much, he's heard and seen worse in his career. He drives back to headquarters to leave the recording for transcribing before heading home.

'Betcha that was a big surprise for you yesterday, Detective Bailey,' Miller says to Frank the following morning.

Frank decides to be honest with him, and give Miller the acknowledgement he craves at the same time. 'I did have my suspicions about you being involved in the fire Martin, but I couldn't work out how you could've done it after reading all the reports. Very clever I must say.'

This is clearly what Miller wants to hear as his emaciated body perks up and his face splits into a wide crooked grin. Frank can see glimpses of the child in Miller and suspects praise was something he lacked in his life. He doesn't seem such an ugly person when he smiles with the innocence of a child. But he's not an innocent child Frank reminds himself and Miller's actions as an adult are certainly far from innocent. More like evil.

'Are you ready to carry on now?' he asks Miller, wondering what revelations will be coming his way today.

Miller nods and Frank presses the recording button.

49

Marty's Story
Sydney 1974

Libby changed after her parent's death. In the first few weeks she was cryin' all the time. Then she went real quiet. We had a lot of stuff to sort out with her father's lawyer and the farm. In the end we passed it all over to him to deal with as Libby was too upset and couldn't cope with goin' up there all the time. We couldn't really afford it anyway. It was a long drive in those days. Libby left her job after the fire. I don't think she could cope with workin' for a bit and we were broke.

In late November we both got temporary jobs and our situation improved a bit. Of course, I was quite flush with the money I took from the farm, but I couldn't let her know that. I'd stuffed it into me pocket when I grabbed it without lookin' at it, but when I counted it out later it was over a thousand bucks. That was a lot of money back then. Mum must've just been paid in cash for sellin' some of the beef cattle or pigs they had on the farm.

I asked Brett to mind the money, tellin' him that old

man Fallon had given it to me as a startin' point on the money he was goin' to lend us – to keep me goin' so I could get out and look at places without havin' to worry about work. He believed it of course. Poor old Brett would never do any thievin' like that himself so he couldn't imagine anyone else doin' it. I told him I didn't want Libby to know about the money though and he agreed to keep quiet. I told him it'd probably upset her too much and she was upset enough. Brett knew that.

Lookin' at houses and potential car yards had to go on hold. We weren't able to do anythin'. We had to wait for something called probate to go through.

Things between Libby and me weren't great. Since her parents' death, she hadn't really wanted me to touch her most nights, whereas before she couldn't get enough, you know what I mean? I'm quite well endowed and she'd loved havin' sex before. I dunno why she went off me like that. I worked real hard to make everythin' good between us, but unless we were havin' a drink and a laugh with our mate Brett, she was a bit of a misery guts. I know her parents had died, but a fella's got needs, you know. I woulda thought it would make her feel better.

Weeks passed by and things didn't get a lot better. Although we had a bit of money from casual work, our Christmas was miserable, but she perked up a bit in the New Year; seventy-five this was by then. We talked about a house and the car yard again and she seemed real keen on it for a while. She got a new job in a college and we celebrated her twenty-first birthday in style and got close again. Then a week after her birthday she started askin' me a lot of questions. About the night of the fire. She'd seen my muddy gumboots – which I'd completely forgotten about and hadn't worn since. They were still in the boot of the car and she'd been lookin' in there for something the day before. She asked me where I'd been wearin' them to get mud all over them like that. I fobbed her off tellin' her it must've been from a different day we'd been at the farm. She claimed that she'd cleaned our gummies the week *before* we'd gone up there on that weekend of the fire. They should've been clean as we didn't walk around the property after finding out about the fire. The police wouldn't let us. And if I'd seen her parents as I claimed, I would've walked in from the front gate not wearing them. She reckoned she knew it was farm mud because she could smell the cow shit on them. I must've walked through some when I went across the paddocks.

I played all innocent with her about it, but I could tell she was gettin' suspicious. Things really went downhill from there. It was the middle of February by this time. Libby was hardly talkin' to me, unless Brett was around. She'd put on a bit of a show for him. I couldn't find a job that wasn't too physical for me with me old injury and I had to dip into the money I'd taken from the farm, just so I could afford a few beers.

In the second week of March someone made an offer on the farm and Libby accepted it. The lawyer sent her the contract which she signed and sent it back to him. We thought that was it then, but he had other things he wanted to discuss with her. So in April we went up there on a Thursday after Libby finished work. She'd arranged to have the Friday off. We spent the night at the same friend's house we'd stayed at in October. I shoulda known it would all end in disaster.

The lawyer wanted to see her on her own so I don't know what they discussed. After we left Raymond Terrace, Libby wanted to go and see the farm one last time. It was just like I told your Sergeant back then. She also had a few things in one of the sheds she wanted to collect. On the way Libby told me how much money *she* might be gettin' from the estate and that *she'd* be gettin' it in about another month or so. I'd noticed she said 'she', not 'we'. It was a bloody fortune! For us anyway. She told me that if anythin' happened to her before the estate was settled, I wouldn't get the money, it would go to her family in England. I don't know why she told me that, but it's a good thing she did considerin' what happened later. As I said she'd been suspicious about the fire and maybe she thought I was plannin' to do somethin' to her. But it was never like that. I loved her.

As we were drivin' along Nobles Road, I said that we should start lookin' at places immediately if we were gettin' the money in a month's time. And that's when she made her big announcement. She said she didn't want to buy a place with me. That she was gunna leave me and move to Melbourne to join up with her friends down there.

I was so angry I just exploded and called her a fuckin' bitch. She started attackin' me, punchin' me around my head and hittin' me. She caused the accident really. I was so busy protectin' meself, neither of us saw the other car. Our car was swervin' all over the place and then suddenly there was this big *bang*!

50

Frank waits for Miller to start talking again. He can see he's crying. He's not sure who the tears are for. Libby or himself? Perhaps both. He leaves the recorder running and when nothing is forthcoming from Miller asks, 'Are you okay to continue Martin. Would you like a break or to finish there for today?'

Miller doesn't answer and so he stops the recording and calls for the guard.

'I don't think we'll be doing any further work today,' he tells him. 'Mr. Miller might need some quiet time here for a bit I think.'

'Salright,' Miller sobs. 'I'll be alright in a mo. Can you come back this arvo? I wanna get this out of the way.'

Frank agrees and arranges a time to re-commence proceedings. He leaves the prison and drives into Cessnock to find somewhere to have lunch.

'Sorry 'bout that this mornin'' Miller says when their session resumes. 'It's just that the memory of everythin' came floodin' back to me and it was a bit too much.'

Frank starts the recording equipment and waits for

Miller to pick up where they left off this morning.

51

Marty's Story
April 1975

When the cars crashed Libby went flyin' through the windscreen, smashed headfirst into the trunk of a tree and then fell to the ground. No seat belt you see. I was thrown forward and hit the steerin' wheel hard. Just as I said happened. I told you the truth all those years ago when your sergeant questioned me. The only difference is what happened next.

I realised that we'd hit a car and I could see it was the little red car we'd seen on the road before. The one that Farrell woman owned. Her car was movin' towards the river and I could see she was lyin' on the bonnet. I jumped out and ran over and pulled her off as the car began to slide backwards into the river. I saved her life really. She woulda been a gonner for sure if she'd ended up in the river, as she was unconscious.

I had her on the ground. Libby was lyin' nearby and looked real bad. I thought the knock to her head might be fatal. I looked from one to the other and thought, they could be almost twins. Shape, size, height almost the same. I knew their faces were different when you really looked hard at them. But both of them were cut on the face from the glass. I pulled a big chunk of glass out of the woman's face which I threw into the river. There was blood pouring out of the wound. I ripped up the bottom part of my shirt to tie around her head and staunch the flow.

That Lizzie woman had gone through the windscreen of her car, like Libby. It was then the idea came to me.

Libby had said that she had to be alive when the estate was settled. If the real Libby stayed alive, she was gunna take off and try to make sure I didn't get a cent of it. But it had to *seem* like she was alive. I thought Libby might die due to her bash on the head. Despite the blood, the other one looked better. She started coming around a bit and was moaning whereas Libby was totally silent. But I couldn't pass that woman off as Libby unless she was in a worse condition. Otherwise, she woulda remembered who she was.

I saw a lot of injuries in Vietnam. People shot, blown apart, and bad head injuries from bein' thrown into the air after explosions and landin' bad. I knew what it could do to people. Some people with brain injuries never really recovered; they became dribblin' vegetables and had to be put in homes for the rest of their lives. Some recovered but lost their memories. Either of those options would suit me. I decided to take a gamble. I knew I had to be quick. There wasn't much time.

I bashed the back of the woman's head several times against the road. Hard. It had to look like she'd hit the windscreen and the car bonnet with the front of her head and then hit the rear of her head landing on the road. She *had* hit both sides of her head but I needed to make it worse. She lapsed into unconsciousness again. I took a rug from the car and placed it against the front of her head, rolled her over and bashed her head a few times on the road. I rolled her back and did the same on the other side. I wanted to cause enough injuries so that she might be a bit of a vegetable. I then took the jacket off the woman and swapped it with the one Libby was wearin', rippin' a hole in the sleeve just like her one had. The woman had an injury on her arm. I put the rug into the back seat of the car after shakin' it out and then laid this woman on it.

I finished Libby off with the scarf she was wearin' and then crushed her neck bones even more, just to be sure. I took Libby's weddin' ring and a fancy medallion thing she'd got for her eighteenth birthday from her parents off her and put them on the other woman, takin' off the huge bloody engagement ring she was wearin' first. We were outside the Fallon farm entrance. Libby had the keys in her bag for the sheds. I found the keys, and carried her and that woman's jacket into the yard, past the old house site that had since been demolished and on to one of the sheds. I unlocked the shed and found an old large canvas tarpaulin that Fallon sometimes used to use on the buildin' sites and wrapped Libby and the jacket in it. I locked everythin' up and ran back to our car, smearing gravel and dirt over any tell-tale blood drops on the way, then headed off to Maitland Hospital. My car had no windscreen and it was pretty damaged. It started raining lightly making it difficult to see but thankfully I made it there before the heavens opened. The rain was a godsend really as I knew it would wipe out most of the blood at the crash scene. At the hospital I reported the accident and they contacted the police.

I was worried that I'd bashed the woman's head too hard when the docs said she was in a bad way when we first got there. They took her off and she came back with her head wrapped in bandages and dressins on her face and one of her arms. She was in a coma. With her face so swollen, no one would be able to tell it wasn't Libby, in case someone came along who knew her. Like the lawyer. I was worried he'd turn up. But he never came, even though the police told him about her after my interview. He told me he'd spoken with the police and hospital staff when I phoned him a week later to update him on Libby's condition. I wanted to know what was happenin' with the money from the sale but he wouldn't tell me anythin'. Said Libby was his client, not me.

As soon as I got the chance, I nipped off to see a mate in Maitland some days later. He was a fella I used to work with. I asked him if I could borrow his car that night as ours was a write off. I told me mate I needed his car to collect our things which we'd left in Newcastle before the accident. I said I needed clean clothes. I even wore my ripped and bloody shirt over a clean t-shirt from the day of the accident to his place so that it would seem more real. He offered to drive me at first, but I said I really wanted to be on me own so he finally agreed to lend me his car.

I hadn't wanted to go back to the farm straight away as I knew there'd be too many people about. The police, emergency services and that woman's family maybe. It was night time when I went and I was careful. If anyone was about, I was gunna say that I'd come to see if I could help look for the missin' woman. I'd collected my bag that I'd left at the hospital reception by then after strippin' off the messy shirt. Luckily there was no one about at the Fallon farm. They had moved to lookin' further downriver by then I think.

I collected Libby's body and took it up to Blackbutt Reserve. I knew it well from when Brett and I were younger. I knew there was a place I could put her where she'd never be discovered. And if she ever was discovered it would be long after she'd rotted away and you'd never be able to identify her. Who would've thought that this DNA stuff would've been discovered?

I had one of Fallon's torches with me I'd collected from the shed, so I was able to just about manage it. Almost broke my ankle though findin' my way through that bloody reserve place carryin' such a heavy load.

I returned the car to me mate, who then offered to put me up any night I wanted. I did go and stay with him as the weeks dragged on, but I also went back to Sydney a couple of times.

There was a bit of disaster at the hospital the day after I moved Libby's body though. I'd gone off to Sydney later that night, catchin' the last train down. I didn't know that this woman was allergic to seafood and they gave her some fish, didn't they? I played all innocent and shocked. Libby wasn't allergic to seafood – but she didn't like it and wouldn't eat it. Luckily, they saved her otherwise it would have all been for nuthin'.

When Libby, or I should say the Farrell sheila, first woke up, she couldn't speak, walk or move her arms around properly. I was really pleased as I thought I'd done enough to give her permanent brain damage. I spoke to the doc and he thought she might have brain damage, but said we had to wait and see, that she might fully recover. That was a bit worryin' I can tell you.

I spent day after day talkin' to her, tellin' her about her life. She seemed very confused and I wanted to confuse her even more. Really convince her that she was Libby. I knew she knew Libby, she'd met me, and so I thought everythin' about Libby might be familiar to her. Of course, it was a bit of a laugh that they had the same initials. One was Libby Fallon, and one Lizzie Farrell. And both had the same full name, Elizabeth. Who woulda thought that would happen eh? Never in a million years.

I didn't tell the woman that anyone else was involved in the accident. I said some cows had been on the road and we'd swerved to avoid them and hit the gates to their old farm. I told the staff I didn't want anyone mentionin' it to Libby as she didn't know the other woman had died and it would probably really upset her as they'd been childhood friends. She'd enough to cope with. They were good about that and didn't say a word to her.

I played the part of the lovin' husband. Well as lovin' as I can ever be. I never had any love growin' up in that kiddie's home.

We had a bunch of horrible women who looked after us at the home. The only time they touched us was to clean us up when we was little, and then they were bloody rough with us. Or they'd whack us if we did somethin' against their bloody rules. No comfort if we hurt ourselves or were sick. They'd just tell us to stop cryin' and pull ourselves together.

We didn't get properly seen to when we were sick either. That's how I ended up with a crooked smile. When I was about ten, I had a bad ear pain and I told them, but they took no notice of me. When one side of me face dropped and I couldn't feel anythin' there, they finally got a doc in to see me. *He* got it wrong as well. He gave me antibiotics but it didn't get better. I ended up in hospital with the most awful pain. Me face got better after a time and I could talk and eat without dribblin', but it never went back to what it was before. I was left with a crooked smile. Permanent nerve damage or somethin' they said.

There was also a bunch of clowns in suits that ran the place and loved nuthin' better that beltin' us. So I didn't really know how to be a lovin' husband. I realised that when I met the love of my life the followin' year. She taught me a lot. But I'm goin' off track you know…

I spoke to this woman who was supposed to be Libby as though she was Libby. Some days I'd even forget that she wasn't her. Libby'd told me that this Lizzie woman came from quite a posh, educated family in Sydney, so I had to invent a reason why she might have a la-de-da accent, in case she was ever able to talk again. I'd heard her a bit when she was talkin' to Libby on Nobles Road the previous year, so I knew she did speak well. I made up a story about her wantin' a job in David Jones in Newcastle and that she'd wanted to posh her accent up to get the job. It worked.

The only problem was Brett. I knew that if she started talkin' again and he heard her, he'd know it wasn't Libby. I wasn't too worried about how she looked. That could be explained away with the damage to her face and havin' no hair. She looked enough like Libby anyway. But the voice could be a problem. When she did start talkin', I told Brett that the Doc at the hospital spoke with a plummy accent and that when Libby first started talkin' again, she'd imitated him. I explained about her losin' her memory and not rememberin' anythin', includin' me. He fell for it of course. No-one would ever think that I'd swap me wife for someone else, would they? I did the same thing with the lawyer. He'd heard Libby's voice of course, so I had to make the same excuse with him too. He told me he'd checked with the hospital and they seemed to confirm what I'd said.

Another thing that was a bit of a problem were the tits. This woman had bigger tits that Libby. Not enormous or anythin', but noticeably bigger. I was worried that Brett might notice that too, but if he did, he never said anythin'. I had to throw out all Libby's bras and make out that she went around with no bras except goin' to work and seein' her family. She was left with only the bra she was wearin' when I took her into the hospital. It's lucky she didn't lose that as well, as they cut all her clothes off, except the bra and pants. She had no injuries in that area of her body. I threw her pants out as they were so different to Libby's.

I could see that the woman didn't really believe I was her husband. And I can understand that. Although she couldn't remember who she was, or anythin' much about her life, she would've known someone like her wouldn't've married someone like me. But I finally managed to convince her and she began to accept we was married. Don't think she was too happy about it though.

I avoided touchin' the woman too much and just gave her the odd peck at the hospital or held her hand. Didn't want to scare her off. I spent weeks up there at the hospital apart from my odd trips to Sydney. On the first trip I made to Sydney, I sold the woman's engagement ring. I'd guessed it was her engagement ring as the papers said her fiancé was helpin' in the search for her. Big bloody diamond ring it was. I got a good price for it. Kept me goin' for a while and I was able to pay the rent and electricity owed on the flat.

I saw Brett in Sydney and told him about the accident. I told him part of the truth – that Libby caused it. And I told him about Libby's big announcement that she was gunna leave me which led to the fight and the crash. I told him that since she'd woken up that she couldn't remember anythin' and that I hoped we could start afresh. I made him promise not to say anythin' to Libby.

I was a bit worried about the papers at the time. They put a picture of Elizabeth Farrell in there and I was worried that someone at the hospital might notice the resemblance, even though her face was swollen and she had most of her head and face covered up. But no-one did, so it was fine.

Libby, I mean the woman, started to get better and I kept naggin' the hospital to let me take her home as we needed to get back to Sydney. They finally did let her go, but not before I cleared the place out a bit. I got rid of all the letters from her cousin – or so I thought. I took our telly around to Brett's sayin' that I didn't want Libby to see anythin' about the accident anywhere or she might become upset; seein' that it was her fault. I hocked our radio for a few extra bucks as well. Couldn't have anythin' in the place where she might hear her real name mentioned. The news had died down by then, but it was a bit less than a month so there were still odd comments comin' up about the woman.

Just before *Libby* came home, I had to go to the inquest. With what I, and that stupid sergeant told them, they decided the Farrell woman was to blame for the accident. They believed it was likely that she'd drowned and her body swept out to sea with the strong currents. The verdict was accidental death.

The insurance paid out on our old car and I bought another second-hand car with Brett's expert help. I collected the woman from the hospital and took her home.

52

Cessnock Prison
August 2003

Miller stops talking at this point. Frank wants to ask him questions but decides against it. He is already feeling angry with everything Miller has told him and is worried he'll react too personally. He'd suspected that Miller had hidden his wife's remains in one of the outbuildings on the Fallon farm. During the investigation they'd visited the old farm but the current owners had demolished the old outbuildings and built one vary large barn to replace it. He packs things up and tells Miller he'll see him tomorrow.

Frank receives a call from the Cessnock Correctional Centre in the morning to inform him that Miller is too unwell to take part in sessions that day. He agrees to call the following morning to check his condition before setting out.

He decides that he should take the transcribed pages of Miller's confession to date with him to the next session they have for him to sign every page.

The next morning, he receives the green light for the

confession sessions to resume, and enters the room with a folder of the transcribed pages. He asks Miller to read and sign them before they begin recording for the day. Miller admits he's a slow reader and it is some time before they can resume.

Frank has another two sessions with Miller before his confession is complete. Miller recounts what it was like for him when he took Beth back to the Sydney flat. It covers much of the same ground he'd heard from Beth but from Miller's perspective. Miller admits that he couldn't stand living with Beth – she was so different to his wife Libby so he began plotting and planning *her* death to keep himself sane. The one thing he omits to mention is how he raped Beth on her last night at the flat. Miller express his rage at how Beth managed to dupe him and escape. He then goes on to talk about his trip to the UK where he made the attempt on Beth's life.

If Miller thought Frank might feel sympathetic towards him from the outcome of his trip to London, he was badly mistaken. It took all of Frank's strength to remain emotionally detached from everything Miller was telling him and to say nothing. When Miller reaches the part about Susan Kennedy's death Frank is able to engage with Miller wearing his detective hat again. It seems that it was *his* visit to Miller at the car yard that triggered events leading to Susan Kennedy's death. Miller learned from Brett Saunders that Susan had been around looking for him and making comments Miller found suspicious. He tracked her down and after observing her habits broke into her flat. There he found loads of notes pertaining to things he'd said when they were together and he'd had a few drinks under his belt. He decided she had to go and so after removing all the notes and photographs of himself from Susan's albums, he implemented a swift plan that led to her death.

When Miller finally finishes his confession, he seems to drift off into a trance-like state. Frank is tempted to say something to him, but decides it can wait until Miller has signed all the transcribed notes.

'Thank you, Martin,' he says. 'I'll get everything typed up and back to you for reading tomorrow afternoon.'

Miller doesn't answer him as he leaves.

53

The following afternoon Frank returns to the Cessnock Correctional Centre with the final pages of Miller's confession. Miller is waiting for him by the time he enters the room; he looks more drawn and haggard today; a ghostly figure on the verge of death.

Frank spent several hours tossing and turning in bed last night thinking of all the things he wanted to say to Miller. Looking at him now though, Frank doesn't have the heart to launch into his judgemental spiel. He decides to rein his emotions and thoughts in, and remain professional.

He passes Miller the pages and asks him to read through them, signing and dating each one. There is a further statement he has to complete and sign on the final page. When he hands the pages back to Frank and they are safely slotted into his file and placed in a brief case he has brought along today, he finally turns to Miller and says, 'It was Elizabeth Farrell's ex-fiancé who suggested I question you, not Susan Kennedy.'

'What? Why on earth would he say that?' Miller asks with a puzzled expression.

'He knew you'd lied about the car accident. He thought

if you'd lied about what happened that day, you might be capable of anything. He knew you were the last person to see Elizabeth Farrell and so the most likely person to have laid hands on her jacket. The jacket we found with your wife's remains.'

'Ah, okey doke. I got it wrong. Still Susan *was* up to somethin' wasn't she? Otherwise, she wouldn't've had all those notes. We'll never know now though, will we?'

'No.' Frank can't help himself and blurts out, 'I'm disappointed that you've not taken responsibility for *anything* you've done Martin. You might have confessed to your crimes, but in doing so you blamed *others* for your actions whereas it was you who destroyed many lives.'

'Well, I'm the one who's sufferin', aren't I? I'm the one who lost me legs and spent years in jail. I'm the one who's still banged up and dyin' of cancer.'

'Yes, you are. I'm sorry that you had such a bad start in life Martin. The disadvantages you had because of it. And I'm sorry you chose the path you did. For you, and all your victims.'

'No use in cryin' over spilt milk is there? It's done and I'm done.'

'Yes. And so are we,' Frank says standing. 'Thank you for doing this. I don't think we'll be meeting again. Goodbye Martin.'

As he drives away from the prison, Frank reflects on what he's learned about Miller in the confession sessions. He knew life for some kids in homes had been dreadful. There'd been a lot of publicity come out in the press since the late eighties about such things. Miller had only given him a tiny glimpse of what it had been like for him, but Frank's sure that there are many more horror stories he could've told.

When he'd been investigating Miller a few years back he'd discovered from records that Miller's mother had died a few days after giving birth to him alone in her tiny cottage in late nineteen forty-eight. Miller himself was only saved after a neighbour heard him crying and went to investigate. Miller's mother had been a Polish immigrant who'd come to Australia after the war. It was probably her who Miller had inherited his fair hair from.

Miller's father, another immigrant from Scotland, had died in a mining accident six months before his birth. There had been a delay in him being put up for adoption while a search went on for surviving relatives in Poland and Scotland. When none were traced, he was eventually adopted shortly before his third birthday by a local childless couple, but the wife was diagnosed with cancer a few months after Miller's fourth birthday. The husband, unable, or unwilling to look after a child on his own, returned him to the home after his wife died when Miller was six, just before the infamous Hunter River floods that decimated Maitland in February 'fifty-five. His return to the home and the dramatic evacuation during the floods would have been further traumatic events for a young child.

Miller still carried the name of the couple who'd adopted him. His birth name was McAllister. He's surprised that Miller never changed his name back to McAllister as an adult. Perhaps he never knew his birth name, or was ever told about his background. He'd never mentioned it.

Maybe he was never interested enough to find out.

He remembers Beth Carey telling him on the plane trip to Australia that Miller told her he'd taken drugs in Vietnam. Perhaps that caused further damage to his already damaged soul. Who knows what these things do to us? Frank had only ever tried a little marijuana in his youth. He liked the pleasant experiences he had with it at first, but on subsequent bouts, perhaps from a bad batch, he'd not liked the sensation of being out of control and never tried it again. It was the same with alcohol for him. A few drunken experiences and the ensuing hangovers that followed turned him off for life. He only ever has alcohol in moderation these days. But he does like to have his relaxing tipples of an evening when he's not working silly long hours. That is his drug.

As Beth springs into his mind, he wonders whether the Chief Super will let her have access to Miller's confession. Or know the details of what it contains. He thinks she deserves to, but that will not be his decision to make.

Three weeks later Frank receives a phone call from the Governor of Cessnock, informing him that Miller has died. He'd succumbed to his illness sooner than expected. As Miller had said, he was done; done with his life.

Epilogue
December 2004, Hunter Valley, NSW

Beth thinks they chose the ideal location for the wedding reception. She couldn't remember what it had been like in the seventies when she and Steve had provided the catering for wine tasting events, but she'd been told that the event room the winery hired out for special functions today was a far cry from what it had been like back then. She looks across at her family and smiles. She could never have imagined that she would be sitting here today, marrying a man she loves. She keeps thinking she'll have to pinch herself to make sure it's real, not just a dream.

When she returned to Australia at her grandmother's passing in 2003, she contacted Frank Bailey to let him know she was staying at her grandmother's house in Maitland. He very kindly attended the funeral and came to the 'wake' she laid on at Gran's house. It was a matter of weeks after that the call had come in from the Cessnock Correctional Services requesting that Frank take down Martin Miller's confession.

Frank's Chief Superintendent had given permission for Beth to read the completed transcripts. She noted Miller had instinctively acted to save her following the accident and then destroyed his heroic feat with his subsequent actions by causing her further injuries and all that followed. Reading about some of Miller's experiences as a child, with Frank additionally filling her in on Miller's birth and background, greatly upset her. She'd always felt slightly sorry for Miller and could now understand why she'd irritated him so much. They were worlds apart in their outlook on life. His had been skewed from an early age. She was grateful that she'd not the misfortune to have his experiences. Although she still can't remember much of her upbringing, she knows that she came from a happy, loving family. The stories her father and brothers have told her, the family photo albums and the 8mm film reels they've played for her, bore witness to that fact.

To read what Miller had done to her and Libby on the day of the accident, and killing Libby's parents with the fire had horrified Beth and she'd felt great anger towards Miller's callous actions. She'd spent an entire evening pacing around the lounge venting her anger and distress after reading it. It still upset her to think about it, but she's let it go. It was all in the past now.

Like her relationship with Steve. It came to an end after Miller's trial in 2001. Steve rang her in 2002 to say he was marrying a woman who was expecting his child. He assured her he was in love with the woman and that he was happy. Relieved to hear his news, she wished him well.

Their son Matt had travelled around Australia, having fantastic adventures and finally returned to Brisbane where he regularly saw his father and half siblings. Early in December last year Matt married a young woman called Sophie. She seems a lovely young woman and Beth is happy for them. They're expecting their first child.

Ali is living in Sydney with Stefan, Helen and Paul's son. A qualified lawyer now, following in his father's footsteps, Stefan moved to Sydney, where he and Ali had started seeing each other.

'I suspect they'll be the next two to tie the knot,' Helen had whispered to her earlier, referring to Ali and Stefan. But Ali has told her they're not rushing into anything, so a marriage isn't on the cards for them just yet.

Helen and her husband Paul, have come over to attend the wedding and are staying at her grandmother's house. *No, my house,* Beth corrects herself. Gran left Beth her house.

Beth's thoughts are interrupted by her husband. There's no question about today's marriage being legal and above board. 'The limousine is here Mrs. Bailey. Are you ready to leave?'

'I certainly am,' Beth replies, reaching out to accept Frank's outstretched hand.

Acknowledgements

I drafted the first copy of A Convenient Accident in 2016. At the time I had a working title but soon learned that another book had been released with the same title. I chose other titles, but while I hesitated to submit the manuscript to anyone, various other books were brought out using the titles I'd chosen. I then chose another title which I was not happy with and after sitting on it for some time drew up a list of alternatives that I sent out to friends to vote on. *A Convenient Accident* won and guess what — no other author has (as yet) used that title. So it stuck.

Most authors dismiss their early titles and put them away to revisit another day. I have done that repeatedly with *A convenient Accident* over the years. To begin with, it was far too long and had to be pruned dramatically. I wrote further 'books' featuring the same detectives which I felt were far better (not yet published). However, *A Convenient Accident* is an important milestone in Frank Bailey's life so it had to come first.

Still not confident that it was up to publication standards I submitted the manuscript to be evaluated through The Literary Consultancy. It was assessed by author Doug Johnstone who, while praising many aspects of the manuscript, pointed out the shortfalls. I have worked on the manuscript to improve things. But as we authors know, our 'books' are our 'babies' and we can't bring ourselves to make some alterations. So on my head be it. I'd like to thank the TLC and Doug Johnston for their invaluable feedback.

But first and foremost, I'd like to thank Judy and Laura.

A Convenient Accident

My two main beta readers through the years. Their honest feedback always proves valuable. Thanks too to Bianca Alice who absolutely adored Frank. I hope you will too.

About the Author

L.E. Luttrell was born in Sydney, Australia and spent the first 21 years of her life there before moving to the UK. After working in publishing (in the UK) for a few years she went on to study and trained as a teacher. From the 90s she spent many years working in secondary education, although she's also had numerous other part time jobs. A frustrated architect/builder, L.E. Luttrell has spent much of her adult life moving house and wielding various tools while renovating properties.

L.E. Luttrell lives in Merseyside England, but also spends time travelling between there, Wales (UK) and Australia.

Follow on:

www.leluttrell.com

: L.E. Luttrell – Author

: @LLuttrellauthor

Go to: www.lelutrell.com and sign up the the VIP list to receive a **FREE BOOK**